BY TRUMAN CAPOTE

Other Voices, Other Rooms

A Tree of Night

Local Color

The Grass Harp

The Muses Are Heard

Breakfast at Tiffany's

Observations (with Richard Avedon)

Selected Writings

In Cold Blood

A Christmas Memory

The Thanksgiving Visitor

The Dogs Bark

Music for Chameleons

One Christmas

Three by Truman Capote

Answered Prayers: The Unfinished Novel

A Capote Reader

The Complete Stories of Truman Capote

Too Brief a Treat: The Letters of Truman Capote
(edited by Gerald Clarke)

Summer Crossing

Portraits and Observations: The Essays of Truman Capote

BREAKFAST AT TIFFANY'S
& OTHER VOICES, OTHER ROOMS

BREAKFAST AT TIFFANY'S

& OTHER VOICES, OTHER ROOMS

TRUMAN CAPOTE

MODERN LIBRARY

NEW YORK

TRUMAN CAPOTE

Truman Capote was born Truman Streckfus Persons on September 30, 1924, in New Orleans. His early years were affected by an unsettled family life. He was turned over to the care of his mother's family in Monroeville, Alabama; his father was imprisoned for fraud; his parents divorced and then fought a bitter custody battle over Truman. Eventually he moved to New York City to live with his mother and her second husband, a Cuban businessman whose name he adopted. The young Capote got a job as a copyboy at *The New Yorker* in the early forties, but was fired for inadvertently offending Robert Frost. The publication of his early stories in *Harper's Bazaar* established his literary reputation when he was in his twenties. His novel *Other Voices, Other Rooms* (1948), a Gothic coming-of-age story that Capote described as "an attempt to exorcise demons," and his novella *The Grass Harp* (1951), a gentler fantasy rooted in his Alabama years, consolidated his precocious fame.

From the start of his career Capote associated himself with a wide range of writers and artists, high-society figures, and international celebrities, gaining frequent media attention for his exuberant social life. He collected his stories in *A Tree of Night* (1949) and published the novella *Breakfast at Tiffany's* (1958), but devoted his energies increasingly to the stage—adapting *The*

Grass Harp into a play and writing the musical *House of Flowers* (1954)—and to journalism, of which the earliest examples are "Local Color" (1950) and "The Muses Are Heard" (1956). He made a brief foray into the movies to write the screenplay for John Huston's *Beat the Devil* (1954).

Capote's interest in the murder of a family in Kansas led to the prolonged investigation that provided the basis for *In Cold Blood* (1966), his most successful and acclaimed book. By "treating a real event with fictional techniques," Capote intended to create a new synthesis: something both "immaculately factual" and a work of art. However its genre was defined, from the moment it began to appear in serialized form in *The New Yorker* the book exerted a fascination among a wider readership than Capote's writing had ever attracted before. The abundantly publicized masked ball at the Plaza Hotel with which he celebrated the completion of *In Cold Blood* was an iconic event of the 1960s, and for a time Capote was a constant presence on television and in magazines, even trying his hand at movie acting in *Murder by Death*.

He worked for many years on *Answered Prayers,* an ultimately unfinished novel that was intended to be the distillation of everything he had observed in his life among the rich and famous; an excerpt from it published in *Esquire* in 1975 appalled many of Capote's wealthy friends for its revelation of intimate secrets, and he found himself excluded from the world he had once dominated. In his later years he published two collections of fiction and essays, *The Dogs Bark* (1973) and *Music for Chameleons* (1980). He died on August 25, 1984, after years of problems with drugs and alcohol.

The Complete Stories of Truman Capote and *Too Brief a Treat: The Letters of Truman Capote* were published in 2004. In 2005, *Summer Crossing,* his long-lost first novel, was published for the first time around the world.

CONTENTS

Biographical Note   vii

BREAKFAST AT TIFFANY'S   3

OTHER VOICES, OTHER ROOMS   89

BREAKFAST AT TIFFANY'S

For Jack Dunphy

I am always drawn back to places where I have lived, the houses and their neighborhoods. For instance, there is a brownstone in the East Seventies where, during the early years of the war, I had my first New York apartment. It was one room crowded with attic furniture, a sofa and fat chairs upholstered in that itchy, particular red velvet that one associates with hot days on a train. The walls were stucco, and a color rather like tobacco-spit. Everywhere, in the bathroom too, there were prints of Roman ruins freckled brown with age. The single window looked out on a fire escape. Even so, my spirits heightened whenever I felt in my pocket the key to this apartment; with all its gloom, it still was a place of my own, the first, and my books were there, and jars of pencils to sharpen, everything I needed, so I felt, to become the writer I wanted to be.

It never occurred to me in those days to write about Holly Golightly, and probably it would not now except for a conversation I had with Joe Bell that set the whole memory of her in motion again.

Holly Golightly had been a tenant in the old brownstone; she'd occupied the apartment below mine. As for Joe Bell, he ran a bar around the corner on Lexington Avenue; he still does.

Both Holly and I used to go there six, seven times a day, not for
a drink, not always, but to make telephone calls: during the war
a private telephone was hard to come by. Moreover, Joe Bell was
good about taking messages, which in Holly's case was no small
favor, for she had a tremendous many.

Of course this was a long time ago, and until last week I
hadn't seen Joe Bell in several years. Off and on we'd kept in
touch, and occasionally I'd stopped by his bar when passing
through the neighborhood; but actually we'd never been strong
friends except in as much as we were both friends of Holly Golightly. Joe Bell hasn't an easy nature, he admits it himself, he
says it's because he's a bachelor and has a sour stomach. Anyone
who knows him will tell you he's a hard man to talk to. Impossible if you don't share his fixations, of which Holly is one. Some
others are: ice hockey, Weimaraner dogs, *Our Gal Sunday* (a soap
serial he has listened to for fifteen years), and Gilbert and
Sullivan—he claims to be related to one or the other, I can't
remember which.

And so when, late last Tuesday afternoon, the telephone
rang and I heard "Joe Bell here," I knew it must be about Holly.
He didn't say so, just: "Can you rattle right over here? It's
important," and there was a croak of excitement in his froggy
voice.

I took a taxi in a downpour of October rain, and on my
way I even thought she might be there, that I would see Holly
again.

But there was no one on the premises except the proprietor.
Joe Bell's is a quiet place compared to most Lexington Avenue
bars. It boasts neither neon nor television. Two old mirrors reflect the weather from the streets; and behind the bar, in a niche
surrounded by photographs of ice-hockey stars, there is always

a large bowl of fresh flowers that Joe Bell himself arranges with matronly care. That is what he was doing when I came in.

"Naturally," he said, rooting a gladiola deep into the bowl, "naturally I wouldn't have got you over here if it wasn't I wanted your opinion. It's peculiar. A very peculiar thing has happened."

"You heard from Holly?"

He fingered a leaf, as though uncertain of how to answer. A small man with a fine head of coarse white hair, he has a bony, sloping face better suited to someone far taller; his complexion seems permanently sunburned: now it grew even redder. "I can't say exactly heard from her. I mean, I don't know. That's why I want your opinion. Let me build you a drink. Something new. They call it a White Angel," he said, mixing one-half vodka, one-half gin, no vermouth. While I drank the result, Joe Bell stood sucking on a Tums and turning over in his mind what he had to tell me. Then: "You recall a certain Mr. I. Y. Yunioshi? A gentleman from Japan."

"From California," I said, recalling Mr. Yunioshi perfectly. He's a photographer on one of the picture magazines, and when I knew him he lived in the studio apartment on the top floor of the brownstone.

"Don't go mixing me up. All I'm asking, you know who I mean? Okay. So last night who comes waltzing in here but this selfsame Mr. I. Y. Yunioshi. I haven't seen him, I guess it's over two years. And where do you think he's been those two years?"

"Africa."

Joe Bell stopped crunching on his Tums, his eyes narrowed. "So how did you know?"

"Read it in Winchell." Which I had, as a matter of fact.

He rang open his cash register, and produced a manila envelope. "Well, see did you read this in Winchell."

In the envelope were three photographs, more or less the same, though taken from different angles: a tall delicate Negro man wearing a calico skirt and with a shy, yet vain smile, displaying in his hands an odd wood sculpture, an elongated carving of a head, a girl's, her hair sleek and short as a young man's, her smooth wood eyes too large and tilted in the tapering face, her mouth wide, overdrawn, not unlike clown-lips. On a glance it resembled most primitive carving; and then it didn't, for here was the spit-image of Holly Golightly, at least as much of a likeness as a dark still thing could be.

"Now what do you make of that?" said Joe Bell, satisfied with my puzzlement.

"It looks like her."

"Listen, boy," and he slapped his hand on the bar, "it *is* her. Sure as I'm a man fit to wear britches. The little Jap knew it was her the minute he saw her."

"He saw her? In Africa?"

"Well. Just the statue there. But it comes to the same thing. Read the facts for yourself," he said, turning over one of the photographs. On the reverse was written: Wood Carving, S Tribe, Tococul, East Anglia, Christmas Day, 1956.

He said, "Here's what the Jap says," and the story was this: On Christmas day Mr. Yunioshi had passed with his camera through Tococul, a village in the tangles of nowhere and of no interest, merely a congregation of mud huts with monkeys in the yards and buzzards on the roofs. He'd decided to move on when he saw suddenly a Negro squatting in a doorway carving monkeys on a walking stick. Mr. Yunioshi was impressed and asked to see more of his work. Whereupon he was shown the carving of the girl's head: and felt, so he told Joe Bell, as if he were falling in a dream. But when he offered to buy it the Negro cupped his private parts in his hand (apparently a tender gesture, comparable to tapping one's heart) and said no. A pound of salt and ten dollars, a wristwatch and two pounds of salt and twenty dollars, nothing swayed him. Mr. Yunioshi was in all events determined to learn how the carving came to be made. It cost him his salt and his watch, and the incident was conveyed in African and pig-English and finger-talk. But it would seem that in the spring of that year a party of three white persons had appeared out of the brush riding horseback. A young woman and two men. The men, both red-eyed with fever, were forced for several weeks to stay shut and shivering in an isolated hut, while the young woman, having presently taken a fancy to the woodcarver, shared the woodcarver's mat.

"I don't credit that part," Joe Bell said squeamishly. "I know she had her ways, but I don't think she'd be up to anything as much as that."

"And then?"

"Then nothing," he shrugged. "By and by she went like she come, rode away on a horse."

"Alone, or with the two men?"

Joe Bell blinked. "With the two men, I guess. Now the Jap, he asked about her up and down the country. But nobody else had ever seen her." Then it was as if he could feel my own sense of letdown transmitting itself to him, and he wanted no part of it. "One thing you got to admit, it's the only *definite* news in I don't know how many"—he counted on his fingers: there weren't enough—"years. All I hope, I hope she's rich. She must be rich. You got to be rich to go mucking around in Africa."

"She's probably never set foot in Africa," I said, believing it; yet I could see her there, it was somewhere she would have gone. And the carved head: I looked at the photographs again.

"You know so much, where is she?"

"Dead. Or in a crazy house. Or married. I think she's married and quieted down and maybe right in this very city."

He considered a moment. "No," he said, and shook his head. "I'll tell you why. If she was in this city I'd have seen her. You take a man that likes to walk, a man like me, a man's been walking in the streets going on ten or twelve years, and all those years he's got his eye out for one person, and nobody's ever her, don't it stand to reason she's not there? I see pieces of her all the time, a flat little bottom, any skinny girl that walks fast and straight—" He paused, as though too aware of how intently I was looking at him. "You think I'm round the bend?"

"It's just that I didn't know you'd been in love with her. Not like that."

I was sorry I'd said it; it disconcerted him. He scooped up the photographs and put them back in their envelope. I looked at my watch. I hadn't any place to go, but I thought it was better to leave.

"Hold on," he said, gripping my wrist. "Sure I loved her. But it wasn't that I wanted to touch her." And he added, without smiling: "Not that I don't think about that side of things. Even at my age, and I'll be sixty-seven January ten. It's a peculiar fact—but, the older I grow, that side of things seems to be on my mind more and more. I don't remember thinking about it so much even when I was a youngster and it's every other minute. Maybe the older you grow and the less easy it is to put thought into action, maybe that's why it gets all locked up in your head and becomes a burden. Whenever I read in the paper about an old man disgracing himself, I know it's because of this burden. But"—he poured himself a jigger of whiskey and swallowed it neat—"I'll never disgrace myself. And I swear, it never crossed my mind about Holly. You can love somebody without it being like that. You keep them a stranger, a stranger who's a friend."

Two men came into the bar, and it seemed the moment to leave. Joe Bell followed me to the door. He caught my wrist again. "Do you believe it?"

"That you didn't want to touch her?"

"I mean about Africa."

At that moment I couldn't seem to remember the story, only the image of her riding away on a horse. "Anyway, she's gone."

"Yeah," he said, opening the door. "Just gone."

Outside, the rain had stopped, there was only a mist of it in the air, so I turned the corner and walked along the street where the brownstone stands. It is a street with trees that in the summer make cool patterns on the pavement; but now the leaves were yellowed and mostly down, and the rain had made them slippery, they skidded underfoot. The brownstone is midway in the block, next to a church where a blue tower-clock tolls the hours. It has been sleeked up since my day; a smart black door has replaced the old frosted glass, and gray elegant shutters frame the windows. No one I remember still lives there except Madame Sapphia Spanella, a husky coloratura who every afternoon went roller-skating in Central Park. I know she's still there because I went up the steps and looked at the mailboxes. It was one of these mailboxes that had first made me aware of Holly Golightly.

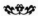

I'd been living in the house about a week when I noticed that the mailbox belonging to Apt. 2 had a name-slot fitted with a curious card. Printed, rather Cartier-formal, it read: *Miss Holi-*

day Golightly; and, underneath, in the corner, *Traveling.* It nagged me like a tune: *Miss Holiday Golightly, Traveling.*

One night, it was long past twelve, I woke up at the sound of Mr. Yunioshi calling down the stairs. Since he lived on the top floor, his voice fell through the whole house, exasperated and stern. "Miss Golightly! I must protest!"

The voice that came back, welling up from the bottom of the stairs, was silly-young and self-amused. "Oh, darling, I *am* sorry. I lost the goddamn key."

"You cannot go on ringing my bell. You must please, please have yourself a key made."

"But I lose them all."

"I work, I have to sleep," Mr. Yunioshi shouted. "But always you are ringing my bell . . ."

"Oh, *don't* be angry, you *dear* little man: I *won't* do it again. And if you promise not to be angry"—her voice was coming nearer, she was climbing the stairs—"I might let you take those pictures we mentioned."

By now I'd left my bed and opened the door an inch. I could hear Mr. Yunioshi's silence: hear, because it was accompanied by an audible change of breath.

"When?" he said.

The girl laughed. "Sometime," she answered, slurring the word.

"Any time," he said, and closed his door.

I went out into the hall and leaned over the banister, just enough to see without being seen. She was still on the stairs, now she reached the landing, and the ragbag colors of her boy's hair, tawny streaks, strands of albino-blond and yellow, caught the hall light. It was a warm evening, nearly summer, and she wore a slim cool black dress, black sandals, a pearl choker. For all her chic thinness, she had an almost breakfast-cereal air of health, a soap and lemon cleanness, a rough pink darkening in the cheeks. Her mouth was large, her nose upturned. A pair of dark glasses blotted out her eyes. It was a face beyond child-hood, yet this side of belonging to a woman. I thought her any-where between sixteen and thirty; as it turned out, she was shy two months of her nineteenth birthday.

She was not alone. There was a man following behind her. The way his plump hand clutched at her hip seemed somehow improper; not morally, aesthetically. He was short and vast, sun-lamped and pomaded, a man in a buttressed pin-stripe suit with a red carnation withering in the lapel. When they reached her door she rummaged her purse in search of a key, and took no notice of the fact that his thick lips were nuzzling the nape of her neck. At last, though, finding the key and opening her door, she turned to him cordially: "Bless you, darling—you were sweet to see me home."

"Hey, baby!" he said, for the door was closing in his face.

"Yes, Harry?"

"Harry was the other guy. I'm Sid. Sid Arbuck. You like me."

"I worship you, Mr. Arbuck. But good night, Mr. Arbuck."

Mr. Arbuck stared with disbelief as the door shut firmly. "Hey, baby, let me in, baby. You like me, baby. I'm a liked guy. Didn't I pick up the check, five people, *your* friends, I never seen them before? Don't that give me the right you should like me? You like me, baby."

He tapped on the door gently, then louder; finally he took several steps back, his body hunched and lowering, as though he meant to charge it, crash it down. Instead, he plunged down the stairs, slamming a fist against the wall. Just as he reached the bottom, the door of the girl's apartment opened and she poked out her head.

"Oh, Mr. *Ar*buck . . ."

He turned back, a smile of relief oiling his face: she'd only been teasing.

"The next time a girl wants a little powder-room change," she called, not teasing at all, "take my advice, darling: *don't* give her twenty cents!"

She kept her promise to Mr. Yunioshi; or I assume she did not ring his bell again, for in the next days she started ringing mine, sometimes at two in the morning, three and four: she had no qualms at what hour she got me out of bed to push the buzzer that released the downstairs door. As I had few friends, and none who would come around so late, I always knew that it was her. But on the first occasions of its happening, I went to my door, half-expecting bad news, a telegram; and Miss Golightly would call up: "Sorry, darling—I forgot my key."

Of course we'd never met. Though actually, on the stairs, in the street, we often came face-to-face; but she seemed not quite to see me. She was never without dark glasses, she was always well groomed, there was a consequential good taste in the plain-ness of her clothes, the blues and grays and lack of luster that made her, herself, shine so. One might have thought her a pho-tographer's model, perhaps a young actress, except that it was obvious, judging from her hours, she hadn't time to be either.

Now and then I ran across her outside our neighborhood. Once a visiting relative took me to "21," and there, at a superior table, surrounded by four men, none of them Mr. Arbuck, yet all of them interchangeable with him, was Miss Golightly, idly, publicly combing her hair; and her expression, an unrealized yawn, put, by example, a dampener on the excitement I felt over dining at so swanky a place. Another night, deep in the summer, the heat of my room sent me out into the streets. I walked down Third Avenue to Fifty-first Street, where there was an antique store with an object in its window I admired: a palace of a bird cage, a mosque of minarets and bamboo rooms yearning to be filled with talkative parrots. But the price was three hundred and fifty dollars. On the way home I noticed a cab-driver crowd gathered in front of P. J. Clarke's saloon, apparently attracted there by a happy group of whiskey-eyed Australian army officers baritoning, "Waltzing Matilda." As they sang they took turns spin-dancing a girl over the cobbles under the El; and the girl, Miss Golightly, to be sure, floated round in their arms light as a scarf.

But if Miss Golightly remained unconscious of my existence, except as a doorbell convenience, I became, through the summer, rather an authority on hers. I discovered, from observing the trash-basket outside her door, that her regular reading consisted of tabloids and travel folders and astrological charts; that she smoked an esoteric cigarette called Picayunes; survived on cottage cheese and melba toast; that her vari-colored hair was somewhat self-induced. The same source made it evident that she received V-letters by the bale. They were always torn into strips like bookmarks. I used occasionally to pluck myself a bookmark in passing. *Remember* and *miss you* and *rain* and *please write* and *damn* and *goddamn* were the words that recurred most often on these slips; those, and *lonesome* and *love.*

Also, she had a cat and she played the guitar. On days when the sun was strong, she would wash her hair, and together with the cat, a red tiger-striped tom, sit out on the fire escape thumbing a guitar while her hair dried. Whenever I heard the music, I would go stand quietly by my window. She played very well, and sometimes sang too. Sang in the hoarse, breaking tones of a boy's adolescent voice. She knew all the show hits, Cole Porter and Kurt Weill; especially she liked the songs from *Oklahoma!,* which were new that summer and everywhere. But there were moments when she played songs that made you wonder where she learned them, where indeed she came from. Harsh-tender wandering tunes with words that smacked of pineywoods or prairie. One went: *Don't wanna sleep, Don't wanna die, Just wanna go a-travelin' through the pastures of the sky;* and this one seemed to gratify her the most, for often she continued it long after her hair had dried, after the sun had gone and there were lighted windows in the dusk.

But our acquaintance did not make headway until September, an evening with the first ripple-chills of autumn running through it. I'd been to a movie, come home and gone to bed with a bourbon nightcap and the newest Simenon: so much my idea of comfort that I couldn't understand a sense of unease that multiplied until I could hear my heart beating. It was a feeling I'd read about, written about, but never before experienced. The feeling of being watched. Of someone in the room. Then: an abrupt rapping at the window, a glimpse of ghostly gray: I spilled the bourbon. It was some little while before I could bring myself to open the window, and ask Miss Golightly what she wanted.

"I've got the most terrifying man downstairs," she said, stepping off the fire escape into the room. "I mean he's sweet when he isn't drunk, but let him start lapping up the vino, and oh God quel beast! If there's one thing I loathe, it's men who bite." She loosened a gray flannel robe off her shoulder to show me evidence of what happens if a man bites. The robe was all she was wearing. "I'm sorry if I frightened you. But when the beast got so tiresome I just went out the window. I think he thinks I'm in the bathroom, not that I give a damn what he thinks, the hell with him, he'll get tired, he'll go to sleep, my God he should, eight martinis before dinner and enough wine to wash an elephant. Listen, you can throw me out if you want to. I've got a gall barging in on you like this. But that fire escape was damned icy. And you looked so cozy. Like my brother Fred. We used to sleep four in a bed, and he was the only one that ever let me hug him on a cold night. By the way, do you mind if I call you Fred?" She'd come completely into the room now, and she paused there, staring at me. I'd never seen her before not wearing dark glasses, and it was obvious now that they were prescription lenses, for without them her eyes had an assessing squint, like a jeweler's. They were large eyes, a little blue, a little green, dotted with bits of brown: vari-colored, like her hair; and, like her hair, they gave out a lively warm light. "I suppose you think I'm very brazen. Or *très fou*. Or something."

"Not at all."

She seemed disappointed. "Yes, you do. Everybody does. I don't mind. It's useful."

She sat down on one of the rickety red-velvet chairs, curved her legs underneath her, and glanced round the room, her eyes puckering more pronouncedly. "How can you bear it? It's a chamber of horrors."

"Oh, you get used to anything," I said, annoyed with myself, for actually I was proud of the place.

"I don't. I'll never get used to anything. Anybody that does, they might as well be dead." Her dispraising eyes surveyed the room again. "What do you *do* here all day?"

I motioned toward a table tall with books and paper. "Write things."

"I thought writers were quite old. Of course Saroyan isn't old. I met him at a party, and really he isn't old at all. In fact," she mused, "if he'd give himself a closer shave . . . by the way, is Hemingway old?"

"In his forties, I should think."

"That's not bad. I can't get excited by a man until he's forty-two. I know this idiot girl who keeps telling me I ought to go to a head-shrinker; she says I have a father complex. Which is so much *merde*. I simply *trained* myself to like older men, and it was the smartest thing I ever did. How old is W. Somerset Maugham?"

"I'm not sure. Sixty-something."

"That's not bad. I've never been to bed with a writer. No, wait: do you know Benny Shacklett?" She frowned when I shook my head. "That's funny. He's written an awful lot of radio stuff. But quel rat. Tell me, are you a real writer?"

"It depends on what you mean by real."

"Well, darling, does anyone *buy* what you write?"

"Not yet."

"I'm going to help you," she said. "I can, too. Think of all the people I know who know people. I'm going to help you because you look like my brother Fred. Only smaller. I haven't seen him since I was fourteen, that's when I left home, and he was already six-feet-two. My other brothers were more your size, runts. It was the peanut butter that made Fred so tall. Everybody thought it was dotty, the way he gorged himself on peanut butter; he didn't care about anything in this world except horses and pea-nut butter. But he wasn't dotty, just sweet and vague and terribly slow; he'd been in the eighth grade three years when I ran away.

Poor Fred. I wonder if the Army's generous with their peanut butter. Which reminds me, I'm starving."

I pointed to a bowl of apples, at the same time asked her how and why she'd left home so young. She looked at me blankly, and rubbed her nose, as though it tickled: a gesture, seeing often repeated, I came to recognize as a signal that one was trespassing. Like many people with a bold fondness for volunteering intimate information, anything that suggested a direct question, a pinning-down, put her on guard. She took a bite of apple, and said: "Tell me something you've written. The story part."

"That's one of the troubles. They're not the kind of stories you *can* tell."

"Too dirty?"

"Maybe I'll let you read one sometime."

"Whiskey and apples go together. Fix me a drink, darling. Then you can read me a story yourself."

Very few authors, especially the unpublished, can resist an invitation to read aloud. I made us both a drink and, settling in a chair opposite, began to read to her, my voice a little shaky with a combination of stage fright and enthusiasm: it was a new story, I'd finished it the day before, and that inevitable sense of shortcoming had not had time to develop. It was about two women who share a house, schoolteachers, one of whom, when the other becomes engaged, spreads with anonymous notes a scandal that prevents the marriage. As I read, each glimpse I stole of Holly made my heart contract. She fidgeted. She picked apart the butts in an ashtray, she mooned over her fingernails, as though longing for a file; worse, when I did seem to have her interest, there was actually a telltale frost over her eyes, as if she were wondering whether to buy a pair of shoes she'd seen in some window.

"Is that the *end?*" she asked, waking up. She floundered for something more to say. "Of course I like dykes themselves. They don't scare me a bit. But stories about dykes bore the bejesus out of me. I just can't put myself in their shoes. Well really, darling," she said, because I was clearly puzzled, "if it's not about a couple of old bull-dykes, what the hell *is* it about?"

But I was in no mood to compound the mistake of having read the story with the further embarrassment of explaining it. The same vanity that had led to such exposure, now forced me to mark her down as an insensitive, mindless show-off.

"Incidentally," she said, "do you happen to *know* any nice lesbians? I'm looking for a roommate. Well, don't laugh. I'm so disorganized, I simply can't afford a maid; and really, dykes are wonderful homemakers, they love to do all the work, you never have to bother about brooms and defrosting and sending out the laundry. I had a roommate in Hollywood, she played in Westerns, they called her the Lone Ranger; but I'll say this for her, she was better than a man around the house. Of course people couldn't help but think I must be a bit of a dyke myself. And of course I am. Everyone is: a bit. So what? That never discouraged a man yet, in fact it seems to goad them on. Look at the Lone Ranger, married twice. Usually dykes only get married once, just for the name. It seems to carry such cachet later on to be called Mrs. Something Another. That's not true!" She was staring at an alarm clock on the table. "It can't be four-thirty!"

The window was turning blue. A sunrise breeze bandied the curtains.

"What is today?"

"Thursday."

"Thursday." She stood up. "My God," she said, and sat down again with a moan. "It's too gruesome."

I was tired enough not to be curious. I lay down on the bed and closed my eyes. Still it was irresistible: "What's gruesome about Thursday?"

"Nothing. Except that I can never remember when it's coming. You see, on Thursdays I have to catch the eight forty-five. They're so particular about visiting hours, so if you're there by ten that gives you an hour before the poor men eat lunch. Think of it, lunch at eleven. You *can* go at two, and I'd so much rather, but he likes me to come in the morning, he says it sets him up for the rest of the day. I've *got* to stay awake," she said, pinching her cheeks until the roses came, "there isn't time to sleep, I'd look consumptive, I'd sag like a tenement, and that wouldn't be fair: a girl can't go to Sing Sing with a green face."

"I suppose not." The anger I felt at her over my story was ebbing; she absorbed me again.

"All the visitors *do* make an effort to look their best, and it's very tender, it's sweet as hell, the way the women wear their prettiest everything, I mean the old ones and the really poor ones too, they make the dearest effort to look nice and smell nice too, and I love them for it. I love the kids too, especially the colored ones. I mean the kids the wives bring. It should be sad, seeing the kids there, but it isn't, they have ribbons in their hair and lots of shine on their shoes, you'd think there was going to be ice cream; and sometimes that's what it's like in the visitors' room, a party. Anyway it's not like the movies: you know, grim whisperings through a grille. There isn't any grille, just a counter between you and them, and the kids can stand on it to be hugged; all you have to do to kiss somebody is lean across. What I like most, they're so happy to see each other, they've saved up so much to talk about, it isn't possible to be dull, they keep laughing and holding hands. It's different afterwards," she said. "I see them on the train. They sit so quiet watching the river go by." She stretched a strand of hair to the corner of her mouth and nibbled it thoughtfully. "I'm keeping you awake. Go to sleep."

"Please. I'm interested."

"I know you are. That's why I want you to go to sleep. Because if I keep on, I'll tell you about Sally. I'm not sure that would be quite cricket." She chewed her hair silently. "They never *told* me not to tell anyone. In so many words. And it *is* funny. Maybe you could put it in a story with different names and whatnot. Listen, Fred," she said, reaching for another apple, "you've got to cross your heart and kiss your elbow—"

Perhaps contortionists can kiss their elbow; she had to accept an approximation.

"Well," she said, with a mouthful of apple, "you may have read about him in the papers. His name is Sally Tomato, and I speak Yiddish better than he speaks English; but he's a darling old man, terribly pious. He'd look like a monk if it weren't for the gold teeth; he says he prays for me every night. Of course he was never my lover; as far as that goes, I never knew him until he was already in jail. But I adore him now, after all I've been going to see him every Thursday for seven months, and I think I'd go even if he didn't pay me. This one's mushy," she said, and aimed the rest of the apple out the window. "By the way, I *did* know Sally by sight. He used to come to Joe Bell's bar, the one around the corner: never talked to anybody, just stand there, like the kind of man who lives in hotel rooms. But it's funny to remember back and realize how closely he must have been watching me, because right after they sent him up (Joe Bell showed me his picture in the paper. Blackhand. Mafia. All that mumbo jumbo: but they gave him five years) along came this telegram from a lawyer. It said to contact him immediately for information to my advantage."

"You thought somebody had left you a million?"

"Not at all. I figured Bergdorf was trying to collect. But I took the gamble and went to see this lawyer (if he *is* a lawyer, which I doubt, since he doesn't seem to have an office, just an answering service, and he always wants to meet you in Hamburg Heaven: that's because he's fat, he can eat ten hamburgers and two bowls of relish and a whole lemon meringue pie). He asked me how I'd like to cheer up a lonely old man, at the same time pick up a hundred a week. I told him look, darling, you've got the wrong Miss Golightly, I'm not a nurse that does tricks on the side. I wasn't impressed by the honorarium either; you can do as well as that on trips to the powder room: any gent with the slightest chic will give you fifty for the girl's john, and I always ask for cab fare too, that's another fifty. But then he told me his client was Sally Tomato. He said dear old Sally had long admired me *à la distance,* so wouldn't it be a good deed if I went to visit him once a week. Well, I couldn't say no: it was too romantic."

"I don't know. It doesn't sound right."

She smiled. "You think I'm lying?"

"For one thing, they can't simply let *any*one visit a prisoner."

"Oh, they don't. In fact they make quite a boring fuss. I'm supposed to be his niece."

"And it's as simple as that? For an hour's conversation he gives you a hundred dollars?"

"He doesn't, the lawyer does. Mr. O'Shaughnessy mails it to me in cash as soon as I leave the weather report."

"I think you could get into a lot of trouble," I said, and switched off a lamp; there was no need of it now, morning was in the room and pigeons were gargling on the fire escape.

"How?" she said seriously.

"There must be something in the law books about false identity. After all, you're *not* his niece. And what about this weather report?"

She patted a yawn. "But it's nothing. Just messages I leave with the answering service so Mr. O'Shaughnessy will know for sure that I've been up there. Sally tells me what to say, things like, oh, 'there's a hurricane in Cuba' and 'it's snowing in Palermo.' Don't worry, darling," she said, moving to the bed, "I've taken care of myself a long time." The morning light seemed refracted through her: as she pulled the bed covers up to my chin she gleamed like a transparent child; then she lay down beside me. "Do you mind? I only want to rest a moment. So let's don't say another word. Go to sleep."

I pretended to, I made my breathing heavy and regular. Bells in the tower of the next-door church rang the half-hour, the hour. It was six when she put her hand on my arm, a fragile touch careful not to waken. "Poor Fred," she whispered, and it seemed she was speaking to me, but she was not. "Where are you, Fred? Because it's cold. There's snow in the wind." Her cheek came to rest against my shoulder, a warm damp weight.

"Why are you crying?"

She sprang back, sat up. "Oh, for God's sake," she said, starting for the window and the fire escape, "I *hate* snoops."

❧

The next day, Friday, I came home to find outside my door a grand-luxe Charles & Co. basket with her card: *Miss Holiday*

Golightly, Traveling: and scribbled on the back in a freakishly awkward, kindergarten hand: *Bless you darling Fred. Please forgive the other night. You were an angel about the whole thing. Mille tendresse—Holly. P.S. I won't bother you again.* I replied, *Please do,* and left this note at her door with what I could afford, a bunch of street-vendor violets. But apparently she'd meant what she said; I neither saw nor heard from her, and I gathered she'd gone so far as to obtain a downstairs key. At any rate she no longer rang my bell. I missed that; and as the days merged I began to feel toward her certain far-fetched resentments, as if I were being neglected by my closest friend. A disquieting loneliness came into my life, but it induced no hunger for friends of longer acquaintance: they seemed now like a salt-free, sugarless diet. By Wednesday thoughts of Holly, of Sing Sing and Sally Tomato, of worlds where men forked over fifty dollars for the powder room, were so constant that I couldn't work. That night I left a message in her mailbox: *Tomorrow is Thursday.* The next morning rewarded me with a second note in the play-pen script: *Bless you for reminding me. Can you stop for a drink tonight 6-ish?*

I waited until ten past six, then made myself delay five minutes more.

A creature answered the door. He smelled of cigars and Knize cologne. His shoes sported elevated heels; without these added inches, one might have taken him for a Little Person. His bald freckled head was dwarf-big: attached to it were a pair of pointed, truly elfin ears. He had Pekingese eyes, unpitying and slightly bulged. Tufts of hair sprouted from his ears, from his nose; his jowls were gray with afternoon beard, and his handshake almost furry.

"Kid's in the shower," he said, motioning a cigar toward a sound of water hissing in another room. The room in which we stood (we were standing because there was nothing to sit on) seemed as though it were being just moved into; you expected to smell wet paint. Suitcases and unpacked crates were the only furniture. The crates served as tables. One supported the mixings of a martini; another a lamp, a Libertyphone, Holly's red cat and a bowl of yellow roses. Bookcases, covering one wall, boasted a half-shelf of literature. I warmed to the room at once, I liked its fly-by-night look.

The man cleared his throat. "You expected?"

He found my nod uncertain. His cold eyes operated on me, made neat, exploratory incisions. "A lot of characters come here, they're not expected. You know the kid long?"

"Not very."

"So you don't know the kid long?"

"I live upstairs."

The answer seemed to explain enough to relax him. "You got the same layout?"

"Much smaller."

He tapped ash on the floor. "This is a dump. This is unbelievable. But the kid don't know how to live even when she's got the dough." His speech had a jerky metallic rhythm, like a teletype. "So," he said, "what do you think: is she or ain't she?"

"Ain't she what?"

"A phony."

"I wouldn't have thought so."

"You're wrong. She is a phony. But on the other hand you're right. She isn't a phony because she's a *real* phony. She believes all this crap she believes. You can't talk her out of it. I've tried with tears running down my cheeks. Benny Polan, respected everywhere, Benny Polan tried. Benny had it on his mind to marry her, she don't go for it, Benny spent maybe thousands sending her to head-shrinkers. Even the famous one, the one can only speak German, boy, did he throw in the towel. You can't talk her out of these"—he made a fist, as though to crush an intangible—"ideas. Try it sometime. Get her to tell you some of the stuff she believes. Mind you," he said, "I like the kid. Everybody does, but there's lots that don't. I do. I sincerely like the kid. I'm sensitive, that's why. You've got to be sensitive to appreciate her: a streak of the poet. But I'll tell you the truth. You can beat your brains out for her, and she'll hand you horse-shit on a platter. To give an example—who is she like you see her today? She's strictly a girl you'll read where she ends up at the bottom of a bottle of Seconals. I've seen it happen more times than you've got toes: and those kids, they weren't even nuts. She's nuts."

"But young. And with a great deal of youth ahead of her."

"If you mean future, you're wrong again. Now a couple of years back, out on the Coast, there was a time it could've been different. She had something working for her, she had them in-terested, she could've really rolled. But when you walk out on a thing like that, you don't walk back. Ask Luise Rainer. And Rainer was a star. Sure, Holly was no star; she never got out of the still department. But that was before *The Story of Dr. Wassell*. Then she could've really rolled. I know, see, cause I'm the guy was giving her the push." He pointed his cigar at himself. "O.J. Berman."

He expected recognition, and I didn't mind obliging him, it was all right by me, except I'd never heard of O.J. Berman. It developed that he was a Hollywood actor's agent.

"I'm the first one saw her. Out at Santa Anita. She's hanging around the track every day. I'm interested: professionally. I find out she's some jock's regular, she's living with the shrimp. I get the jock told Drop It if he don't want conversation with the vice boys: see, the kid's fifteen. But stylish: she's okay, she comes across. Even when she's wearing glasses *this* thick; even when she opens her mouth and you don't know if she's a hillbilly or an Okie or what. I still don't. My guess, nobody'll ever know where she came from. She's such a goddamn liar, maybe she don't know herself any more. But it took us a year to smooth out that accent. How we did it finally, we gave her French lessons: after she could imitate French, it wasn't so long she could imitate English. We modeled her along the Margaret Sullavan type, but she could pitch some curves of her own, people were interested, big ones, and to top it all, Benny Polan, a respected guy, Benny wants to marry her. An agent could ask for more? Then wham! *The Story of Dr. Wassell.* You see that picture? Cecil B. DeMille. Gary Cooper. Jesus. I kill myself, it's all set: they're going to test her for the part of Dr. Wassell's nurse. One of his nurses, anyway. Then wham! The phone rings." He picked a telephone out of the air and held it to his ear. "She says, this is Holly, I say honey, you sound far away, she says I'm in New York, I say what the hell are you doing in New York when it's Sunday and you got the test tomorrow? She says I'm in New York cause I've never been to New York. I say get your ass on a plane and get back here, she says I don't want it. I say what's your angle, doll? She says you got to want it to be good and I don't want it, I say well, what the hell do you want, and she says when I find out you'll be the first to know. See what I mean: horseshit on a platter."

The red cat jumped off its crate and rubbed against his leg. He lifted the cat on the toe of his shoe and gave him a toss, which was hateful of him except he seemed not aware of the cat but merely his own irritableness.

"*This* is what she wants?" he said, flinging out his arms. "A lot of characters they aren't expected? Living off tips. Running around with bums. So maybe she could marry Rusty Trawler? You should pin a medal on her for that?"

He waited, glaring.

"Sorry, I don't know him."

"You don't know Rusty Trawler, you can't know much about the kid. Bad deal," he said, his tongue clucking in his huge head. "I was hoping you maybe had influence. Could level with the kid before it's too late."

"But according to you, it already is."

He blew a smoke ring, let it fade before he smiled; the smile altered his face, made something gentle happen. "I could get it rolling again. Like I told you," he said, and now it sounded true, "I sincerely like the kid."

"What scandals are you spreading, O.J.?" Holly splashed into the room, a towel more or less wrapped round her and her wet feet dripping footmarks on the floor.

"Just the usual. That you're nuts."

"Fred knows that already."

"But you don't."

"Light me a cigarette, darling," she said, snatching off a bathing cap and shaking her hair. "I don't mean you, O.J. You're such a slob. You always nigger-lip."

She scooped up the cat and swung him onto her shoulder. He perched there with the balance of a bird, his paws tangled in her hair as if it were knitting yarn; and yet, despite these amiable antics, it was a grim cat with a pirate's cutthroat face; one eye was gluey-blind, the other sparkled with dark deeds.

"O.J. is a slob," she told me, taking the cigarette I'd lighted. "But he does know a terrific lot of phone numbers. What's David O. Selznick's number, O.J.?"

"Lay off."

"It's not a joke, darling. I want you to call him up and tell him what a genius Fred is. He's written barrels of the most marvelous stories. Well, don't blush, Fred: you didn't say you were a genius, I did. Come on, O.J. What are you going to do to make Fred rich?"

"Suppose you let me settle that with Fred."

"Remember," she said, leaving us, "I'm his agent. Another thing: if I holler, come zipper me up. And if anybody knocks, let them in."

A multitude did. Within the next quarter-hour a stag party had taken over the apartment, several of them in uniform. I counted two Naval officers and an Air Force colonel; but they were outnumbered by graying arrivals beyond draft status. Except for a lack of youth, the guests had no common theme, they seemed strangers among strangers; indeed, each face, on entering, had struggled to conceal dismay at seeing others there. It was as if the hostess had distributed her invitations while zigzagging through various bars; which was probably the case. After the initial frowns, however, they mixed without grumbling, especially O.J. Berman, who avidly exploited the new company to avoid discussing my Hollywood future. I was left abandoned by the bookshelves; of the books there, more than half were about horses, the rest baseball. Pretending an interest in *Horseflesh and How to Tell It* gave me sufficiently private opportunity for sizing Holly's friends.

Presently one of these became prominent. He was a middle-aged child that had never shed its baby fat, though some gifted tailor had almost succeeded in camouflaging his plump and spankable bottom. There wasn't a suspicion of bone in his body; his face, a zero filled in with pretty miniature features, had an unused, a virginal quality: it was as if he'd been born, then expanded, his skin remaining unlined as a blown-up balloon, and his mouth, though ready for squalls and tantrums, a spoiled sweet puckering. But it was not appearance that singled him out; preserved infants aren't all that rare. It was, rather, his conduct; for he was behaving as though the party were his: like an energetic octopus, he was shaking martinis, making introductions, manipulating the phonograph. In fairness, most of his activities were dictated by the hostess herself: *Rusty, would you mind; Rusty, would you please.* If he was in love with her, then clearly he had his jealousy in check. A jealous man might have lost control, watching her as she skimmed around the room, carrying her cat in one hand but leaving the other free to straighten a tie or remove lapel lint; the Air Force colonel wore a medal that came in for quite a polish.

The man's name was Rutherfurd ("Rusty") Trawler. In 1908 he'd lost both his parents, his father the victim of an anarchist and his mother of shock, which double misfortune had made Rusty an orphan, a millionaire, and a celebrity, all at the age of five. He'd been a stand-by of the Sunday supplements ever since, a consequence that had gathered hurricane momentum when, still a schoolboy, he had caused his godfather-custodian to be arrested on charges of sodomy. After that, marriage and divorce sustained his place in the tabloid-sun. His first wife had taken herself, and her alimony, to a rival of Father Divine's. The second wife seems unaccounted for, but the third had sued him in New York State with a full satchel of the kind of testimony that entails. He himself divorced the last Mrs. Trawler, his principal complaint stating that she'd started a mutiny aboard his yacht, said mutiny resulting in his being deposited on the Dry Tortugas. Though he'd been a bachelor since, apparently before the war he'd proposed to Unity Mitford, at least he was supposed to have sent her a cable offering to marry her if Hitler didn't. This was said to be the reason Winchell always referred to him as a Nazi; that, and the fact that he attended rallies in Yorkville.

I was not told these things. I read them in *The Baseball Guide*, another selection off Holly's shelf which she seemed to use for a scrapbook. Tucked between the pages were Sunday features, together with scissored snippings from gossip columns. *Rusty Trawler and Holly Golightly two-on-the-aisle at "One Touch of Venus" preem.* Holly came up from behind, and caught me reading: *Miss Holiday Golightly, of the Boston Golightlys, making every day a holiday for the 24-karat Rusty Trawler.*

"Admiring my publicity, or are you just a baseball fan?" she said, adjusting her dark glasses as she glanced over my shoulder.

I said, "What was this week's weather report?"

She winked at me, but it was humorless: a wink of warning, "I'm all for horses, but I loathe baseball," she said, and the sub-message in her voice was saying she wished me to forget she'd ever mentioned Sally Tomato. "I hate the sound of it on a radio, but I have to listen, it's part of my research. There're so few things men can talk about. If a man doesn't like baseball, then he must like horses, and if he doesn't like either of them, well, I'm in trouble anyway: he don't like girls. And how are you making out with O.J.?"

"We've separated by mutual agreement."

"He's an opportunity, believe me."

"I do believe you. But what have I to offer that would strike him as an opportunity?"

She persisted. "Go over there and make him think he isn't funny-looking. He really can help you, Fred."

"I understand you weren't too appreciative." She seemed puzzled until I said: *"The Story of Doctor Wassell."*

"He's still harping?" she said, and cast across the room an affectionate look at Berman. "But he's got a point, I *should* feel guilty. Not because they would have given me the part or because I would have been good: they wouldn't and I wouldn't. If I do feel guilty, I guess it's because I let him go on dreaming when I wasn't dreaming a bit. I was just vamping for time to make a few self-improvements: I knew damn well I'd never be a movie star. It's too hard; and if you're intelligent, it's too embarrassing. My complexes aren't inferior enough: being a movie star and having a big fat ego are supposed to go hand-in-hand; actually, it's essential not to have any ego at all. I don't mean I'd mind being rich and famous. That's very much on my schedule, and someday I'll try to get around to it; but if it happens, I'd like to have my ego tagging along. I want to still be me when I wake up one fine morning and have breakfast at Tiffany's. You need a glass," she said, noticing my empty hands. "Rusty! Will you bring my friend a drink?"

She was still hugging the cat. "Poor slob," she said, tickling his head, "poor slob without a name. It's a little inconvenient, his not having a name. But I haven't any right to give him one: he'll have to wait until he *belongs* to somebody. We just sort of took up by the river one day, we don't belong to each other: he's an independent, and so am I. I don't want to own anything until I know I've found the place where me and things belong together. I'm not quite sure where that is just yet. But I know what it's like." She smiled, and let the cat drop to the floor. "It's like Tiffany's," she said. "Not that I give a hoot about jewelry. Diamonds, yes. But it's tacky to wear diamonds before you're forty; and even that's risky. They only look right on the really old girls. Maria Ouspenskaya. Wrinkles and bones, white hair and diamonds: I can't wait. But that's not why I'm mad about Tiffany's. Listen. You know those days when you've got the mean reds?"

"Same as the blues?"

"No," she said slowly. "No, the blues are because you're getting fat or maybe it's been raining too long. You're sad, that's all. But the mean reds are horrible. You're afraid and you sweat like hell, but you don't know what you're afraid of. Except something bad is going to happen, only you don't know what it is. You've had that feeling?"

"Quite often. Some people call it *angst*."

"All right. *Angst*. But what do you do about it?"

"Well, a drink helps."

"I've tried that. I've tried aspirin, too. Rusty thinks I should smoke marijuana, and I did for a while, but it only makes me giggle. What I've found does the most good is just to get into a taxi and go to Tiffany's. It calms me down right away, the quietness and the proud look of it; nothing very bad could happen to you there, not with those kind men in their nice suits, and that lovely smell of silver and alligator wallets. If I could find a real-life place that made me feel like Tiffany's, then I'd buy some furniture and give the cat a name. I've thought maybe after the war, Fred and I—" She pushed up her dark glasses, and her eyes, the differing colors of them, the grays and wisps of blue and green, had taken on a far-seeing sharpness. "I went to

Mexico once. It's wonderful country for raising horses. I saw one place near the sea. Fred's good with horses."

Rusty Trawler came carrying a martini; he handed it over without looking at me. "I'm hungry," he announced, and his voice, retarded as the rest of him, produced an unnerving brat-whine that seemed to blame Holly. "It's seven-thirty, and I'm hungry. You know what the doctor said."

"Yes, Rusty. I know what the doctor said."

"Well, then break it up. Let's go."

"I want you to behave, Rusty." She spoke softly, but there was a governess threat of punishment in her tone that caused an odd flush of pleasure, of gratitude, to pink his face.

"You don't love me," he complained, as though they were alone.

"Nobody loves naughtiness."

Obviously she'd said what he wanted to hear; it appeared to both excite and relax him. Still he continued, as though it were a ritual: "Do you love me?"

She patted him. "Tend to your chores, Rusty. And when I'm ready, we'll go eat wherever you want."

"Chinatown?"

"But that doesn't mean sweet and sour spareribs. You know what the doctor said."

As he returned to his duties with a satisfied waddle, I couldn't resist reminding her that she hadn't answered his question. "*Do you love him?*"

"I told you: you can make yourself love anybody. Besides, he had a stinking childhood."

"If it was so stinking, why does he cling to it?"

"Use your head. Can't you see it's just that Rusty feels safer in diapers than he would in a skirt? Which is really the choice, only he's awfully touchy about it. He tried to stab me with a butter knife because I told him to grow up and face the issue, settle down and play house with a nice fatherly truck driver. Meantime, I've got him on my hands; which is okay, he's harmless, he thinks girls are dolls literally."

"Thank God."

"Well, if it were true of most men, I'd hardly be thanking God."

"I meant thank God you're not going to marry Mr. Trawler."

She lifted an eyebrow. "By the way, I'm not pretending I don't know he's rich. Even land in Mexico costs something. Now," she said, motioning me forward, "let's get hold of O.J."

I held back while my mind worked to win a postponement. Then I remembered: "Why *Traveling?*"

"On my card?" she said, disconcerted. "You think it's funny?"

"Not funny. Just provocative."

She shrugged. "After all, how do I know where I'll be living tomorrow? So I told them to put *Traveling*. Anyway, it was a waste of money, ordering those cards. Except I felt I owed it to them to buy some little *some*thing. They're from Tiffany's." She reached for my martini, I hadn't touched it; she drained it in two swallows, and took my hand. "Quit stalling. You're going to make friends with O.J."

An occurrence at the door intervened. It was a young woman, and she entered like a wind-rush, a squall of scarves and jangling gold. "H-H-Holly," she said, wagging a finger as she advanced, "you miserable h-h-hoarder. Hogging all these simply r-r-riveting m-m-men!"

She was well over six feet, taller than most men there. They straightened their spines, sucked in their stomachs; there was a general contest to match her swaying height.

Holly said, "What are you doing here?" and her lips were taut as drawn string.

"Why, n-n-nothing, sugar. I've been upstairs working with Yunioshi. Christmas stuff for the *Ba-ba-zaar*. But you sound vexed, sugar?" She scattered a roundabout smile. "You b-b-boys not vexed at me for butting in on your p-p-party?"

Rusty Trawler tittered. He squeezed her arm, as though to admire her muscle, and asked her if she could use a drink.

"I surely could," she said. "Make mine bourbon."

Holly told her, "There *isn't* any." Whereupon the Air Force colonel suggested he run out for a bottle.

"Oh, I declare, don't let's have a f-f-fuss. I'm happy with ammonia. Holly, honey," she said, slightly shoving her, "don't you bother about me. I can introduce myself." She stooped toward O.J. Berman, who, like many short men in the presence of tall women, had an aspiring mist in his eye. "I'm Mag W-w-wildwood, from Wild-w-w-wood, Arkansas. That's hill country."

It seemed a dance, Berman performing some fancy footwork to prevent his rivals cutting in. He lost her to a quadrille of partners who gobbled up her stammered jokes like popcorn tossed to pigeons. It was a comprehensible success. She was a triumph over ugliness, so often more beguiling than real beauty, if only because it contains paradox. In this case, as opposed to the scrupulous method of plain good taste and scientific grooming, the trick had been worked by exaggerating defects; she'd made them ornamental by admitting them boldly. Heels that emphasized her height, so steep her ankles trembled; a flat tight bodice that indicated she could go to a beach in bathing trunks; hair that was pulled straight back, accentuating the spareness, the starvation of her fashion-model face. Even the stutter, certainly genuine but still a bit laid on, had been turned to advantage. It was the master stroke, that stutter; for it contrived to make her banalities sound somehow original, and secondly, despite her tallness, her assurance, it served to inspire in male listeners a protective feeling. To illustrate: Berman had to be pounded on the back because she said, "Who can tell me w-w-where is the j-j-john?"; then, completing the cycle, he offered an arm to guide her himself.

"That," said Holly, "won't be necessary. She's been here before. She knows where it is." She was emptying ashtrays, and after Mag Wildwood had left the room, she emptied another, then said, sighed rather: "It's really very sad." She paused long enough to calculate the number of inquiring expressions; it was sufficient. "And so mysterious. You'd think it would show more. But heaven knows, she *looks* healthy. So, well, *clean.* That's the extraordinary part. Wouldn't you," she asked with concern, but of no one in particular, "wouldn't you say she *looked* clean?"

Someone coughed, several swallowed. A Naval officer, who had been holding Mag Wildwood's drink, put it down.

"But then," said Holly, "I hear so many of these Southern girls have the same trouble." She shuddered delicately, and went to the kitchen for more ice.

Mag Wildwood couldn't understand it, the abrupt absence of warmth on her return; the conversations she began behaved like green logs, they fumed but would not fire. More unforgivably, people were leaving without taking her telephone number. The Air Force colonel decamped while her back was turned, and this was the straw too much: he'd asked her to dinner. Suddenly she was blind. And since gin to artifice bears the same relation as tears to mascara, her attractions at once dissembled. She took it out on everyone. She called her hostess a Hollywood degenerate. She invited a man in his fifties to fight. She told Berman,

Hitler was right. She exhilarated Rusty Trawler by stiff-arming him into a corner. "You know what's going to happen to you?" she said, with no hint of a stutter. "I'm going to march you over to the zoo and feed you to the yak." He looked altogether willing, but she disappointed him by sliding to the floor, where she sat humming.

"You're a bore. Get up from there," Holly said, stretching on a pair of gloves. The remnants of the party were waiting at the door, and when the bore didn't budge Holly cast me an apologetic glance. "Be an angel, would you, Fred? Put her in a taxi. She lives at the Winslow."

"Don't. Live Barbizon. Regent 4-5700. Ask for Mag Wildwood."

"You *are* an angel, Fred."

They were gone. The prospect of steering an Amazon into a taxi obliterated whatever resentment I felt. But she solved the problem herself. Rising on her own steam, she stared down at me with a lurching loftiness. She said, "Let's go Stork. Catch lucky balloon," and fell full-length like an axed oak. My first thought was to run for a doctor. But examination proved her pulse fine and her breathing regular. She was simply asleep. After finding a pillow for her head, I left her to enjoy it.

The following afternoon I collided with Holly on the stairs. *"You"* she said, hurrying past with a package from the druggist. "There she is, on the verge of pneumonia. A hang-over out to here. And the mean reds on top of it." I gathered from this that Mag Wildwood was still in the apartment, but she gave me no chance to explore her surprising sympathy. Over the weekend, mystery deepened. First, there was the Latin who came to my door: mistakenly, for he was inquiring after Miss Wildwood. It took a while to correct his error, our accents seemed mutually incoherent, but by the time we had I was charmed. He'd been put together with care, his brown head and bullfighter's figure had an exactness, a perfection, like an apple, an orange, something nature has made just right. Added to this, as decoration, were an English suit and a brisk cologne and, what is still more unlatin, a bashful manner. The second event of the day involved him again. It was toward evening, and I saw him on my way out to dinner. He was arriving in a taxi; the driver helped him totter into the house with a load of suitcases. That gave me something to chew on: by Sunday my jaws were quite tired.

Then the picture became both darker and clearer.

Sunday was an Indian summer day, the sun was strong, my window was open, and I heard voices on the fire escape. Holly and Mag were sprawled there on a blanket, the cat between them. Their hair, newly washed, hung lankly. They were busy, Holly varnishing her toenails, Mag knitting on a sweater. Mag was speaking.

"If you ask me, I think you're l-l-lucky. At least there's one thing you can say for Rusty. He's an American."

"Bully for him."

"*Sugar.* There's a war on."

"And when it's over, you've seen the last of me, boy."

"I don't feel that way. I'm p-p-proud of my country. The men in my family were great soldiers. There's a statue of Papadaddy Wildwood smack in the center of Wildwood."

"Fred's a soldier," said Holly. "But I doubt if he'll ever be a statue. Could be. They say the more stupid you are the braver. He's pretty stupid."

"Fred's that boy upstairs? I didn't realize he was a soldier. But he *does* look stupid."

"Yearning. Not stupid. He wants awfully to be on the inside staring out: anybody with their nose pressed against a glass is liable to look stupid. Anyhow, he's a different Fred. Fred's my brother."

"You call your own f-f-flesh and b-b-blood stupid?"

"If he is he is."

"Well, it's poor taste to say so. A boy that's fighting for you and me and all of us."

"What is this: a bond rally?"

"I just want you to know where I stand. I appreciate a joke, but underneath I'm a s-s-serious person. Proud to be an American. That's why I'm sorry about José." She put down her knitting needles. "You *do* think he's terribly good-looking, don't you?" Holly said Hmn, and swiped the cat's whiskers with her lacquer brush. "If only I could get used to the idea of m-m-marrying a Brazilian. And *being* a B-b-brazilian myself. It's such a canyon to cross. Six thousand miles, and not knowing the language—"

"Go to Berlitz."

"Why on earth would they be teaching P-p-portuguese? It isn't as though anyone spoke it. No, my only chance is to try and make José forget politics and become an American. It's such a useless thing for a man to want to be: the p-p-president of *Brazil*." She sighed and picked up her knitting. "I must be madly in love. You saw us together. Do you think I'm madly in love?"

"Well. Does he bite?"

Mag dropped a stitch. "Bite?"

"You. In bed."

"Why, no. *Should* he?" Then she added, censoriously: "But he does laugh."

"Good. That's the right spirit. I like a man who sees the humor; most of them, they're all pant and puff."

Mag withdrew her complaint; she accepted the comment as flattery reflecting on herself. "Yes. I suppose."

"Okay. He doesn't bite. He laughs. What else?"

Mag counted up her dropped stitch and began again, knit, purl, purl.

"I said—"

"I heard you. And it isn't that I don't want to tell you. But it's so difficult to remember. I don't d-d-dwell on these things. The way you seem to. They go out of my head like a dream. I'm sure that's the n-n-normal attitude."

"It may be normal, darling; but I'd rather be natural." Holly paused in the process of reddening the rest of the cat's whiskers. "Listen. If you can't remember, try leaving the lights on."

"Please understand me, Holly. I'm a very-very-very *conventional* person."

"Oh, balls. What's wrong with a decent look at a guy you like? Men are beautiful, a lot of them are, José is, and if you don't even want to *look* at him, well, I'd say he's getting a pretty cold plate of macaroni."

"L-l-lower your voice."

"You can't possibly be in love with him. Now. Does that answer your question?"

"No. Because I'm not a cold plate of m-m-macaroni. I'm a warm-hearted person. It's the basis of my character."

"Okay. You've got a warm heart. But if I were a man on my way to bed, I'd rather take along a hot-water bottle. It's more tangible."

"You won't hear any squawks out of José," she said complacently, her needles flashing in the sunlight. "What's more, I *am* in love with him. Do you realize I've knitted ten pairs of Argyles in less than three months? And this is the second sweater." She stretched the sweater and tossed it aside. "What's the point, though? Sweaters in Brazil. I ought to be making s-s-sun helmets."

Holly lay back and yawned. "It must be winter sometime."

"It *rains,* that I know. Heat. Rain. J-j-jungles."

"Heat. Jungles. Actually, I'd like that."

"Better you than me."

"Yes," said Holly, with a sleepiness that was not sleepy. "Better me than you."

❦

On Monday, when I went down for the morning mail, the card on Holly's box had been altered, a name added: Miss Golightly and Miss Wildwood were now traveling together. This might have held my interest longer except for a letter in my own mailbox. It was from a small university review to whom I'd sent a story. They liked it; and, though I must understand they could not afford to pay, they intended to publish. Publish: that meant *print*. Dizzy with excitement is no mere phrase. I had to tell someone: and, taking the stairs two at a time, I pounded on Holly's door.

I didn't trust my voice to tell the news; as soon as she came to the door, her eyes squinty with sleep, I thrust the letter at her. It seemed as though she'd had time to read sixty pages before she handed it back. "I wouldn't let them do it, not if they don't pay you," she said, yawning. Perhaps my face explained she'd misconstrued, that I'd not wanted advice but congratulations: her mouth shifted from a yawn into a smile. "Oh, I see. It's wonderful. Well, come in," she said. "We'll make a pot of coffee and celebrate. No. I'll get dressed and take you to lunch."

Her bedroom was consistent with her parlor: it perpetuated the same camping-out atmosphere; crates and suitcases, everything packed and ready to go, like the belongings of a criminal who feels the law not far behind. In the parlor there was no conventional furniture, but the bedroom had the bed itself, a double one at that, and quite flashy: blond wood, tufted satin.

She left the door of the bathroom open, and conversed from there; between the flushing and the brushing, most of what she said was unintelligible, but the gist of it was: she *supposed* I knew Mag Wildwood had moved in, and wasn't that *convenient?* because if you're going to *have* a roommate, and she *isn't* a dyke, then the next best thing is a *perfect* fool, which Mag *was,* because then you can dump the lease on them *and* send them out for the laundry.

One could see that Holly had a laundry problem; the room was strewn, like a girl's gymnasium.

"—and you know, she's quite a successful model: isn't that *fan*tastic? But a good thing," she said, hobbling out of the bathroom as she adjusted a garter. "It ought to keep her out of my hair most of the day. And there shouldn't be too much trouble on the man front. She's engaged. Nice guy, too. Though there's a tiny difference in height: I'd say a foot, her favor. Where the hell—" She was on her knees poking under the bed. After she'd found what she was looking for, a pair of lizard shoes, she had to search for a blouse, a belt, and it was a subject to ponder, how, from such wreckage, she evolved the eventual effect: pampered, calmly immaculate, as though she'd been attended by Cleopatra's maids. She said, "Listen," and cupped her hand under my chin, "I'm glad about the story. Really I am."

That Monday in October, 1943. A beautiful day with the buoyancy of a bird. To start, we had Manhattans at Joe Bell's; and, when he heard of my good luck, champagne cocktails on the house. Later, we wandered toward Fifth Avenue, where there was a parade. The flags in the wind, the thump of military bands and military feet, seemed to have nothing to do with war, but to be, rather, a fanfare arranged in my personal honor.

We ate lunch at the cafeteria in the park. Afterwards, avoiding the zoo (Holly said she couldn't bear to see anything in a cage), we giggled, ran, sang along the paths toward the old wooden boathouse, now gone. Leaves floated on the lake; on the shore, a park-man was fanning a bonfire of them, and the smoke, rising like Indian signals, was the only smudge on the quivering air. Aprils have never meant much to me, autumns seem that season of beginning, spring; which is how I felt sitting with Holly on the railings of the boathouse porch. I thought of the future, and spoke of the past. Because Holly wanted to know about my childhood. She talked of her own, too; but it was elusive, nameless, placeless, an impressionistic recital, though the impression received was contrary to what one expected, for she gave an almost voluptuous account of swimming and summer, Christmas trees, pretty cousins and parties: in short, happy in a way that she was not, and never, certainly, the background of a child who had run away.

Or, I asked, wasn't it true that she'd been out on her own since she was fourteen? She rubbed her nose. "That's true. The other isn't. But really, darling, you made such a tragedy out of *your* childhood I didn't feel I should compete."

She hopped off the railing. "Anyway, it reminds me: I ought to send Fred some peanut butter." The rest of the afternoon we were east and west worming out of reluctant grocers cans of peanut butter, a wartime scarcity; dark came before we'd rounded up a half-dozen jars, the last at a delicatessen on Third Avenue. It was near the antique shop with the palace of a bird cage in its window, so I took her there to see it, and she enjoyed the point, its fantasy: "But still, it's a cage."

Passing a Woolworth's, she gripped my arm: "Let's steal something," she said, pulling me into the store, where at once there seemed a pressure of eyes, as though we were already under suspicion. "Come on. Don't be chicken." She scouted a counter piled with paper pumpkins and Halloween masks. The saleslady was occupied with a group of nuns who were trying on masks. Holly picked up a mask and slipped it over her face; she chose another and put it on mine; then she took my hand and we walked away. It was as simple as that. Outside, we ran a few blocks, I think to make it more dramatic; but also because, as I'd discovered, successful theft exhilarates. I wondered if she'd often stolen. "I used to," she said. "I mean I had to. If I wanted anything. But I still do it every now and then, sort of to keep my hand in."

We wore the masks all the way home.

I have a memory of spending many hither and yonning days with Holly; and it's true, we did at odd moments see a great deal of each other; but on the whole, the memory is false. Because toward the end of the month I found a job: what is there to add?

The less the better, except to say it was necessary and lasted from nine to five. Which made our hours, Holly's and mine, extremely different.

Unless it was Thursday, her Sing Sing day, or unless she'd gone horseback riding in the park, as she did occasionally, Holly was hardly up when I came home. Sometimes, stopping there, I shared her wake-up coffee while she dressed for the evening. She was forever on her way out, not always with Rusty Trawler, but usually, and usually, too, they were joined by Mag Wildwood and the handsome Brazilian, whose name was José Ybarra-Jaegar: his mother was German. As a quartet, they struck an unmusical note, primarily the fault of Ybarra-Jaegar, who seemed as out of place in their company as a violin in a jazz band. He was intelligent, he was presentable, he appeared to have a serious link with his work, which was obscurely governmental, vaguely important, and took him to Washington several days a week. How, then, could he survive night after night in La Rue, El Morocco, listening to the Wildwood ch-ch-chatter and staring into Rusty's raw baby-buttocks face? Perhaps, like most of us in a foreign country, he was incapable of placing people, selecting a frame for their picture, as he would at home; therefore all Americans had to be judged in a pretty equal light, and on this basis his companions appeared to be tolerable examples of local color and national character. That would explain much; Holly's determination explains the rest.

Late one afternoon, while waiting for a Fifth Avenue bus, I noticed a taxi stop across the street to let out a girl who ran up the steps of the Forty-second Street public library. She was through the doors before I recognized her, which was pardonable, for Holly and libraries were not an easy association to make. I let curiosity guide me between the lions, debating on the way whether I should admit following her or pretend coincidence. In the end I did neither, but concealed myself some tables away from her in the general reading room, where she sat behind her dark glasses and a fortress of literature she'd gathered at the desk. She sped from one book to the next, intermittently lingering on a page, always with a frown, as if it were printed upside down. She had a pencil poised above paper—nothing seemed to catch her fancy, still now and then, as though for the hell of it, she made laborious scribblings. Watching her, I remembered a girl I'd known in school, a grind, Mildred Grossman. Mildred: with her moist hair and greasy spectacles, her stained fingers that dissected frogs and carried coffee to picket lines, her flat eyes that only turned toward the stars to estimate their chemical tonnage. Earth and air could not be more opposite than Mildred and Holly, yet in my head they acquired a Siamese twinship, and the thread of thought that had sewn them together ran like this: the average personality reshapes frequently, every few years even our bodies undergo a complete overhaul—desirable or not, it is a natural thing that we should change. All right, here were two people who never would. That is what Mildred Grossman had in common with Holly Golightly. They would never change because they'd been given their character too soon; which, like sudden riches, leads to a lack of proportion: the one had splurged herself into a top-heavy realist, the other a lopsided romantic. I imagined them in a restaurant of the future, Mildred still studying the menu for its nutritional values, Holly still gluttonous for everything on it. It would never be different. They would walk through life and out of it with the same determined step that took small notice of those cliffs at the left. Such profound observations made me forget where I was; I came to, startled to find myself in the gloom of the library, and surprised all over again to see Holly there. It was after seven, she was freshening her lipstick and perking up her appearance from what she deemed correct for a library to what, by adding a bit of scarf, some earrings, she considered suitable for the Colony. When she'd left, I wandered over to the table where her books remained; they were what I had wanted to see. *South by Thunderbird. Byways of Brazil. The Political Mind of Latin America.* And so forth.

On Christmas Eve she and Mag gave a party. Holly asked me to come early and help trim the tree. I'm still not sure how they maneuvered that tree into the apartment. The top branches were crushed against the ceiling, the lower ones spread wall-to-wall; altogether it was not unlike the yuletide giant we see in Rockefeller Plaza. Moreover, it would have taken a Rockefeller to decorate it, for it soaked up baubles and tinsel like melting snow. Holly suggested she run out to Woolworth's and steal some balloons; she did: and they turned the tree into a fairly good show. We made a toast to our work, and Holly said: "Look in the bedroom. There's a present for you."

I had one for her, too: a small package in my pocket that felt even smaller when I saw, square on the bed and wrapped with a red ribbon, the beautiful bird cage.

"But, Holly! It's dreadful!"

"I couldn't agree more; but I thought you wanted it."

"The money! Three hundred and fifty dollars!"

She shrugged. "A few extra trips to the powder room. Promise me, though. Promise you'll never put a living thing in it."

I started to kiss her, but she held out her hand. "Gimme," she said, tapping the bulge in my pocket.

"I'm afraid it isn't much," and it wasn't: a St. Christopher's medal. But at least it came from Tiffany's.

❧❀❧

Holly was not a girl who could keep anything, and surely by now she has lost that medal, left it in a suitcase or some hotel drawer. But the bird cage is still mine. I've lugged it to New Orleans, Nantucket, all over Europe, Morocco, the West Indies. Yet I seldom remember that it was Holly who gave it to me, because at one point I chose to forget: we had a big falling-out, and among the objects rotating in the eye of our hurricane were the bird cage and O.J. Berman and my story, a copy of which I'd given Holly when it appeared in the university review.

Sometime in February, Holly had gone on a winter trip with Rusty, Mag and José Ybarra-Jaegar. Our altercation happened soon after she returned. She was brown as iodine, her hair was sun-bleached to a ghost-color, she'd had a wonderful time: "Well, first of all we were in Key West, and Rusty got mad at some sailors, or vice versa, *any*way he'll have to wear a spine brace the rest of his life. Dearest Mag ended up in the hospital, too. First-degree sunburn. Disgusting: all blisters and citronella. We couldn't stand the smell of her. So José and I left them in the hospital and went to Havana. He says wait till I see Rio; but as far as I'm concerned Havana can take my money right now. We had an irresistible guide, most of him Negro and the rest of him Chinese, and while I don't go much for one or the other, the combination was fairly riveting: so I let him play kneesie under the table, because frankly I didn't find him at all banal; but then one night he took us to a blue movie, and what do you suppose? There *he* was *on* the screen. Of course when we got back to Key West, Mag was positive I'd spent the whole time sleeping with José. So was Rusty: but he doesn't care about that, he simply wants to hear the details. Actually, things were pretty tense until I had a heart-to-heart with Mag."

We were in the front room, where, though it was now nearly March, the enormous Christmas tree, turned brown and scentless, its balloons shriveled as an old cow's dugs, still occupied most of the space. A recognizable piece of furniture had been added to the room: an army cot; and Holly, trying to preserve her tropic look, was sprawled on it under a sun lamp.

"And you convinced her?"

"That I hadn't slept with José? God, yes. I simply told—but you know: made it sound like an *ag*onized confession—simply told her I was a dyke."

"She couldn't have believed that."

"The hell she didn't. Why do you think she went out and bought this army cot? Leave it to me: I'm always top banana in the shock department. Be a darling, darling, rub some oil on my back." While I was performing this service, she said: "O.J. Berman's in town, and listen, I gave him your story in the magazine. He was quite impressed. He thinks maybe you're worth helping. But he says you're on the wrong track. Negroes and children: who cares?"

"Not Mr. Berman, I gather."

"Well, I agree with him. I read that story twice. Brats and niggers. Trembling leaves. *Description.* It doesn't *mean* anything."

My hand, smoothing oil on her skin, seemed to have a temper of its own: it yearned to raise itself and come down on her buttocks. "Give me an example," I said quietly. "Of something that means something. In your opinion."

"*Wuthering Heights,*" she said, without hesitation.

The urge in my hand was growing beyond control. "But that's unreasonable. You're talking about a work of genius."

"It was, wasn't it? *My wild sweet Cathy*. God, I cried buckets. I saw it ten times."

I said, "Oh" with recognizable relief, "oh" with a shameful, rising inflection, "the *movie*."

Her muscles hardened, the touch of her was like stone warmed by the sun. "Everybody has to feel superior to somebody," she said. "But it's customary to present a little proof before you take the privilege."

"I don't compare myself to you. Or Berman. Therefore I can't feel superior. We want different things."

"Don't you want to make money?"

"I haven't planned that far."

"That's how your stories sound. As though you'd written them without knowing the end. Well, I'll tell you: you'd better make money. You have an expensive imagination. Not many people are going to buy you bird cages."

"Sorry."

"You will be if you hit me. You wanted to a minute ago: I could feel it in your hand; and you want to now."

I did, terribly; my hand, my heart was shaking as I recapped the bottle of oil. "Oh no, I wouldn't regret that. I'm only sorry you wasted your money on me: Rusty Trawler is too hard a way of earning it."

She sat up on the army cot, her face, her naked breasts coldly blue in the sun-lamp light. "It should take you about four seconds to walk from here to the door. I'll give you two."

I went straight upstairs, got the bird cage, took it down and left it in front of her door. That settled that. Or so I imagined until the next morning when, as I was leaving for work, I saw the cage perched on a sidewalk ashcan waiting for the garbage collector. Rather sheepishly, I rescued it and carried it back to my room, a capitulation that did not lessen my resolve to put Holly Golightly absolutely out of my life. She was, I decided, "a crude exhibitionist," "a time waster," "an utter fake": someone never to be spoken to again.

And I didn't. Not for a long while. We passed each other on the stairs with lowered eyes. If she walked into Joe Bell's, I walked out. At one point, Madame Sapphia Spanella, the coloratura and roller-skating enthusiast who lived on the first floor, circulated a petition among the brownstone's other tenants asking them to join her in having Miss Golightly evicted: she was, said Madame Spanella, "morally objectionable" and the "perpetrator of all-night gatherings that endanger the safety and sanity of her neighbors." Though I refused to sign, secretly I felt Madame Spanella had cause to complain. But her petition failed, and as April approached May, the open-windowed, warm spring nights were lurid with the party sounds, the loud-playing phonograph and martini laughter that emanated from Apt. 2.

It was no novelty to encounter suspicious specimens among Holly's callers, quite the contrary; but one day late that spring, while passing through the brownstone's vestibule, I noticed a *very* provocative man examining her mailbox. A person in his early fifties with a hard, weathered face, gray forlorn eyes. He wore an old sweat-stained gray hat, and his cheap summer suit, a pale blue, hung too loosely on his lanky frame; his shoes were brown and brand-new. He seemed to have no intention of ringing Holly's bell. Slowly, as though he were reading Braille, he kept rubbing a finger across the embossed lettering of her name.

That evening, on my way to supper, I saw the man again. He was standing across the street, leaning against a tree and staring up at Holly's windows. Sinister speculations rushed through my head. Was he a detective? Or some underworld agent connected with her Sing Sing friend, Sally Tomato? The situation revived my tenderer feelings for Holly; it was only fair to interrupt our feud long enough to warn her that she was being watched. As I walked to the corner, heading east toward the Hamburg Heaven at Seventy-ninth and Madison, I could feel the man's attention focused on me. Presently, without turning my head, I knew that he was following me. Because I could hear him whistling. Not any ordinary tune, but the plaintive, prairie melody Holly sometimes played on her guitar: *Don't wanna sleep, don't wanna die, just wanna go a-travelin' through the pastures of the sky.* The whistling continued across Park Avenue and up Madison. Once, while waiting for a traffic light to change, I watched him out of the corner of my eye as he stooped to pet a sleazy Pomeranian. "That's a fine animal you got there," he told the owner in a hoarse, countrified drawl.

Hamburg Heaven was empty. Nevertheless, he took a seat right beside me at the long counter. He smelled of tobacco and sweat. He ordered a cup of coffee, but when it came he didn't touch it. Instead, he chewed on a toothpick and studied me in the wall mirror facing us.

"Excuse me," I said, speaking to him via the mirror, "but what do you want?"

The question didn't embarrass him; he seemed relieved to have had it asked. "Son," he said, "I need a friend."

He brought out a wallet. It was as worn as his leathery hands, almost falling to pieces; and so was the brittle, cracked, blurred snapshot he handed me. There were seven people in the picture, all grouped together on the sagging porch of a stark wooden house, and all children, except for the man himself, who had his arm around the waist of a plump blond little girl with a hand shading her eyes against the sun.

"That's me," he said, pointing at himself. "That's her . . ." he tapped the plump girl. "And this one over here," he added, indicating a tow-headed beanpole, "that's her brother, Fred."

I looked at "her" again: and yes, now I could see it, an embryonic resemblance to Holly in the squinting, fat-cheeked child. At the same moment, I realized who the man must be.

"You're Holly's *father*."

He blinked, he frowned. "Her name's not Holly. She was a Lulamae Barnes. Was," he said, shifting the toothpick in his mouth, "till she married me. I'm her husband. Doc Golightly. I'm a horse doctor, animal man. Do some farming, too. Near Tulip, Texas. Son, why are you laughin'?"

It wasn't real laughter: it was nerves. I took a swallow of water and choked; he pounded me on the back. "This here's no humorous matter, son. I'm a tired man. I've been five years lookin' for my woman. Soon as I got that letter from Fred, saying where she was, I bought myself a ticket on the Greyhound. Lulamae belongs home with her husband and her churren."

"Children?"

"*Them's* her churren," he said, almost shouted. He meant the four other young faces in the picture, two barefooted girls and a pair of overalled boys. Well, of course: the man was deranged. "But Holly can't be the mother of those children. They're older than she is. Bigger."

"Now, son," he said in a reasoning voice, "I didn't claim they was her natural-born churren. Their own precious mother, precious woman, Jesus rest her soul, she passed away July 4th, Independence Day, 1936. The year of the drought. When I married Lulamae, that was in December, 1938, she was going on fourteen. Maybe an ordinary person, being only fourteen, wouldn't know their right mind. But you take Lulamae, she was an exceptional woman. She knew good-and-well what she was doing when she promised to be my wife and the mother of my churren. She plain broke our hearts when she ran off like she done." He sipped his cold coffee, and glanced at me with a searching earnestness. "Now, son, do you doubt me? Do you believe what I'm saying is so?"

I did. It was too implausible not to be fact; moreover, it dovetailed with O.J. Berman's description of the Holly he'd first encountered in California: "You don't know whether she's a hillbilly or an Okie or what." Berman couldn't be blamed for not guessing that she was a child-wife from Tulip, Texas.

"Plain broke our hearts when she ran off like she done," the horse doctor repeated. "She had no cause. All the housework was done by her daughters. Lulamae could just take it easy: fuss in front of mirrors and wash her hair. Our own cows, our own garden, chickens, pigs: son, that woman got positively fat. While her brother growed into a giant. Which is a sight different from how they come to us. 'Twas Nellie, my oldest girl, 'twas Nellie brought 'em into the house. She come to me one morning, and said: 'Papa, I got two wild yunguns locked in the kitchen. I caught 'em outside stealing milk and turkey eggs.' That was Lulamae and Fred. Well, you never saw a more pitiful something. Ribs sticking out everywhere, legs so puny they can't hardly stand, teeth wobbling so bad they can't chew mush. Story was: their mother died of the TB, and their papa done the same—and all the churren, a whole raft of 'em, they been sent off to live with different mean people. Now Lulamae and her brother, them two been living with some mean, no-count people a hundred miles east of Tulip. She had good cause to run off from that house. She didn't have none to leave mine. 'Twas her home." He leaned his elbows on the counter and, pressing his closed eyes with his fingertips, sighed. "She plumped out to be a real pretty woman. Lively, too. Talky as a jaybird. With something smart to say on every subject: better than the radio. First thing you know, I'm out picking flowers. I tamed her a crow and taught it to say her name. I showed her how to play the guitar. Just to look at her made the tears spring to my eyes. The night I proposed, I cried like a baby. She said: 'What you want to cry for, Doc? 'Course we'll be married. I've never been married before.' Well, I had to laugh, hug and squeeze her: *never been married before!*" He chuckled, chewed on his toothpick a moment. "Don't tell me that woman wasn't happy!" he said, challengingly. "We all doted on her. She didn't have to lift a finger, 'cept to eat a piece of pie. 'Cept to comb her hair and send away for all the magazines. We must've had a hunnerd dollars' worth of magazines come into that house. Ask me, that's what done it. Looking at show-off pictures. Reading dreams. That's what started her walking down the road. Every day she'd walk a little further: a mile, and come home. Two miles, and come home. One day she just kept on." He put his hands over his eyes again; his breathing made a ragged noise. "The crow I give her went wild and flew away. All summer you could hear him. In the yard. In the garden. In the woods. All summer that damned bird was calling: Lulamae, Lulamae."

He stayed hunched over and silent, as though listening to the long-ago summer sound. I carried our checks to the cashier.

While I was paying, he joined me. We left together and walked over to Park Avenue. It was a cool, blowy evening; swanky awnings flapped in the breeze. The quietness between us continued until I said: "But what about her brother? He didn't leave?"

"No, sir," he said, clearing his throat. "Fred was with us right till they took him in the Army. A fine boy. Fine with horses. He didn't know what got into Lulamae, how come she left her brother and husband and churren. After he was in the Army, though, Fred started hearing from her. The other day he wrote me her address. So I come to get her. I know she's sorry for what she done. I know she wants to go home." He seemed to be asking me to agree with him. I told him that I thought he'd find Holly, or Lulamae, somewhat changed. "Listen, son," he said, as we reached the steps of the brownstone, "I advised you I need a friend. Because I don't want to surprise her. Scare her none. That's why I've held off. Be my friend: let her know I'm here."

The notion of introducing Mrs. Golightly to her husband had its satisfying aspects; and, glancing up at her lighted windows, I hoped her friends were there, for the prospect of watching the Texan shake hands with Mag and Rusty and José was more satisfying still. But Doc Golightly's proud earnest eyes and sweat-stained hat made me ashamed of such anticipations. He followed me into the house and prepared to wait at the bottom of the stairs. "Do I look nice?" he whispered, brushing his sleeves, tightening the knot of his tie.

Holly was alone. She answered the door at once; in fact, she was on her way out—white satin dancing pumps and quantities of perfume announced gala intentions. "Well, idiot," she said, and playfully slapped me with her purse. "I'm in too much of a hurry to make up now. We'll smoke the pipe tomorrow, okay?"

"Sure, Lulamae. If you're still around tomorrow."

She took off her dark glasses and squinted at me. It was as though her eyes were shattered prisms, the dots of blue and gray and green like broken bits of sparkle. "*He* told you that," she said in a small, shivering voice. "Oh, please. *Where* is he?" She ran past me into the hall. "Fred!" she called down the stairs. "Fred! Where are you, darling?"

I could hear Doc Golightly's footsteps climbing the stairs. His head appeared above the banisters, and Holly backed away from him, not as though she were frightened, but as though she were retreating into a shell of disappointment. Then he was standing in front of her, hangdog and shy. "Gosh, Lulamae," he began, and hesitated, for Holly was gazing at him vacantly, as though she couldn't place him. "Gee, honey," he said, "don't they feed you up here? You're so skinny. Like when I first saw you. All wild around the eye."

Holly touched his face; her fingers tested the reality of his chin, his beard stubble. "Hello, Doc," she said gently, and kissed him on the cheek. "Hello, Doc," she repeated happily, as he lifted her off her feet in a rib-crushing grip. Whoops of relieved laughter shook him. "Gosh, Lulamae. Kingdom come."

Neither of them noticed me when I squeezed past them and went up to my room. Nor did they seem aware of Madame Sapphia Spanella, who opened her door and yelled: "Shut up! It's a disgrace. Do your whoring elsewhere."

❧❀❧

"*Divorce* him? Of course I never divorced him. I was only fourteen, for God's sake. It couldn't have been *legal*." Holly tapped an empty martini glass. "Two more, my darling Mr. Bell."

Joe Bell, in whose bar we were sitting, accepted the order reluctantly. "You're rockin' the boat kinda early," he complained, crunching on a Tums. It was not yet noon, according to the black mahogany clock behind the bar, and he'd already served us three rounds.

"But it's Sunday, Mr. Bell. Clocks are slow on Sundays. Besides, I haven't been to bed yet," she told him, and confided to me: "Not to sleep." She blushed, and glanced away guiltily. For the first time since I'd known her, she seemed to feel a need to justify herself: "Well, I had to. Doc really loves me, you know. And I love him. He may have looked old and tacky to *you*. But you don't know the sweetness of him, the confidence he can give to birds and brats and fragile things like that. Anyone who ever gave you confidence, you owe them a lot. I've always remembered Doc in my prayers. Please stop smirking!" she demanded, stabbing out a cigarette. "I *do* say my prayers."

"I'm not smirking. I'm smiling. You're the most amazing person."

"I suppose I am," she said, and her face, wan, rather bruised-looking in the morning light, brightened; she smoothed her tousled hair, and the colors of it glimmered like a shampoo advertisement. "I must look fierce. But who wouldn't? We spent the rest of the night roaming around in a bus station. Right up till the last minute Doc thought I was going to go with him. Even though I kept telling him: But, Doc, I'm not fourteen any more, and I'm not Lulamae. But the terrible part is (and I realized it while we were standing there) I am. I'm still stealing turkey eggs and running through a brier patch. Only now I call it having the mean reds."

Joe Bell disdainfully settled the fresh martinis in front of us.

"Never love a wild thing, Mr. Bell," Holly advised him. "That was Doc's mistake. He was always lugging home wild things. A hawk with a hurt wing. One time it was a full-grown bobcat with a broken leg. But you can't give your heart to a wild thing: the more you do, the stronger they get. Until they're strong enough to run into the woods. Or fly into a tree. Then a taller tree. Then the sky. That's how you'll end up, Mr. Bell. If you let yourself love a wild thing. You'll end up looking at the sky."

"She's drunk," Joe Bell informed me.

"Moderately," Holly confessed. "But Doc knew what I meant. I explained it to him very carefully, and it was something he could understand. We shook hands and held on to each other and he wished me luck." She glanced at the clock. "He must be in the Blue Mountains by now."

"What's she talkin' about?" Joe Bell asked me.

Holly lifted her martini. "Let's wish the Doc luck, too," she said, touching her glass against mine. "Good luck: and believe me, dearest Doc—it's better to look at the sky than live there. Such an empty place; so vague. Just a country where the thunder goes and things disappear."

TRAWLER MARRIES FOURTH. I was on a subway somewhere in Brooklyn when I saw that headline. The paper that bannered it belonged to another passenger. The only part of the text that I could see read: *Rutherfurd "Rusty" Trawler, the millionaire playboy often accused of pro-Nazi sympathies, eloped to Greenwich yesterday with a beautiful*—Not that I wanted to read any more. Holly had married him: well, well. I wished I were under the wheels of the train. But I'd been wishing that before I spotted the headline. For a headful of reasons. I hadn't seen Holly, not really, since our drunken Sunday at Joe Bell's bar. The intervening weeks had given me my own case of the mean reds. First off, I'd been fired from my job: deservedly, and for an amusing misdemeanor too complicated to recount here. Also, my draft board was displaying an uncomfortable interest; and, having so recently escaped the regimentation of a small town, the idea of entering another form of disciplined life made me desperate. Between the uncertainty of my draft status and a lack of specific experience, I couldn't seem to find another job. That was what I was doing on a subway in Brooklyn: returning from a discouraging interview with an editor of the now defunct newspaper, *PM*. All this, combined with the city heat of the summer, had reduced me to a state of nervous inertia. So I more than half meant it when I wished I were under the wheels of the train. The headline made the desire quite positive. If Holly could marry that "absurd foetus," then the army of wrongness rampant in the world might as well march over me. Or, and the question is apparent, was my outrage a little the result of being in love with Holly myself? A little. For I *was* in love with her. Just as I'd once been in love with my mother's elderly colored cook and a postman who let me follow him on his rounds and a whole family named McKendrick. That category of love generates jealousy, too.

When I reached my station I bought a paper; and, reading the tail-end of that sentence, discovered that Rusty's bride was: *a beautiful cover girl from the Arkansas hills, Miss Margaret Thatcher Fitzhue Wildwood.* Mag! My legs went so limp with relief I took a taxi the rest of the way home.

Madame Sapphia Spanella met me in the hall, wild-eyed and wringing her hands. "Run," she said. "Bring the police. She is killing somebody! Somebody is killing her!"

It sounded like it. As though tigers were loose in Holly's apartment. A riot of crashing glass, of rippings and fallings and overturned furniture. But there were no quarreling voices inside the uproar, which made it seem unnatural. "Run," shrieked Madame Spanella, pushing me. "Tell the police murder!"

I ran; but only upstairs to Holly's door. Pounding on it had one result: the racket subsided. Stopped altogether. But pleadings to let me in went unanswered, and my efforts to break down the door merely culminated in a bruised shoulder. Then below I heard Madame Spanella commanding some newcomer to go for the police. "Shut up," she was told, "and get out of my way."

It was José Ybarra-Jaegar. Looking not at all the smart Brazilian diplomat; but sweaty and frightened. He ordered me out of his way, too. And, using his own key, opened the door. "In here, Dr. Goldman," he said, beckoning to a man accompanying him.

Since no one prevented me, I followed them into the apartment, which was tremendously wrecked. At last the Christmas tree had been dismantled, very literally: its brown dry branches sprawled in a welter of torn-up books, broken lamps and phonograph records. Even the icebox had been emptied, its contents tossed around the room: raw eggs were sliding down the walls, and in the midst of the debris Holly's no-name cat was calmly licking a puddle of milk.

In the bedroom, the smell of smashed perfume bottles made me gag. I stepped on Holly's dark glasses; they were lying on the floor, the lenses already shattered, the frames cracked in half.

Perhaps that is why Holly, a rigid figure on the bed, stared at José so blindly, seemed not to see the doctor, who, testing her pulse, crooned: "You're a tired young lady. Very tired. You want to go to sleep, don't you? Sleep."

Holly rubbed her forehead, leaving a smear of blood from a cut finger. "Sleep," she said, and whimpered like an exhausted, fretful child. "He's the only one would ever let me. Let me hug him on cold nights. I saw a place in Mexico. With horses. By the sea."

"With horses by the sea," lullabied the doctor, selecting from his black case a hypodermic.

José averted his face, queasy at the sight of a needle. "Her sickness is only grief?" he asked, his difficult English lending the question an unintended irony. "She is grieving only?"

"Didn't hurt a bit, now did it?" inquired the doctor, smugly dabbing Holly's arm with a scrap of cotton.

She came to sufficiently to focus the doctor. "*Everything* hurts. Where are my glasses?" But she didn't need them. Her eyes were closing of their own accord.

"She is only grieving?" insisted José.

"Please, sir," the doctor was quite short with him, "if you will leave me alone with the patient."

José withdrew to the front room, where he released his temper on the snooping, tiptoeing presence of Madame Spanella. "Don't touch me! I'll call the police," she threatened as he whipped her to the door with Portuguese oaths.

He considered throwing me out, too; or so I surmised from his expression. Instead, he invited me to have a drink. The only unbroken bottle we could find contained dry vermouth. "I have a worry," he confided. "I have a worry that this should cause scandal. Her crashing everything. Conducting like a crazy. I must have no public scandal. It is too delicate: my name, my work."

He seemed cheered to learn that I saw no reason for a "scandal"; demolishing one's own possessions was, presumably, a private affair.

"It is only a question of grieving," he firmly declared. "When the sadness came, first she throws the drink she is drinking. The bottle. Those books. A lamp. Then I am scared. I hurry to bring a doctor."

"But why?" I wanted to know. "Why should she have a fit over Rusty? If I were her, I'd celebrate."

"Rusty?"

I was still carrying my newspaper, and showed him the headline.

"Oh, that." He grinned rather scornfully. "They do us a grand favor, Rusty and Mag. We laugh over it: how they think they break our hearts when all the time we *want* them to run away. I assure you, we were laughing when the sadness came." His eyes searched the litter on the floor; he picked up a ball of yellow paper. "This," he said.

It was a telegram from Tulip, Texas: *Received notice young Fred killed in action overseas stop your husband and children join in the sorrow of our mutual loss stop letter follows love Doc.*

❧❦❧

Holly never mentioned her brother again: except once. Moreover, she stopped calling me Fred. June, July, all through the warm months she hibernated like a winter animal who did not know spring had come and gone. Her hair darkened, she put on weight. She became rather careless about her clothes: used to rush round to the delicatessen wearing a rain-slicker and nothing underneath. José moved into the apartment, his name replacing Mag Wildwood's on the mailbox. Still, Holly was a good deal alone, for José stayed in Washington three days a week. During his absences she entertained no one and seldom left the apartment—except on Thursdays, when she made her weekly trip to Ossining.

Which is not to imply that she had lost interest in life; far from it, she seemed more content, altogether happier than I'd ever seen her. A keen sudden un-Holly-like enthusiasm for homemaking resulted in several un-Holly-like purchases: at a Parke-Bernet auction she acquired a stag-at-bay hunting tapestry and, from the William Randolph Hearst estate, a gloomy pair of Gothic "easy" chairs; she bought the complete Modern Library, shelves of classical records, innumerable Metropolitan Museum reproductions (including a statue of a Chinese cat that her own cat hated and hissed at and ultimately broke), a Waring mixer and a pressure cooker and a library of cook books. She spent whole hausfrau afternoons slopping about in the sweatbox of her midget kitchen: "José says I'm better than the Colony. Really, who would have dreamed I had such a great natural talent? A month ago I couldn't scramble eggs." And still couldn't, for that matter. Simple dishes, steak, a proper salad, were beyond her. Instead, she fed José, and occasionally myself, *outré* soups (brandied black terrapin poured into avocado shells), Nero-ish novelties (roasted pheasant stuffed with pomegranates and persimmons) and other dubious innovations (chicken and saffron rice served with a chocolate sauce: "An East Indian classic, *my* dear"). Wartime sugar and cream rationing restricted her imagination when it came to sweets—nevertheless, she once managed something called Tobacco Tapioca: best not describe it.

Nor describe her attempts to master Portuguese, an ordeal as tedious to me as it was to her, for whenever I visited her an album of Linguaphone records never ceased rotating on the phonograph. Now, too, she rarely spoke a sentence that did not begin, "After we're married—" or "When we move to Rio—" Yet José had never suggested marriage. She admitted it. "But, after all, he *knows* I'm preggers. Well, I am, darling. Six weeks

gone. I don't see why *that* should surprise you. It didn't me. Not
un peu bit. I'm delighted. I want to have at least nine. I'm sure
some of them will be rather dark—José has a touch of *le nègre,* I
suppose you guessed that? Which is fine by me: what could be
prettier than a quite coony baby with bright green beautiful
eyes? I wish, please don't laugh—but I wish I'd been a virgin for
him, for José. Not that I've warmed the multitudes some people
say: I don't blame the bastards for *saying* it, I've always thrown
out such a jazzy line. Really, though, I toted up the other night,
and I've only had eleven lovers—not counting anything that
happened before I was thirteen because, after all, that just *doesn't*
count. Eleven. Does that make me a whore? Look at Mag Wildwood. Or Honey Tucker. Or Rose Ellen Ward. They've had the
old clap-yo'-hands so many times it amounts to applause. Of
course I haven't anything *against* whores. Except this: some of
them may have an honest tongue but they all have dishonest
hearts. I mean, you can't bang the guy and cash his checks and
at least not *try* to believe you love him. I never have. Even Benny
Shacklett and all those rodents. I sort of hypnotized myself into
thinking their sheer rattiness had a certain allure. Actually, except for Doc, if you want to count Doc, José is my first non-rat
romance. Oh, he's not my idea of the absolute finito. He tells
little lies and he worries what people *think* and he takes about
fifty baths a day: men ought to smell *some*what. He's too prim,
too cautious to be my guy ideal; he always turns his back to get
undressed and he makes too much noise when he eats and I
don't like to see him run because there's something funny-
looking about him when he runs. If I were free to choose from
everybody alive, just snap my fingers and say come here you, I
wouldn't pick José. Nehru, he's nearer the mark. Wendell
Willkie. I'd settle for Garbo any day. Why not? A person ought

to be able to marry men or women or—listen, if you came to me and said you wanted to hitch up with Man O' War, I'd respect your feeling. No, I'm serious. Love should be allowed. I'm all for it. Now that I've got a pretty good idea what it is. Because I *do* love José—I'd stop smoking if he asked me to. He's *friendly,* he can laugh me out of the mean reds, only I don't have them much any more, except sometimes, and even then they're not so hideola that I gulp Seconal or have to haul myself to Tiffany's: I take his suit to the cleaner, or stuff some mushrooms, and I feel fine, just great. Another thing, I've thrown away my horoscopes. I must have spent a dollar on every goddamn star in the goddamn planetarium. It's a bore, but the answer is good things only happen to you if you're good. Good? Honest is more what I mean. Not law-type honest—I'd rob a grave, I'd steal two-bits off a dead man's eyes if I thought it would contribute to the day's enjoyment—but unto-thyself-type honest. Be anything but a coward, a pretender, an emotional crook, a whore: I'd rather have cancer than a dishonest heart. Which isn't being pious. Just practical. Cancer *may* cool you, but the other's sure to. Oh, screw it, cookie—hand me my guitar and I'll sing you a *fado* in *the* most perfect Portuguese."

Those final weeks, spanning end of summer and the beginning of another autumn, are blurred in memory, perhaps because our understanding of each other had reached that sweet depth where two people communicate more often in silence than in words: an affectionate quietness replaces the tensions, the unrelaxed chatter and chasing about that produce a friendship's more showy, more, in the surface sense, dramatic moments. Frequently, when *he* was out of town (I'd developed hostile attitudes toward *him,* and seldom used his name) we spent entire evenings together during which we exchanged less than a hundred words; once, we walked all the way to China-town, ate a chow-mein supper, bought some paper lanterns and stole a box of joss sticks, then moseyed across the Brooklyn Bridge, and on the bridge, as we watched seaward-moving ships pass between the cliffs of burning skyline, she said: "Years from now, years and years, one of those ships will bring me back, me and my nine Brazilian brats. Because yes, they *must* see this, these lights, the river—I love New York, even though it isn't mine, the way something has to be, a tree or a street or a house, something, anyway, that belongs to me because I belong to it." And I said: "Do shut up," for I felt infuriatingly left out—a tug-boat in dry-dock while she, glittery voyager of secure destina-tion, steamed down the harbor with whistles whistling and confetti in the air.

So the days, the last days, blow about in memory, hazy, au-tumnal, all alike as leaves: until a day unlike any other I've lived.

❧❀❧

It happened to fall on the 30th of September, my birthday, a fact which had no effect on events, except that, expecting some form of monetary remembrance from my family, I was eager for the postman's morning visit. Indeed, I went downstairs and waited for him. If I had not been loitering in the vestibule, then Holly would not have asked me to go horseback riding; and would not, consequently, have had the opportunity to save my life.

"Come on," she said, when she found me awaiting the post-man. "Let's walk a couple of horses around the park." She was wearing a windbreaker and a pair of blue jeans and tennis shoes; she slapped her stomach, drawing attention to its flatness: "Don't

think I'm out to lose the heir. But there's a horse, my darling old
Mabel Minerva—I can't go without saying good-bye to Mabel
Minerva."

"Good-bye?"

"A week from Saturday. José bought the tickets." In rather a
trance, I let her lead me down to the street. "We change planes
in Miami. Then over the sea. Over the Andes. Taxi!"

Over the Andes. As we rode in a cab across Central Park it
seemed to me as though I, too, were flying, desolately floating
over snow-peaked and perilous territory.

"But you can't. After all, what about. Well, what about. Well,
you can't *really* run off and leave everybody."

"I don't think anyone will miss me. I have no friends."

"I will. Miss you. So will Joe Bell. And oh—millions. Like
Sally. Poor Mr. Tomato."

"I loved old Sally," she said, and sighed. "You know I haven't
been to see him in a month? When I told him I was going away,
he was an angel. *Actually*"—she frowned—"he seemed *delighted*
that I was leaving the country. He said it was all for the best.
Because sooner or later there might be trouble. If they found
out I wasn't his real niece. That fat lawyer, O'Shaughnessy,
O'Shaughnessy sent me five hundred dollars. In cash. A wedding present from Sally."

I wanted to be unkind. "You can expect a present from me,
too. When, and if, the wedding happens."

She laughed. "He'll marry me, all right. In church. And with
his family there. That's why we're waiting till we get to Rio."

"Does he know you're married already?"

"What's the matter with you? Are you trying to ruin the day?
It's a beautiful day: leave it alone!"

"But it's perfectly possible—"

"It *isn't* possible. I've told you, that wasn't legal. It *couldn't* be." She rubbed her nose, and glanced at me sideways. "Mention that to a living soul, darling. I'll hang you by your toes and dress you for a hog."

The stables—I believe they have been replaced by television studios—were on West Sixty-sixth street. Holly selected for me an old sway-back black and white mare: "Don't worry, she's safer than a cradle." Which, in my case, was a necessary guarantee, for ten-cent pony rides at childhood carnivals were the limit of my equestrian experience. Holly helped hoist me into the saddle, then mounted her own horse, a silvery animal that took the lead as we jogged across the traffic of Central Park West and entered a riding path dappled with leaves denuding breezes danced about.

"See?" she shouted. "It's great!"

And suddenly it was. Suddenly, watching the tangled colors of Holly's hair flash in the red-yellow leaf light, I loved her enough to forget myself, my self-pitying despairs, and be content that something she thought happy was going to happen. Very gently the horses began to trot, waves of wind splashed us, spanked our faces, we plunged in and out of sun and shadow pools, and joy, a glad-to-be-alive exhilaration, jolted through me like a jigger of nitrogen. That was one minute; the next introduced farce in grim disguise.

For all at once, like savage members of a jungle ambush, a band of Negro boys leapt out of the shrubbery along the path. Hooting, cursing, they launched rocks and thrashed at the horse's rumps with switches.

Mine, the black and white mare, rose on her hind legs, whinnied, teetered like a tightrope artist, then blue-streaked down the path, bouncing my feet out of the stirrups and leaving me scarcely attached. Her hooves made the gravel stones spit sparks. The sky careened. Trees, a lake with little-boy sailboats, statues went by licketysplit. Nursemaids rushed to rescue their charges from our awesome approach; men, bums and others, yelled: "Pull in the reins!" and "Whoa, boy, whoa!" and "Jump!" It was only later that I remembered these voices; at the time I was simply conscious of Holly, the cowboy-sound of her racing behind me, never quite catching up, and over and over calling encouragements. Onward: across the park and out into Fifth Avenue: stampeding against the noonday traffic, taxis, buses that screechingly swerved. Past the Duke mansion, the Frick Museum, past the Pierre and the Plaza. But Holly gained ground; moreover, a mounted policeman had joined the chase: flanking my runaway mare, one on either side, their horses performed a pincer movement that brought her to a steamy halt. It was then, at last, that I fell off her back. Fell off and picked myself up and stood there, not altogether certain where I was. A crowd gathered. The policeman huffed and wrote in a book: presently he was most sympathetic, grinned and said he would arrange for our horses to be returned to their stable.

Holly put us in a taxi. "Darling. How do you feel?"

"Fine."

"But you haven't *any* pulse," she said, feeling my wrist.

"Then I must be dead."

"No, idiot. This is serious. Look at me."

The trouble was, I couldn't see her; rather, I saw several Hollys, a trio of sweaty faces so white with concern that I was both touched and embarrassed. "Honestly. I don't feel anything. Except ashamed."

"Please. Are you sure? Tell me the truth. You might have been killed."

"But I wasn't. And thank you. For saving my life. You're wonderful. Unique. I love you."

"Damn fool." She kissed me on the cheek. Then there were four of her, and I fainted dead away.

❦

That evening, photographs of Holly were front-paged by the late edition of the *Journal-American* and by the early editions of both the *Daily News* and the *Daily Mirror*. The publicity had nothing to do with runaway horses. It concerned quite another matter, as the headlines revealed: PLAYGIRL ARRESTED IN NARCOTICS SCANDAL (*Journal-American*), ARREST DOPE-SMUGGLING ACTRESS (*Daily News*), DRUG RING EXPOSED, GLAMOUR GIRL HELD (*Daily Mirror*).

Of the lot, the *News* printed the most striking picture: Holly, entering police headquarters, wedged between two muscular detectives, one male, one female. In this squalid context even her clothes (she was still wearing her riding costume, windbreaker and blue jeans) suggested a gang-moll hooligan: an impression dark glasses, disarrayed coiffure and a Picayune cigarette dangling from sullen lips did not diminish. The caption read: *Twenty-year-old Holly Golightly, beautiful movie starlet and café society celebrity D.A. alleges to be key figure in international drug-smuggling racket linked to racketeer Salvatore "Sally" Tomato. Dets. Patrick Connor and Sheilah Fezzonetti (L. and R.) are shown escorting her into 67th St. Precinct. See story on Pg. 3.* The story, featuring a photograph of a man identified as Oliver "Father" O'Shaughnessy (shielding his face with a fedora), ran three full columns. Here, somewhat condensed, are the pertinent paragraphs: *Members of café society were stunned today by the arrest of gorgeous Holly Golightly, twenty-year-old Hollywood starlet and highly publicized girl-about-New York. At the same time, 2 P.M., police nabbed Oliver O'Shaughnessy, 52, of the Hotel Seabord, W. 49th St., as he exited from a Hamburg Heaven on Madison Ave. Both are alleged by District Attorney Frank L. Donovan to be important figures in an international drug ring dominated by the notorious Mafia-führer Salvatore "Sally" Tomato, currently in Sing Sing serving a five-year rap for political brib-ery. . . . O'Shaughnessy, a defrocked priest variously known in crimeland circles as "Father" and "The Padre," has a history of arrests dating back to 1934, when he served two years for operating a phony Rhode Island mental institution, The Monastery. Miss Golightly, who has no previous criminal record, was arrested in her luxurious apartment at a swank East Side address. . . . Although the D.A.'s office has issued no formal statement, responsible sources insist the blond and beautiful actress, not long ago the constant companion of multimillionaire Rutherfurd Trawler, has been acting as "liaison" between the imprisoned Tomato and his chief-lieutenant, O'Shaughnessy. . . . Posing as a relative of Tomato's, Miss Golightly is said to have paid weekly visits to Sing Sing, and on these occasions Tomato supplied her with verbally coded messages which she then transmitted to O'Shaughnessy. Via this link, Tomato, believed to have been born in Cefalu, Sicily, in 1874, was able to keep first-hand control of a world-wide narcotics syndicate with outposts in Mexico, Cuba, Sicily, Tangier, Tehran and Dakar. But the D.A.'s office refused to offer any detail on these allegations or even verify them. . . . Tipped off, a large number of reporters were on hand at the E. 67th St. Precinct station when the accused pair arrived for booking. O'Shaughnessy, a burly red-haired man, refused comment and kicked one cameraman in the groin. But Miss Golightly, a fragile eyeful, even though attired like a tomboy in slacks and leather jacket, appeared relatively unconcerned. "Don't ask me what the hell this is about," she told reporters. "Parce-que je ne sais pas, mes chères. (Because I do not know, my dears). Yes—I have visited Sally Tomato. I used to go to see him every week. What's wrong with that? He believes in God, and so do I.".* . . . Then, under the sub-heading ADMITS OWN DRUG ADDICTION: *Miss Golightly smiled when a reporter asked whether or not she herself is a narcotics user. "I've had a little go at marijuana. It's not half so destructive as brandy. Cheaper, too. Unfortunately, I prefer brandy. No, Mr. Tomato never mentioned drugs to me. It makes me furious, the way these wretched people keep persecuting him. He's a sensitive, a religious person. A darling old man."*

There is one especially gross error in this report: she was not arrested in her "luxurious apartment." It took place in my own bathroom. I was soaking away my horse-ride pains in a tub of scalding water laced with Epsom salts; Holly, an attentive nurse, was sitting on the edge of the tub waiting to rub me with Sloan's liniment and tuck me into bed. There was a knock at the front door. As the door was unlocked, Holly called Come in. In came Madame Sapphia Spanella, trailed by a pair of civilian-clothed detectives, one of them a lady with thick yellow braids roped round her head.

"*Here* she is: the wanted woman!" boomed Madame Spanella, invading the bathroom and leveling a finger, first at Holly's, then my nakedness. "Look. What a whore she is." The male detective seemed embarrassed: by Madame Spanella and by the situation; but a harsh enjoyment tensed the face of his companion—she plumped a hand on Holly's shoulder and, in a surprising baby-child voice, said: "Come along, sister. You're going places." Whereupon Holly coolly told her: "Get them cotton-pickin' hands off of me, you dreary, driveling old bull-dyke." Which rather enraged the lady: she slapped Holly damned hard. So hard, her head twisted on her neck, and the bottle of liniment, flung from her hand, smithereened on the tile floor—where I, scampering out of the tub to enrich the fray, stepped on it and all but severed both big toes. Nude and bleeding a path of bloody footprints, I followed the action as far as the hall. "Don't forget," Holly managed to instruct me as the detectives propelled her down the stairs, "please feed the cat."

❧❧❧

Of course I believed Madame Spanella to blame: she'd several times called the authorities to complain about Holly. It didn't occur to me the affair could have dire dimensions until that evening when Joe Bell showed up flourishing the newspapers. He was too agitated to speak sensibly; he caroused the room hitting his fists together while I read the accounts.

Then he said: "You think it's so? She was mixed up in this lousy business?"

"Well, yes."

He popped a Tums in his mouth and, glaring at me, chewed it as though he were crunching my bones. "Boy, that's rotten. And you meant to be her friend. What a bastard!"

"Just a minute. I didn't say she was involved *knowingly*. She wasn't. But there, she did do it. Carry messages and whatnot—"

He said: "Take it pretty calm, don't you? Jesus, she could get ten years. More." He yanked the papers away from me. "You know her friends. These rich fellows. Come down to the bar, we'll start phoning. Our girl's going to need fancier shysters than I can afford."

I was too sore and shaky to dress myself; Joe Bell had to help. Back at his bar he propped me in the telephone booth with a triple martini and a brandy tumbler full of coins. But I couldn't think who to contact. José was in Washington, and I had no notion where to reach him there. Rusty Trawler? Not that bastard! Only: what other friends of hers did I know? Perhaps she'd been right when she'd said she had none, not really.

I put through a call to Crestview 5-6958 in Beverly Hills, the number long-distance information gave me for O.J. Berman. The person who answered said Mr. Berman was having a massage and couldn't be disturbed: sorry, try later. Joe Bell was incensed—told me I should have said it was a life and death matter; and he insisted on my trying Rusty. First, I spoke to Mr. Trawler's butler—Mr. and Mrs. Trawler, he announced, were at dinner and might he take a message? Joe Bell shouted into the receiver: "This is urgent, mister. Life and death." The outcome was that I found myself talking—listening, rather—to the former Mag Wildwood: "Are you starkers?" she demanded. "My husband and I will positively *sue* anyone who attempts to connect our names with that ro-ro-ro*vol*ting and de-de-de*gen*erate girl. I always *knew* she was a hop-hop-head with no more morals than a hound-bitch in heat. Prison is where she belongs. And my husband agrees one thousand percent. We will positively *sue* anyone who—" Hanging up, I remembered old Doc down in Tulip, Texas; but no, Holly wouldn't like it if I called him, she'd kill me good.

I rang California again; the circuits were busy, stayed busy, and by the time O.J. Berman was on the line I'd emptied so many martinis he had to tell me why I was phoning him: "About the kid, is it? I know already. I spoke already to Iggy Fitelstein. Iggy's the best shingle in New York. I said Iggy you take care of it, send me the bill, only keep my name anonymous, see. Well, I owe the kid something. Not that I owe her *any*thing, you want to come down to it. She's crazy. A phony. But a *real* phony, you know? Anyway, they only got her in ten thousand bail. Don't worry, Iggy'll spring her tonight—it wouldn't surprise me she's home already."

❧❧❧

But she wasn't; nor had she returned the next morning when I went down to feed her cat. Having no key to the apartment, I used the fire escape and gained entrance through a window. The cat was in the bedroom, and he was not alone: a man was there, crouching over a suitcase. The two of us, each thinking the other a burglar, exchanged uncomfortable stares as I stepped through the window. He had a pretty face, lacquered hair, he resembled José; moreover, the suitcase he'd been packing contained the wardrobe José kept at Holly's, the shoes and suits she fussed over, was always carting to menders and cleaners. And I said, certain it was so: "Did Mr. Ybarra-Jaegar send you?"

"I am the cousin," he said with a wary grin and just-penetrable accent.

"Where is José?"

He repeated the question, as though translating it into another language. "Ah, *where* she is! She is waiting," he said and, seeming to dismiss me, resumed his valet activities.

So: the diplomat was planning a powder. Well, I wasn't amazed; or in the slightest sorry. Still, what a heartbreaking stunt: "He ought to be horsewhipped."

The cousin giggled, I'm sure he understood me. He shut the suitcase and produced a letter. "My cousin, she ask me leave that for his chum. You will oblige?"

On the envelope was scribbled: *For Miss H. Golightly—Courtesy Bearer.*

I sat down on Holly's bed, and hugged Holly's cat to me, and felt as badly for Holly, every iota, as she could feel for herself.

"Yes, I will oblige."

And I did: without the least wanting to. But I hadn't the courage to destroy the letter; or the will power to keep it in my pocket when Holly very tentatively inquired if, if by any chance, I'd had news of José. It was two mornings later; I was sitting by her bedside in a room that reeked of iodine and bedpans, a hospital room. She had been there since the night of her arrest. "Well, darling," she'd greeted me, as I tiptoed toward her carrying a carton of Picayune cigarettes and a wheel of new-autumn violets, "I lost the heir." She looked not quite twelve years: her pale vanilla hair brushed back, her eyes, for once minus their dark glasses, clear as rain water—one couldn't believe how ill she'd been.

Yet it was true: "Christ, I nearly cooled. No fooling, the fat woman almost had me. She was yakking up a storm. I guess I couldn't have told you about the fat woman. Since I didn't know about her myself until my brother died. Right away I was wondering where he'd gone, what it meant, Fred's dying; and then I saw her, she was there in the room with me, and she had Fred cradled in her arms, a fat mean red bitch rocking in a rocking chair with Fred on her lap and laughing like a brass band. The mockery of it! But it's all that's ahead for us, my friend: this comedienne waiting to give you the old razz. Now do you see why I went crazy and broke everything?"

Except for the lawyer O.J. Berman had hired, I was the only visitor she had been allowed. Her room was shared by other patients, a trio of triplet-like ladies who, examining me with an interest not unkind but total, speculated in whispered Italian. Holly explained that: "They think you're my downfall, darling. The fellow what done me wrong"; and, to a suggestion that she set them straight, replied: "I can't. They don't speak English. Anyway, I wouldn't dream of spoiling their fun." It was then that she asked about José.

The instant she saw the letter she squinted her eyes and bent her lips in a tough tiny smile that advanced her age immeasurably. "Darling," she instructed me, "would you reach in the drawer there and give me my purse. A girl doesn't read this sort of thing without her lipstick."

Guided by a compact mirror, she powdered, painted every vestige of twelve-year-old out of her face. She shaped her lips with one tube, colored her cheeks from another. She penciled the rims of her eyes, blued the lids, sprinkled her neck with 4711; attached pearls to her ears and donned her dark glasses; thus armored, and after a displeased appraisal of her manicure's shabby condition, she ripped open the letter and let her eyes race through it while her stony small smile grew smaller and harder. Eventually she asked for a Picayune. Took a puff: "Tastes bum. But divine," she said and, tossing me the letter: "Maybe this will come in handy—if you ever write a rat-romance. Don't be hoggy: read it aloud. I'd like to hear it myself."

It began: "My dearest little girl—"

Holly at once interrupted. She wanted to know what I thought of the handwriting. I thought nothing: a tight, highly legible, uneccentric script. "It's him to a T. Buttoned up and constipated," she declared. "Go on."

"My dearest little girl, I have loved you knowing you were not as others. But conceive of my despair upon discovering in such a brutal and public style how very different you are from the manner of woman a man of my faith and career could hope to make his wife. Verily I grief for the disgrace of your present circumstance, and do not find it in my heart to add my condemn to the condemn that surrounds you. So I hope you will find it in your heart not to condemn me. I have my family to protect, and my name, and I am a coward where those institutions enter. Forget me, beautiful child. I am no longer here. I am gone home. But may God always be with you and your child. May God be not the same as—José."

"Well?"

"In a way it seems quite honest. And even touching."

"*Touching?* That square-ball jazz!"

"But after all, he *says* he's a coward; and from his point of view, you must see—"

Holly, however, did not want to admit that she saw; yet her face, despite its cosmetic disguise, confessed it. "All right, he's not a rat without reason. A super-sized, King Kong–type rat like Rusty. Benny Shacklett. But oh gee, golly goddamn," she said, jamming a fist into her mouth like a bawling baby, "I *did* love him. The rat."

The Italian trio imagined a lover's *crise* and, placing the blame for Holly's groanings where they felt it belonged, tut-tutted their tongues at me. I was flattered: proud that any-one should think Holly cared for me. She quieted when I of-fered her another cigarette. She swallowed and said: "Bless you, Buster. And bless you for being such a bad jockey. If I hadn't had to play Calamity Jane I'd still be looking forward to the grub in an unwed mama's home. Strenuous exercise, that's what did the trick. But I've scared *la merde* out of the whole badge-department by saying it was because Miss Dykeroo slapped me. Yessir, I can sue them on several counts, including false arrest."

Until then, we'd skirted mention of her more sinister tribulations, and this jesting reference to them seemed appalling, pathetic, so definitely did it reveal how incapable she was of recognizing the bleak realities before her. "Now, Holly," I said, thinking: be strong, mature, an uncle. "Now, Holly. We can't treat it as a joke. We have to make plans."

"You're too young to be stuffy. Too small. By the way, what business is it of yours?"

"None. Except you're my friend, and I'm worried. I mean to know what you intend doing."

She rubbed her nose, and concentrated on the ceiling. "Today's Wednesday, isn't it? So I suppose I'll sleep until Saturday, really get a good *schluffen*. Saturday morning I'll skip out to the bank. Then I'll stop by the apartment and pick up a nightgown or two and my Mainbocher. Following which, I'll report to Idlewild. Where, as you damn well know, I have a perfectly fine reservation on a perfectly fine plane. And since you're such a friend I'll let you wave me off. *Please* stop shaking your head."

"Holly. Holly. You can't do that."

"*Et pourquoi pas?* I'm not hot-footing after José, if that's what you suppose. According to my census, he's strictly a citizen of Limboville. It's only: why should I waste a perfectly fine ticket? Already paid for? Besides, I've never been to Brazil."

"Just what kind of pills have they been feeding you here? Can't you realize, you're under a criminal indictment. If they catch you jumping bail, they'll throw away the key. Even if you get away with it, you'll never be able to come home."

"Well, so, tough titty. Anyway, home is where you feel at home. I'm still looking."

"No, Holly, it's stupid. You're innocent. You've got to stick it out."

She said, "Rah, team, rah," and blew smoke in my face. She was impressed, however; her eyes were dilated by unhappy visions, as were mine: iron rooms, steel corridors of gradually closing doors. "Oh, screw it," she said, and stabbed out her cigarette. "I have a fair chance they *won't* catch me. Provided *you* keep your *bouche fermez*. Look. Don't despise me, darling." She put her hand over mine and pressed it with sudden immense sincerity. "I haven't much choice. I talked it over with the lawyer: oh, I didn't tell *him* anything *re* Rio—he'd tip the badgers himself, rather than lose his fee, to say nothing of the nickels O.J. put up for bail. Bless O.J.'s heart; but once on the coast I helped him win more than ten thou in a single poker hand: we're square. No, here's the real shake: all the badgers want from me is a couple of free grabs and my services as a state's witness against Sally—nobody has any intention of prosecuting me, they haven't a ghost of a case. Well, I may be rotten to the core, Maude, *but:* testify against a friend I will not. Not if they can prove he doped Sister Kenny. My yardstick is how somebody treats me, and old Sally, all right he wasn't absolutely white with me, say he took a slight advantage, just the same Sally's an okay shooter, and I'd let the fat woman snatch me sooner than help the law-boys pin him down." Tilting her compact mirror above her face, smoothing her lipstick with a crooked pinkie, she said: "And to be honest, that isn't all. Certain shades of limelight wreck a girl's complexion. Even if a jury gave me the Purple Heart, this neighborhood holds no future: they'd still have up every rope from LaRue to Perona's Bar and Grill—take my word, I'd be about as welcome as Mr. Frank E. Campbell. And if you lived off my particular talents, Cookie, you'd understand the kind of bankruptcy I'm describing. Uh, uh, I don't just fancy a fade-out that finds me belly-bumping around Roseland with a pack of West Side hillbillies. While the excellent Madame Trawler sashays her twat in and out of Tiffany's. I couldn't take it. Give me the fat woman any day."

A nurse, soft-shoeing into the room, advised that visiting hours were over. Holly started to complain, and was curtailed by having a thermometer popped in her mouth. But as I took leave, she unstoppered herself to say: "Do me a favor, darling. Call up the *Times,* or whatever you call, and get a list of the fifty richest men in Brazil. I'm *not* kidding. The fifty richest: regardless of race or color. Another favor—poke around my apartment till you find that medal you gave me. The St. Christopher. I'll need it for the trip."

✖✖✖

The sky was red Friday night, it thundered, and Saturday, departing day, the city swayed in a squall-like downpour. Sharks might have swum through the air, though it seemed improbable a plane could penetrate it.

But Holly, ignoring my cheerful conviction that her flight would not go, continued her preparations—placing, I must say, the chief burden of them on me. For she had decided it would be unwise of her to come near the brownstone. Quite rightly, too: it was under surveillance, whether by police or reporters or other interested parties one couldn't tell—simply a man, sometimes men, who hung around the stoop. So she'd gone from the hospital to a bank and straight then to Joe Bell's bar. "She don't figure she was followed," Joe Bell told me when he came with a message that Holly wanted me to meet her there as soon as possible, a half-hour at most, bringing: "Her jewelry. Her guitar. Toothbrushes and stuff. And a bottle of hundred-year-old brandy: she says you'll find it hid down in the bottom of the dirty-clothes basket. Yeah, oh, and the cat. She wants the cat. But hell," he said, "I don't know we should help her at all. She ought to be protected against herself. Me, I feel like telling the cops. Maybe if I go back and build her some drinks, maybe I can get her drunk enough to call it off."

Stumbling, skidding up and down the fire escape between Holly's apartment and mine, wind-blown and winded and wet to the bone (clawed to the bone as well, for the cat had not looked favorably upon evacuation, especially in such inclement weather) I managed a fast, first-rate job of assembling her going-away belongings. I even found the St. Christopher's medal. Everything was piled on the floor of my room, a poignant pyramid of brassières and dancing slippers and pretty things I packed in Holly's only suitcase. There was a mass left over that I had to put in paper grocery bags. I couldn't think how to carry the cat; until I thought of stuffing him in a pillow-case.

Never mind why, but once I walked from New Orleans to Nancy's Landing, Mississippi, just under five hundred miles. It was a light-hearted lark compared to the journey to Joe Bell's bar. The guitar filled with rain, rain softened the paper sacks, the sacks split and perfume spilled on the pavement, pearls rolled in the gutter: while the wind pushed and the cat scratched, the cat screamed—but worse, I was frightened, a coward to equal José: those storming streets seemed aswarm with unseen presences waiting to trap, imprison me for aiding an outlaw.

The outlaw said: "You're late, Buster. Did you bring the brandy?"

And the cat, released, leaped and perched on her shoulder: his tail swung like a baton conducting rhapsodic music. Holly, too, seemed inhabited by melody, some bouncy *bon voyage* oompahpah. Uncorking the brandy, she said: "This was meant to be part of my hope chest. The idea was, every anniversary we'd have a swig. Thank Jesus I never bought the chest. Mr. Bell, sir, three glasses."

"You'll only need two," he told her. "I won't drink to your foolishness."

The more she cajoled him ("Ah, Mr. Bell. The lady doesn't vanish every day. Won't you toast her?"), the gruffer he was: "I'll have no part of it. If you're going to hell, you'll go on your own. With no further help from me." An inaccurate statement: because seconds after he'd made it a chauffeured limousine drew up outside the bar, and Holly, the first to notice it, put down her brandy, arched her eyebrows, as though she expected to see the District Attorney himself alight. So did I. And when I saw Joe Bell blush, I had to think: by God, he *did* call the police. But then, with burning ears, he announced: "It's nothing. One of them Carey Cadillacs. I hired it. To take you to the airport."

He turned his back on us to fiddle with one of his flower arrangements. Holly said: "Kind, dear Mr. Bell. Look at me, sir."

He wouldn't. He wrenched the flowers from the vase and thrust them at her; they missed their mark, scattered on the floor. "Good-bye," he said; and, as though he were going to vomit, scurried to the men's room. We heard the door lock.

The Carey chauffeur was a worldly specimen who accepted our slapdash luggage most civilly and remained rock-faced when, as the limousine swished uptown through a lessening rain, Holly stripped off her clothes, the riding costume she'd never had a chance to substitute, and struggled into a slim black dress. We didn't talk: talk could have only led to argument; and also, Holly seemed too preoccupied for conversation. She hummed to herself, swigged brandy, she leaned constantly forward to peer out the windows, as if she were hunting an address—or, I decided, taking a last impression of a scene she wanted to remember. It was neither of these. But this: "Stop here," she ordered the driver, and we pulled to the curb of a street in Spanish Harlem. A savage, a garish, a moody neighborhood garlanded with poster-portraits of movie stars and Madonnas. Sidewalk litterings of fruit-rind and rotted newspaper were hurled about by the wind, for the wind still boomed, though the rain had hushed and there were bursts of blue in the sky.

Holly stepped out of the car; she took the cat with her. Cradling him, she scratched his head and asked, "What do you think? This ought to be the right kind of place for a tough guy like you. Garbage cans. Rats galore. Plenty of cat-bums to gang around with. So scram," she said, dropping him; and when he did not move away, instead raised his thug-face and questioned her with yellowish pirate-eyes, she stamped her foot: "I said beat it!" He rubbed against her leg. "I said fuck off!" she shouted, then jumped back in the car, slammed the door, and: "Go," she told the driver. "Go. Go."

I was stunned. "Well, you *are*. You *are* a bitch."

We'd traveled a block before she replied. "I told you. We just met by the river one day: that's all. Independents, both of us. We never made each other any promises. We never—" she said, and her voice collapsed, a tic, an invalid whiteness seized her face. The car had paused for a traffic light. Then she had the door open, she was running down the street; and I ran after her.

But the cat was not at the corner where he'd been left. There was no one, nothing on the street except a urinating drunk and two Negro nuns herding a file of sweet-singing children. Other children emerged from doorways and ladies leaned over their window sills to watch as Holly darted up and down the block, ran back and forth chanting: "You. Cat. Where are you? Here, cat." She kept it up until a bumpy-skinned boy came forward dangling an old tom by the scruff of its neck: "You wants a nice kitty, miss? Gimme a dollar."

The limousine had followed us. Now Holly let me steer her toward it. At the door, she hesitated; she looked past me, past the boy still offering his cat ("Halfa dollar. Two-bits, maybe? Two-bits, it ain't much"), and she shuddered, she had to grip my arm to stand up: "Oh, Jesus God. We did belong to each other. He was mine."

Then I made her a promise, I said I'd come back and find her cat: "I'll take care of him, too. I promise."

She smiled: that cheerless new pinch of a smile. "But what about me?" she said, whispered, and shivered again. "I'm very scared, Buster. Yes, at last. Because it could go on forever. Not knowing what's yours until you've thrown it away. The mean reds, they're nothing. The fat woman, she nothing. This, though: my mouth's so dry, if my life depended on it I couldn't spit." She stepped in the car, sank in the seat. "Sorry, driver. Let's go."

TOMATO'S TOMATO MISSING. And: DRUG-CASE AC-TRESS BELIEVED GANGLAND VICTIM. In due time, however, the press reported: FLEEING PLAYGIRL TRACED TO RIO. Apparently no attempt was made by American authorities to recover her, and soon the matter diminished to an occasional gossip-column mention; as a news story, it was revived only once: on Christmas Day, when Sally Tomato died of a heart attack at Sing Sing. Months went by, a winter of them, and not a word from Holly. The owner of the brownstone sold her abandoned possessions, the white-satin bed, the tapestry, her precious Gothic chair; a new tenant acquired the apartment, his name was Quaintance Smith, and he entertained as many gentlemen callers of a noisy nature as Holly ever had— though in this instance Madame Spanella did not object, indeed she doted on the young man and supplied filet mignon whenever he had a black eye. But in the spring a postcard came: it was scribbled in pencil, and signed with a lipstick kiss: *Brazil was beastly but Buenos Aires the best. Not Tiffany's, but almost. Am joined at the hip with duhvine $enor. Love? Think so. Anyhoo am looking for somewhere to live ($enor has wife, 7 brats) and will let you know address when I know it myself. Mille tendresse.* But the address, if it ever existed, never was sent, which made me sad, there was so much I wanted to write her: that I'd *sold* two stories, had read where the Trawlers were countersuing for divorce, was moving out of the brownstone because it was haunted. But mostly, I wanted to tell about her cat. I had kept my promise; I had found him. It took weeks of after-work roaming through those Spanish Harlem streets, and there were many false alarms—flashes of tiger-striped fur that, upon inspection, were not him. But one day, one cold sunshiny Sunday winter afternoon, it was. Flanked by potted plants and framed by clean lace curtains, he was seated in the window of a warm-looking room: I wondered what his name was, for I was certain he had one now, certain he'd arrived somewhere he belonged. African hut or whatever, I hope Holly has, too.

OTHER VOICES, OTHER ROOMS

For Newton Arvin

The heart is deceitful above all things, and desperately wicked.
Who can know it?

JEREMIAH 17:9

PART ONE

ONE

Now a traveler must make his way to Noon City by the best means he can, for there are no buses or trains heading in that direction, though six days a week a truck from the Chuberry Turpentine Company collects mail and supplies in the next-door town of Paradise Chapel: occasionally a person bound for Noon City can catch a ride with the driver of the truck, Sam Radclif. It's a rough trip no matter how you come, for these washboard roads will loosen up even brandnew cars pretty fast; and hitchhikers always find the going bad. Also, this is lonesome country; and here in the swamplike hollows where tiger lilies bloom the size of a man's head, there are luminous green logs that shine under the dark marsh water like drowned corpses; often the only movement on the landscape is winter smoke winding out the chimney of some sorry-looking farmhouse, or a wing-stiffened bird, silent and arrow-eyed, circling over the black deserted pinewoods.

Two roads pass over the hinterlands into Noon City; one from the north, another from the south; the latter, known as the Paradise Chapel Highway, is the better of the pair, though both are much the same: desolate miles of swamp and field and forest stretch along either route, unbroken except for scattered signs advertising Red Dot 5¢ Cigars, Dr. Pepper, NEHI, Grove's Chill Tonic, and 666. Wooden bridges spanning brackish creeks named for long-gone Indian tribes rumble like far-off thunder under a passing wheel; herds of hogs and cows roam the roads at will; now and then a farm-family pauses from work to wave as an auto whizzes by, and watch sadly till it disappears in red dust.

One sizzling day in early June the Turpentine Company's driver, Sam Radclif, a big balding six-footer with a rough, manly face, was gulping a beer at the Morning Star Café in Paradise Chapel when the proprietor came over with his arm around this stranger-boy.

"Hiya, Sam," said the proprietor, a fellow called Sydney Katz. "Got a kid here that'd be obliged if you could give him a ride to Noon City. Been trying to get there since yesterday. Think you can help?"

Radclif eyed the boy over the rim of his beer glass, not caring much for the looks of him. He had his notions of what a "real" boy should look like, and this kid somehow offended them. He was too pretty, too delicate and fair-skinned; each of his features was shaped with a sensitive accuracy, and a girlish tenderness softened his eyes, which were brown and very large. His brown hair, cut short, was streaked with pure yellow strands. A kind of tired, imploring expression masked his thin face, and there was an unyouthful sag about his shoulders. He wore long, wrinkled white linen breeches, a limp blue shirt, the collar of which was open at the throat, and rather scuffed tan shoes.

Wiping a mustache of foam off his upper lip, Radclif said: "What's your name, son?"

"Joel. Jo-el Har-ri-son Knox." He separated the syllables explicitly, as though he thought the driver deaf, but his voice was uncommonly soft.

"That so?" drawled Radclif, placing his dry beer glass on the counter. "A mighty fancy name, Mister Knox."

The boy blushed and turned to the proprietor, who promptly intervened: "This is a fine boy, Sam. Smart as a whip. Knows words you and me never heard of."

Radclif was annoyed. "Here, Katz," he ordered, "fillerup." After the proprietor trundled away to fetch a second beer, Sam said kindly, "Didn't mean to tease you, son. Where bouts you from?"

"New Orleans," he said. "I left there Thursday and got here Friday . . . and that was as far as I could go; no one come to meet me."

"Oh, yeah," said Radclif. "Visiting folks in Noon City?"

The boy nodded. "My father. I'm going to live with him."

Radclif raised his eyes ceilingward, mumbled "Knox" several times, then shook his head in a baffled manner. "Nope, don't think I know anybody by that name. Sure you're in the right place?"

"Oh, yes," said the boy without alarm. "Ask Mister Katz, he's heard about my father, and I showed him the letters and . . . wait." He hurried back among the tables of the gloomy café, and returned toting a huge tin suitcase that, judging by his grimace, was extremely heavy. The suitcase was colorful with faded souvenir stickers from remote parts of the globe: Paris, Cairo, Venice, Vienna, Naples, Hamburg, Bombay, and so forth. It was an odd thing to see on a hot day in a town the size of Paradise Chapel.

"You been all them places?" asked Radclif.

"No-o-o," said the boy, struggling to undo a worn-out leather strap which held the suitcase together. "It belonged to my grandfather; that was Major Knox: you've read about him in history books, I guess. He was a prominent figure in the Civil War. Anyway, this is the valise he used on his wedding trip around the world."

"Round the world, eh?" said Radclif, impressed. "Musta been a mighty rich man."

"Well, that was a long time ago." He rummaged through his neatly packed possessions till he found a slim package of letters. "Here it is," he said, selecting one in a watergreen envelope.

Radclif fingered the letter a moment before opening it; but presently, with clumsy care, he extracted a green sheet of tissue-like paper and, moving his lips, read:

EDW. R. SANSOM, ESQ.

SKULLY'S LANDING

MAY 18, 19—

My dear Ellen Kendall,

I am in your debt for answering my letter so quickly; indeed, by return post. Yes, hearing from me after twelve years must have seemed strange, but I can assure you sufficient reason prompted this long silence. However, reading in the *Times-Picayune,* to the Sunday issue of which we subscribe, of my late wife's passing, may God the Almighty rest her gentle soul, I at once reasoned the honorable thing could only be to again assume my paternal duties, forsaken, lo, these many years. Both the present Mrs Sansom and myself are happy (nay, overjoyed!) to learn you are willing to concede our desire, though, as you remark, your heart will break in doing so. Ah, how well I sympathize with the sorrow such a sacrifice may bring, having experienced similar emotions when, after that final dreadful affair, I was forced to take leave of my only child, whom I treasured, while he was still no more than an infant. But that is all of the lost past. Rest assured, good lady, we here at the Landing have a beautiful home, healthful food, and a cultured atmosphere with which to provide my son.

As to the journey: we are anxious Joel reach here no later than June First. Now when he leaves New Orleans he should travel via train to Biloxi, at which point he must disembark and purchase a bus ticket for Paradise Chapel, a town some twenty miles south of Noon City. We have at present no mechanical vehicle; therefore, I suggest he remain overnight in P.C. where rooms are let above the Morning Star Café, until appropriate arrangements can be made. Enclosed please find a cheque covering such expenses as all this may incur.

YRS. RESPCT.

EDW. R. SANSOM

The proprietor arrived with the beer just as Radclif, frowning puzzledly, sighed and tucked the paper back in its envelope. There were two things about this letter that bothered him; first of all, the handwriting: penned in ink the rusty color of dried blood, it was a maze of curlicues and dainty i's dotted with daintier o's. What the hell kind of a man would write like that? And secondly: "If your Pa's named Sansom, how come you call yourself Knox?"

The boy stared at the floor embarrassedly. "Well," he said, and shot Radclif a swift, accusing look, as if the driver was robbing him of something, "they were divorced, and mother always called me Joel Knox."

"Aw, say, son," said Radclif, "you oughtn't to have let her done that! Remember, your Pa's your Pa no matter what."

The proprietor avoided a yearning glance for help which the boy now cast in his direction by having wandered off to attend another customer. "But I've never seen him," said Joel, dropping the letters into his suitcase and buckling up the strap. "Do you know where this place is? Skully's Landing?"

"The Landing?" Radclif said. "Sure, sure I know all about it." He took a deep swallow of beer, let forth a mighty belch, and grinned. "Yessir, if I was your Pa I'd take down your britches and muss you up a bit." Then, draining the glass, he slapped a half-dollar on the counter, and stood meditatively scratching his hairy chin till a wall clock sounded the hour four: "O.K., son, let's shove," he said, starting briskly towards the door.

After a moment's hesitation the boy lifted his suitcase and followed.

"Come see us again," called the proprietor automatically.

❧❦❧

The truck was a Ford of the pick-up type. Its interior smelled strongly of sun-warmed leather and gasoline fumes. The broken speedometer registered a petrified twenty. Rainstreaks and crushed insects blurred the windshield, of which one section was shattered in a bursting-star pattern. A toy skull ornamented the gear shift. The wheels bump-bumped over the rising, dipping, curving Paradise Chapel Highway.

Joel sat scrunched in a corner of the seat, elbow propped on windowframe, chin cupped in hand, trying hard to keep awake. He hadn't had a proper hour's rest since leaving New Orleans, for when he closed his eyes, as now, certain sickening memories slid through his mind. Of these, one in particular stood out: he was at a grocery counter, his mother waiting next him, and outside in the street January rain was making icicles on the naked tree limbs. Together they left the store and walked silently along the wet pavement, he holding a calico umbrella above his mother, who carried a sack of tangerines. They passed a house where a piano was playing, and the music sounded sad in the grey afternoon, but his mother remarked what a pretty song. And when they reached home she was humming it, but she felt cold and went to bed, and the doctor came, and for over a month he came every day, but she was always cold, and Aunt Ellen was there, always smiling, and the doctor, always smiling, and the uneaten tangerines shriveled up in the icebox; and when it was over he went with Ellen to live in a dingy two-family house near Pontchartrain.

Ellen was a kind, rather gentle woman, and she did the best she knew how. She had five school-aged children, and her husband clerked in a shoe store, so there was not a great deal of money; but Joel wasn't dependent, his mother having left a small legacy. Ellen and her family were good to him, still he resented them, and often felt compelled to do hateful things, such as tease the older cousin, a dumb-looking girl named Louise, because she was a little deaf: he'd cup his ear and cry "Aye? Aye?" and couldn't stop till she broke into tears. He would not joke or join in the rousing after-supper games his uncle inaugurated nightly, and he took odd pleasure in bringing to attention a slip of grammar on anyone's part, but why this was true puzzled him as much as the Kendalls. It was as if he lived those months wearing a pair of spectacles with green, cracked lenses, and had wax-plugging in his ears, for everything seemed to be something it wasn't, and the days melted in a constant dream. Now Ellen liked to read Sir Walter Scott and Dickens and Hans Andersen to the children before sending them upstairs, and one chilly March evening she read "The Snow Queen." Listening to it, it came to Joel that he had a lot in common with Little Kay, whose outlook was twisted when a splinter from the Sprite's evil mirror infected his eye, changing his heart into a lump of bitter ice: suppose, he thought, hearing Ellen's gentle voice and watching the firelight warm his cousins' faces, suppose, like Little Kay, he also were spirited off to the Snow Queen's frozen palace? What living soul would then brave robber barons for his rescue? And there was no one, really no one.

During the last weeks before the letter came he skipped school three days out of five to loaf around the Canal Street docks. He got into a habit of sharing the box-lunch Ellen fixed for him with a giant Negro stevedore who, as they talked together, spun exotic sea-life legends that Joel knew to be lies even as he listened; but this man was a grown-up, and grown-ups were suddenly the only friends he wanted. And he spent solitary hours watching the loading and unloading of banana boats that shipped to Central America, plotting of course a stowaway voyage, for he was certain in some foreign city he could land a good-paying job. However, on his thirteenth birthday, as it happened, the first letter from Skully's Landing arrived.

Ellen had not shown him this letter for several days. It was peculiar, the way she'd behaved, and whenever her eyes had met his there was a look in them he'd never seen before: a frightened, guilty expression. In answering the letter she'd asked assurance that, should Joel find himself discontented, he would be at once allowed to return; a guarantee his education would be cared for; a promise he could spend Christmas holidays with her. But Joel could sense how relieved she was when, following a long correspondence, Major Knox's old honeymoon suitcase was dragged down from the attic.

He was glad to go. He could not think why, nor did he bother wondering, but his father's more or less incredible appearance on a scene strangely deserted twelve years before didn't strike him as in the least extraordinary, inasmuch as he'd counted on some such happening all along. The miracle he'd planned, however, was in the nature of a kind old rich lady who, having glimpsed him on a street-corner, immediately dispatched an envelope stuffed with thousand-dollar bills; or a similar God-like action on the part of some goodhearted stranger. And this stranger, as it turned out, was his father, which to his mind was simply a wonderful piece of luck.

But afterwards, as he lay in a scaling iron bed above the Morning Star Café, dizzy with heat and loss and despair, a different picture of his father and of his situation asserted itself: he did not know what to expect, and he was afraid, for already there were so many disappointments. A panama hat, newly bought in New Orleans and worn with dashing pride, had been stolen in the train depot in Biloxi; then the Paradise Chapel bus had run three hot, sweaty hours behind schedule; and finally, topping everything, there had been no word from Skully's Landing waiting at the café. All Thursday night he'd left the electric light burning in the strange room, and read a movie magazine till he knew the latest doings of the Hollywood stars by heart, for if he let his attention turn inward even a second he would begin to tremble, and the mean tears would not stay back. Toward dawn he'd taken the magazine and torn it to shreds and burned the pieces in an ashtray one by one till it was time to go downstairs.

❧❀❧

"Reach behind and hand me a match, will you, boy?" said Radclif. "Back there on the shelf, see?"

Joel opened his eyes and looked about him dazedly. A perfect tear of sweat was balanced on the tip of his nose. "You certainly have a lot of junk," he said, probing around the shelf, which was littered with a collection of yellowed newspapers, a slashed inner tube, greasy tools, an air pump, a flashlight and . . . a pistol. Alongside the pistol was an open carton of ammunition; bullets the bright copper of fresh pennies. He was tempted to take a whole handful, but ended by artfully dropping just one into his breast pocket. "Here they are."

Radclif popped a cigarette between his lips, and Joel, without being asked, struck a match for him.

"Thanks," said Radclif, a huge drag of smoke creeping out his nostrils. "Say, ever been in this part of the country before?"

"Not exactly, but my mother took me to Gulfport once, and that was nice because of the sea. We passed through there yesterday on the train."

"Like it round here?"

Joel imagined a queerness in the driver's tone. He studied Radclif's blunt profile, wondering if perhaps the theft had been noticed. If so, Radclif gave no sign. "Well, it's . . . you know, different."

"Course I don't see any difference. Lived hereabouts all my life, and it looks like everywhere else to me, ha ha!"

The truck hit suddenly a stretch of wide, hard road, unbor-

dered by tree-shade, though a black skirt of distant pines darkened the rim of a great field that lay to the left. A far-off figure,
whether man or woman you could not tell, rested from hoeing
to wave, and Joel waved back. Farther on, two little white-haired
boys astride a scrawny mule shouted their delight when the
truck passed, burying them in a screen of dust. Radclif honked
and honked the horn at a tribe of hogs that took their time in
getting off the road. He could swear like nobody Joel had ever
heard, except maybe the Negro dockhand.

A while later, scowling thoughtfully, Joel said: "I'd like to ask
you something, o.k.?" He waited till Radclif nodded consent.
"Well, what I wanted to ask was, do you know my . . . Mister
Sansom?"

"Yeah, I know who he is, sure," said Radclif, and swabbed his
forehead with a filthy handkerchief. "You threw me off the track
with those two names, Sansom and Knox. Oh sure, he's the guy
that married Amy Skully." There was an instant's pause before
he added: "But the real fact is, I never laid eyes on him."

Joel chewed his lip, and was silent a moment. He was crazy
with questions he wanted answered, but the idea of asking them
embarrassed him, for to be so ignorant of one's own blood-kin
seemed shameful. Therefore he said what he had to in a very
bold voice: "What about this Skully's Landing? I mean, who all
lives there?"

Radclif squinted his eyes while he considered. "Well," he said
at last, "they've got a coupla niggers out there, and I know them.
Then your daddy's wife, know her: my old lady does dress-
making for her now and again; used to, anyway." He sucked in
cigarette smoke, and flipped the butt out the window. "And the
cousin . . . yes, by God, the cousin!"

"Oh?" said Joel casually, though never once in all the letters had such a person been mentioned, and his eyes begged the driver to amplify. But Radclif merely smiled a curious smile, as if amused by a private joke too secret for sharing.

And that was as far as the matter went.

"Look sharp now," said Radclif presently, "we're coming into town."

A house. A grey clump of Negro cabins. An unpainted clap-board church with a rain-rod steeple, and three Holy panes of ruby glass. A sign: The Lord Jesus Is Coming! Are You Ready? A little black child wearing a big straw hat and clutching tight a pail of blackberries. Over all the sun's stinging glaze. Soon there was a short, unpaved and nameless street, lined with similar one-floored houses, some nicer-looking than others; each had a front porch and a yard, and in some yards grew scraggly rose bushes and crepe myrtle and China trees, from a branch of which very likely dangled a child's play swing made of rope and an old rub-ber tire. There were Japonica trees with waxy black-green pol-ished leaves. And he saw a fat pink girl skipping rope, and an elderly lady ensconced on a sagging porch cooling herself with a palmetto fan. Then a red-barn livery stable: horses, wagons, buggies, mules, men. An abrupt bend in the road: Noon City.

Radclif braked the truck to a halt. He reached across and opened the door next to Joel. "Too bad I can't ride you out to the Landing, son," he said hurriedly. "The company'd raise hell. But you'll make it fine; it's Saturday, lotsa folks living out that-away come into town on Saturday."

Joel was standing alone now, and his blue shirt, damp with sweat, was pasted to his back. Toting the sticker-covered suit-case, he cautiously commenced his first walk in the town.

Noon City is not much to look at. There is only one street, and on it are located a General Merchandise store, a repair shop, a small building which contains two offices, one lodging a lawyer, the other a doctor; a combination barbershop-beautyparlor that is run by a one-armed man and his wife; and a curious, indefinable establishment known as R. V. Lacey's Princely Place where a Texaco gasoline pump stands under the portico. These buildings are grouped so closely together they seem to form a ramshackle palace haphazardly thrown together overnight by a half-wit carpenter. Now across the road in isolation stand two other structures: a jail, and a tall queer tottering ginger-colored house. The jail has not housed a white criminal in over four years, and there is seldom a prisoner of any kind, the Sheriff being a lazy no-good, prone to take his ease with a bottle of liquor, and let trouble-makers and thieves, even the most dangerous type of cutthroats, run free and wild. As to the freakish old house, no one has lived there for God knows how long, and it is said that once three exquisite sisters were raped and murdered here in a gruesome manner by a fiendish Yankee bandit who rode a silvergrey horse and wore a velvet cloak stained scarlet with the blood of Southern womanhood; when told by antiquated ladies claiming one-time acquaintance with the beautiful victims, it is a tale of Gothic splendor. The windows of the house are cracked and shattered, hollow as eyeless sockets; a rotted balcony leans perilously forward, and yellow sunflower birds hide their nests in its secret places; the scaling outer walls are ragged with torn, weather-faded posters that flutter when there is a wind. Among the town kids it is a sign of great valor to enter these black rooms after dark and signal with a matchflame from a window on the topmost floor. However, the porch of this house is in pretty fair condition, and on Saturdays the visiting farm-families make it their head-quarters.

New people rarely settle in Noon City or its outlying parts; after all, jobs are scarce here. On the other hand, seldom do you hear of a person leaving, unless it's to wend his lonesome way up onto the dark ledge above the Baptist church where forsaken tombstones gleam like stone flowers among the weeds.

Saturday is of course the big day. Shortly after daylight a procession of mule-drawn wagons, broken-down flivvers, and buggies begins wheeling in from the countryside, and towards midmorning a considerable congregation is gathered. The men sport their finest shirts and store-bought breeches; the women scent themselves with vanilla flavoring or dime-store perfume, of which the most popular brand is called Love Divine; the girls wear dodads in their cropped hair, inflame their cheeks with a lot of rouge, and carry five-cent paper fans that have pretty pictures painted on them. Though barefoot and probably half-naked, each little child is washed clean and given a few pennies to spend on something like a prize-inside box of molasses pop-corn. Finished poking around in the various stores, the women-folk assemble on the porch of the old house, while their men mosey on over to the livery stable. Swift and eager, saying the same things over and over, their voices hum and weave through the long day. Sickness and weddings and courting and funerals and God are the favorite topics on the porch. Over at the stable the men joke and drink whiskey, talk crops and play jackknife: once in a while there are terrible fights, for many of these men are hot-tempered, and if they hold a grudge against somebody they like to wrestle it out.

When twilight shadows the sky it is as if a soft bell were toll-ing dismissal, for a gloomy hush stills all, and the busy voices fall silent like birds at sunset. The families in their vehicles roll out of town like a sad, funeral caravan, and the only trace they leave is the fierce quiet that follows. The proprietors of the different Noon City establishments remain open an hour longer before bolting their doors and going home to bed; but after eight o'clock not a decent soul is to be seen wandering in this town except, maybe, a pitiful drunk or a young swain promenading with his ladylove.

"Hey, there! You with the suitcase!"

Joel whirled round to find a bandy-legged, little one-armed man glowering at him from the doorway of a barbershop; he seemed too sickly to be the owner of such a hard, deep voice. "Come here, kid," he commanded, jerking a thumb at his aproned chest.

When Joel reached him, the man held out his hand and in the open palm shone a nickel. "See this?" he said. Joel nodded dumbly. "O.K.," said the man, "now look up the road yonder. See that little gal with the red hair?"

Joel saw whom he meant all right. It was a girl with fiery dutchboy hair. She was about his height, and wore a pair of brown shorts and a yellow polo shirt. She was prancing back and forth in front of the tall, curious old house, thumbing her nose at the barber and twisting her face into evil shapes. "Listen," said the barber, "you go collar that nasty youngun for me and this nickel's yours for keeps. Oh-oh! Watch out, here she comes again. . . ."

Whooping like a wild-west Indian, the redhead whipped down the road, a yelling throng of young admirers racing in her wake. She chunked a great fistful of rocks when she came opposite the spot where Joel was standing. The rocks landed with a maddening clatter on the barbershop's tin roof, and the one-armed man, his face an apoplectic color, hollered: "I'll getcha, Idabel! I'll getcha sure as shooting; you just wait!" A flourish of female laughter floated through the screen door behind him, and a waspish-voiced woman shrilled: "Sugar, you quit actin the fool, and hie yourself in here outa that heat." Then, apparently addressing a third party: "I declare but what he ain't no better'n that Idabel; ain't neither one got the sense God gave 'em. Oh shoot, I says to Miz Potter (she was in for a shampoo a week ago today and I'd give a pretty penny to know how she gets that mop so filthy dirty), well, I says: 'Miz Potter, you teach that Idabel at the school,' I says, 'now how come she's so confounded mean?' I says: 'It do seem to me a mystery, and her with that sweet ol sister—speakin of Florabel—and them two twins, and noways alike. Wellsir, Miz Potter answers me: 'Oh, Miz Caulfield, that Idabel sure do give me a peck of trouble and it's my opinion she oughta be in the penitentiary.' Uh huh, that's just what she said. Well, it wasn't no revelation to me cause I always knew she was a freak, no ma'am, never saw that Idabel Thompkins in a dress yet. *Sugar, you come on in here outa that heat....*"

The man made a yoke with his fingers and spit fatly through it. He gave Joel a nasty look, and snapped, "Are you standing there wanting my money for doing nothing whatsoever, is that it, eh?"

"Sugar, you hear me?"

"Hush your mouth, woman," and the screen door whined shut.

Joel shook his head and went on his way. The redheaded girl and her loud gang were gone from sight, and the white afternoon was ripening towards the quiet time of day when the summer sky spills soft color over the drawn land. He smiled with chilly insolence at the interested stares of passers-by, and when he reached the establishment known as R. V. Lacey's Princely Place, he stopped to read a list that was chalked on a tiny, battered blackboard which stood outside the entrance: Miss Roberta V. Lacey Invites You to Come in and Try Our Tasty Fried Catfish and Chicken—Yummy Dixie Ice Cream—Good Delicious Barbecue—Sweet Drinks & Cold Beer.

"Sweet drinks," he said half-aloud, and it seemed as if frosty Coca-Cola was washing down his dry throat. "Cold beer." Yes, a cold beer. He felt the lumpy outline of the change purse in his pocket, then pushed the swinging screen door open and stepped inside.

In the box-shaped room that was R. V. Lacey's Princely Place there were about a dozen people standing around, mostly overalled boys with rawboned, sun-browned faces, and a few young girls. A hubbub of talk faded to nothing when Joel entered and self-consciously sat himself down at a wooden counter which ran the length of the room.

"Why, hello, little one," boomed a muscular woman who immediately strode forward and propped her elbows on the counter before him. She had long ape-like arms that were covered with dark fuzz, and there was a wart on her chin, and decorating this wart was a single antenna-like hair. A peach silk blouse sagged under the weight of her enormous breasts; a zany light sparkled in the red-rimmed eyes she focused on him. "Welcome to Miss Roberta's." Two of her dirty-nailed fingers reached out to give his cheek a painful pinch. "Say now, what can Miss Roberta do for this cute-lookin fella?"

Joel was overwhelmed. "A cold beer," he blurted, deafly ignoring the titter of giggles and guffaws that sounded in the background.

"Can't serve no beer to minors, babylove, even if you are a

mighty cute-lookin fella. Now what you want is a nice NEHI grapepop," said the woman, lumbering away.

The giggles swelled to honest laughter, and Joel's ears turned a humiliated pink. He wondered if the woman was a lunatic. And his eyes scanned the sour-smelling room as if it were a madhouse. There were calendar portraits of toothy bathing beauties on the walls, and a framed certificate which said: This is to certify that Roberta Velma Lacey won Grand Prize in Lying at the annual Double Branches Dog Days Frolic. Hanging from the low ceiling were several poisonous streamers of strategically arranged flypaper, and a couple of naked lightbulbs that were ornamented with shredded ribbons of green-and-red crepe paper. A water pitcher filled with branches of towering pink dogwood sat on the counter.

"Here y'are," said the woman, plunking down a dripping wet bottle of purple sodapop. "I declare, little one, you sure are hot and dusty-lookin." She gave his head a merry pat. "Know somethin, you must be the boy Sam Radclif brung to town, say?"

Joel admitted this with a nod. He took a swallow of the drink, and it was lukewarm. "I want . . . that is, do you know how far it is from here to Skully's Landing?" he said, realizing every ear in the place was tuned to him.

"Ummm," the woman tinkered with her wart, and walled her eyes up into her head till they all but disappeared. "Hey, Romeo, how far you spec it is out to The Skulls," she said, and grinned crazily. "I call it The Skulls on accounta . . ." but she did not finish, for at that moment the Negro boy of whom she'd asked the information, answered: "Two miles, more like three, maybe, ma'am."

"Three miles," she parroted. "But if I was you, babylove, I wouldn't go traipsin over there."

"Me neither," whined a yellow-haired girl.

"Is there anyway I could get a ride out?"

Somebody said, "Ain't Jesus Fever in town?"

Yeah, I saw Jesus—Jesus, he parked round by the Livery—What? Y'all mean old Jesus Fever? Christamighty, I thought he was way gone and buried!—Nah, man. He's past a hundred but alive as you are.—Sure, I seen Jesus—Yeah, Jesus is here . . .

The woman grabbed a flyswatter and slammed it down with savage force. "Shut up that gab. I can't hear a thing this boy says."

Joel felt a little surge of pride, tinged with fright, at being the center of such a commotion. The woman fixed her zany eyes on a point somewhere above his head, and said: "What business you got with The Skulls, babylove?"

Now this again! He sketched the story briefly, omitting all except the simplest events, even to excluding a mention of the letters. He was trying to locate his father, that was the long and short of it. Could she help him?

Well, she didn't know. She stood silent for some time, toying with her wart and staring off into space. "Hey, Romeo," she said finally, "you say Jesus Fever's in town?"

"Yes'm." The boy she called Romeo was colored, and wore a puffy, stained chef's cap. He was stacking dishes in a sink behind the counter.

"Come here, Romeo," she said, beckoning, "I got something to discuss." Romeo joined her promptly in a rear corner. She began whispering excitedly, glancing over her shoulder now and then at Joel, who could not hear what they were saying. It was quiet in the room, and everyone was looking at him. He took out the bullet thefted from Sam Radclif and rolled it nervously in his hands.

Suddenly the door swung open. The skinny girl with fiery, chopped-off red hair swaggered inside, and stopped dead still, her hands cocked on her hips. Her face was flat, and rather impertinent; a network of big ugly freckles spanned her nose. Her eyes, squinty and bright green, moved swiftly from face to face, but showed none a sign of recognition; they paused a cool instant on Joel, then traveled elsewhere.

Hi, Idabel—Whatchasay, Idabel?

"I'm hunting sister," she said. "Anybody seen her?" Her voice was boy-husky, sounding as though strained through some rough material: it made Joel clear his throat.

"Seen her sitting on the porch a while back," said a chinless young man.

The redhead leaned against the wall, and crossed her pencil-thin, bony-kneed legs. A ragged bandage stained with mercurochrome covered her left knee. She pulled out a blue yo-yo and let it unwind slowly to the floor and spin back. "Who's that?" she asked, jerking her head towards Joel. When nobody answered, she looptylooped the yo-yo, shrugged and said: "Who cares, pray tell?" But she continued to watch him cagily from the corners of her eyes. "Hey, hows about a dope on credit, Roberta?" she called.

"*Miss* Roberta," said the woman, momentarily interrupting her confab with Romeo. "I don't need to tell you you have a right smart tongue, Idabel Thompkins, and always did have. And till such time as you learn a few ladylike manners, I'd be obliged if you'd keep outa my place, hear? Besides, since when have you got all this big credit? Ha! March now . . . and don't come back till you put on some decent female clothes."

"You know what you can do," sassed the girl, stomping out the door. "This old dive'll have a mighty long wait before I bring my trade here again, you betcha." Once outside, her silhouette darkened the screen as she paused to peer in at Joel.

❧❧❧

And now dusk was coming on. A sea of deepening green spread the sky like some queer wine, and across this vast green, shadowed clouds were pushed sluggishly by a mild breeze. Presently the trek homeward would commence, and afterwards the stillness of Noon City would be almost a sound itself: the sound a footfall might make among the mossy tombs on the dark ledge. Miss Roberta had lent Romeo as Joel's guide. The two kept duplicate pace; the Negro boy carried Joel's bag; wordlessly they turned the corner by the jail, and there was the stable, a barnlike structure of faded red which Joel had noticed earlier that day. A number of men who looked like a gang of desperadoes in a Western picture-show were congregated near the hitching post, passing a whiskey bottle from hand to hand; a second group, less boisterous, played a game with a jackknife under the dark area of an oak tree. Swarms of dragonflies quivered above a slime-coated water trough; and a scabby hound dog padded back and forth, sniffing the bellies of tied-up mules. One of the whiskey drinkers, an old man with long white hair and a long white beard, was feeling pretty good evidently, for he was clapping his hands and doing a little shuffle-dance to a tune that was probably singing in his head.

The colored boy escorted Joel round the side of the stable to a backlot where wagons and saddled horses were packed so close a swinging tail was certain to strike something. "That's him," said Romeo, pointing his finger, "there's Jesus Fever."

But Joel had seen at once the pygmy figure huddled atop the seatplank of a grey wagon parked on the lot's further rim: a kind of gnomish little Negro whose primitive face was sharp against the drowning green sky. "Don't less us be fraid," said Romeo, leading Joel through the maze of wagons and animals with timid caution. "You best hold tight to my hand, white boy: Jesus Fever, he the oldest ol buzzard you ever put eyes on."

Joel said, "But I'm not afraid," and this was true.

"Shhh!"

As the boys approached, the little pygmy cocked his head at a wary angle; then slowly, with the staccato movements of a mechanical doll, he turned sideways till his eyes, yellow feeble eyes dotted with milky specks, looked down on them with dreamy detachment. He had a funny derby hat perched rakishly on his head, and in the candy-striped ribbon-band was jabbed a speckled turkey feather.

Romeo stood hesitantly waiting, as if expecting Joel to take the lead; but when the white child kept still, he said: "You lucky you come to town, Mister Fever. This here little gentman's Skully kin, and he going out to the Landing for to live."

"I'm Mister Sansom's son," said Joel, though suddenly, gazing up at the dark and fragile face, this didn't seem to mean much. Mr Sansom. And who was he? A nothing, a nobody. A name that did not appear even to have particular significance for the old man whose sunken, blind-looking eyes studied him without expression.

Then Jesus Fever raised the derby a respectful inch. "Say I should find him here: Miss Amy say," he whispered hoarsely. His face was like a black withered apple, and almost destroyed; his polished forehead shone as though a purple light gleamed under the skin; his sickle-curved posture made him look as though his back were broken: a sad little brokeback dwarf crippled with age. Yet, and this impressed Joel's imagination, there was a touch of the wizard in his yellow, spotted eyes: it was a tricky quality that suggested, well, magic and things read in books. "I here yestiday, day fore, cause Miss Amy, she say wait," and he trembled under the impact of a deep breath. "Now I can't talk no whole lot: ain't got the strenth. So up, child. Gettin towards night, and night's misery on my bones."

"Right with you, Mister Jesus," said Joel without enthusiasm. Romeo gave him a boost into the wagon, and handed up the suitcase. It was an old wagon, wobbly and rather like an over-sized peddler's cart; the floor was strewn with dry cornhusks and croquer sacks which smelled sweetly sour.

"Git, John Brown," urged Jesus Fever, gently slapping the reins against a tan mule's back. "Lift them feet, John Brown, lift them feet. . . ."

Slowly the wagon pulled from the lot and groaned up a path onto the road. Romeo ran ahead, gave the mule's rump a mighty whack and darted off; Joel felt a quick impulse to call him back, for it came to him all at once that he did not want to reach Skully's Landing alone. But there was nothing to be done about it now. Out in front of the stable the bearded drunk had quit dancing, and the hound dog was squatting under the water trough scratching fleas. The wagon's rickety wheels made dust clouds that hung in the green air like powdered bronze. A bend in the road: Noon City was gone.

It was night, and the wagon crept over an abandoned country road where the wheels ground softly through deep fine sand, muting John Brown's forlorn hoofclops. Jesus Fever had so far spoken only twice, each time to threaten the mule with some outlandish torture: he was going to skin him raw or split his head with an axe, possibly both. Finally he'd given up and, still hunched upright on the seatplank, fallen asleep. "Much further?" Joel asked once, and there was no answer. The reins lay limply entwined round the old man's wrists, but the mule skillfully guided the wagon unaided.

Relaxed as a rag doll, Joel was stretched on a croquer-sack mattress, his legs dangling over the wagon's end. A vine-like latticework of stars frosted the southern sky, and with his eyes he interlinked these spangled vines till he could trace many ice-white resemblances: a steeple, fantastic flowers, a springing cat, the outline of a human head, and other curious designs like those made by snowflakes. There was a vivid, slightly red three-quarter moon; the evening wind eerily stirred shawls of Spanish moss which draped the branches of passing trees. Here and there in the mellow dark fireflies signaled one another as though messaging in code. He listened contented and untroubled to the remote, singing-saw noise of night insects.

Then presently the music of a childish duet came carrying over the sounds of the lonesome countryside: "What does the robin do then, poor thing . . ." Like specters he saw them hurrying in the moonshine along the road's weedy edge. Two girls. One walked with easy grace, but the other moved as jerky and quick as a boy, and it was she that Joel recognized.

"Hello, there," he said boldly when the wagon overtook them.

Both girls had watched the wagon's approach, and slowed their step perceptibly; but the one who was unfamiliar, as if startled, cried, "Gee Jemima!" She had long, long hair that fell past her hips, and her face, the little he could see of it, smudged as it was in shadow, seemed very friendly, very pretty. "Why, isn't it just grand of you to come along this way and want to give us a ride?"

"Help yourself," he said, and slid over to make a seat.

"I'm Miss Florabel Thompkins," she announced, after she'd hopped agilely up beside him, and pulled her dresshem below her knees. "This is the Skullys' wagon? Sure, that's Jesus Fever ... is he asleep? Well, don't that beat everything." She talked rapidly in a flighty, too birdlike manner, as if mimicking a certain type of old lady. "Come on, sister, there's oodles of room."

The sister trudged on behind the wagon. "I've got two feet and I reckon I'm not such a flirt I can't find the willpower to put one in front of the other, thanks all the same," she said, and gave her shorts an emphatic hitch.

"You're welcome to ride," said Joel weakly, not knowing what else to do; for she was a funny kid, no doubt about it.

"Oh, folderol," said Florabel Thompkins, "don't you pay her no mind. That's just what Mama calls Idabel Foolishness. Let her walk herself knock-kneed for what it means to the great wide world. No use trying to reason with her: she's got willful ways, Idabel has. Ask anybody."

"Huh," was all Idabel said in her defense.

Joel looked from one to the other, and concluded he liked Florabel the best; she was so pretty, at least he imagined her to be, though he could not see her face well enough to judge fairly. Anyway, her sister was a tomboy, and he'd had a special hatred of tomboys ever since the days of Eileen Otis. This Eileen Otis was a beefy little roughneck who had lived on the same block in New Orleans, and she used to have a habit of waylaying him, stripping off his pants, and tossing them high into a tree. That was years gone by, but the memory of her could infuriate him still. He pictured Florabel's redheaded sister as a regular Eileen Otis.

"We've got us a lovely car, you know," said Florabel. "It's a green Chevrolet that six persons can ride in without anybody sitting on anybody's lap, and there are real windowshades you can pull up or down with darling toy babies. Papa won this lovely Chevrolet from a man at a cock-fight, which I think was real smart of him, only Mama says different. Mama's as honest as the day is long, and she don't hold with the cock-fights. But what I'm trying to say is: we don't usually have to hitch rides, and with strangers, too . . . course we do know Jesus Fever . . . kinda. But what's your name? Joel? Joel what? Knox . . . well, Joel Knox, what I'm trying to say is my Papa usually drives us to town in our lovely car. . . ." She jabbered on and on, and he was content to listen till, turning his head, he saw her sister, and thought she was looking at him peculiarly. As this exchange of stares continued, a smileless but amused look that passed between them was lighted by the moon; it was as if each were saying: *I don't think so much of you, either.* ". . . but one time I just happened to slam the door on Idabel's hand," Florabel was still talking of the car, "and now her thumbnail won't grow the least bit: it's all lumpy and black. But she didn't cry or take on, which was very brave on her part; now me, I couldn't stand to have such a nasty old . . . show him your hand, sister."

"You let me alone or I'll show it to you o.k.: in a place you're not expecting."

Florabel sniffed, and glanced peevishly at Joel because he laughed. "It don't pay to treat Idabel like she was a human being," she said ominously. "Ask anybody. The tough way she acts you'd never suppose she came from a well-to-do family like mine, would you?"

Joel held his peace, knowing no matter what he said it would be the wrong thing.

"That's just what I mean," said Florabel, turning the silence to her own advantage, "you'd never suppose. Naturally she is as we're twins: born the same day, me ten minutes first, so I'm elder; both of us twelve, going on thirteen. Florabel and Idabel. Isn't it tacky the way those names kinda rhyme? Only Mama thinks it's real cute, but . . ."

Joel didn't hear the rest, for he suddenly noticed Idabel had stopped trailing the wagon. She was far back and running, running like a pale animal through the lake of weeds lining the wayside towards a flowering island of dogwood that bloomed lividly some distance off like seashore foam on a black beach. But before he could point this out to Florabel, her twin was gone and lost between the shining trees. "Isn't she afraid to be out there all alone in the dark?" he interrupted, and with a gesture indicated where Idabel had disappeared.

"That child is afraid of nothing," stated Florabel flatly. "Don't you fret none over her; she'll catch up when she gets to feeling like it."

"But out in those woods . . ."

"Oh, sister takes her notions and there's no sense in asking why. We were born twins, like I told you, but Mama says the Lord always sends something bad with the good." Florabel yawned and leaned back, the long hair sprawling about her shoulders. "Idabel will take any kind of a dare; even when we were real little she'd go up and poke around the Skullys' and peek in all the windows. One time she even got a good look at Cousin Randolph." Lazily she reached up and seized a firefly that was pulsing goldenly in the air above her head, then: "Do you like living at that place?"

"What place?"

"The Landing, silly."

Joel said: "I may, but I haven't seen it yet." Her face was close to his, and he could tell she was disappointed with the answer. "And you, where's your house?"

She waved an airy hand. "Just a little ways up yonder. It's not far from the Landing, so maybe you could come visit sometime." She tossed the firefly into the air where it hung suspended like a small moon. "Naturally I didn't know whether to think you lived at the Landing or not. Nobody ever sees any of them Skullys. Why, the Lord himself could be living there with none the wiser. Are you kin to . . ." but this was cut short by a terrible, paralyzing wail, and wild crashing in the all-around darkness.

Idabel bounded into the road from the underbrush. She was flailing her arms and howling loud and fierce.

"You darn fool!" her sister screamed, but Joel did nothing, for his heart was lodged somewhere in his throat. Then he turned to check Jesus Fever's reaction, but the old man still snoozed; and strangely the mule had not bolted with fright.

"That was pretty good, eh?" said Idabel. "I'll bet you thought the devil was hot on your trail."

Florabel said: "Not the devil, sister . . . he's inside you." And to Joel: "She'll catch it when I tell Papa, cause she couldn't have got up here without us seeing unless she cut through the hollow, and Papa's told her and told her about that. She's all the time snooping around in there hunting sweetgum: some day a big old moccasin is going to chew off her leg right at the hip, mark my word."

Idabel had returned carrying a spray of dogwood, and now she smelled the blooms exultantly. "I've already been snakebit," she said.

"Yes, that's the truth," her sister admitted. "You should've seen her leg, Joel Knox. It swelled up like a watermelon; all her hair fell out; oh, she was dogsick for two months, and Mama and me had to wait on her hand and foot."

"It's lucky she didn't die," said Joel.

"I would've if I was you and didn't know how to take care of myself," said Idabel.

"She was smart, all right," conceded Florabel. "She just went smack in the chicken yard and snatched up this rooster and ripped him wide open; never heard such squawking. Hot chicken blood draws the poison."

"You ever been snakebit, boy?" Idabel wanted to know.

"No," he said, feeling somehow in the wrong, "but I was nearly run over by a car once."

Idabel seemed to consider this. "Run over by a car," she said, her woolly voice tinged with envy.

"Now you oughtn't to have told her that," snapped Florabel. "She's liable to run straight off and throw herself in the middle of the highway."

Below the road and in the shallow woods a close-by creek's sliding, pebble-tinkling rush underlined the bellowed comments of hidden frogs. The slow-rolling wagon cleared a slope and started down again. Idabel picked the petals from the dogwood spray, dripping them in her path, and tossed the rind aside; she tilted her head and faced the sky and began to hum; then she sang: "When the northwind doth blow, and we shall have snow, what does the robin do then, poor thing?" Florabel took up the tune: "He got to the barn, to keep he-self warm, and hide he-self under he wing, poor thing!" It was a lively song and they sang it over and over till Joel joined to make a trio; their voices pealed clear and sweet, for all three were sopranos, and Florabel vivaciously strummed a mythical banjo. Then a cloud crossed the moon and in the black the singing ended.

Florabel jumped off the wagon. "Our house is over in there," she said, pointing toward what looked to Joel like an empty wilderness. "Don't forget . . . come to visit."

"I will," he called, but already the tide of darkness had washed the twins from sight.

Sometime later a thought of them echoed, receded, left him suspecting they were perhaps what he'd first imagined: apparitions. He touched his cheek, the cornhusks, glanced at the sleeping Jesus—the old man was trancelike but for his body's rubbery response to the wagon's jolting—and was reassured. The guide reins jangled, the hoofbeats of the mule made a sound as drowsy as a fly's bzzz on a summer afternoon. A jungle of stars rained down to cover him in blaze, to blind and close his eyes. Arms akimbo, legs crumpled, lips vaguely parted—he looked as if sleep had struck him with a blow.

Fence posts suddenly loomed; the mule came alive, began to trot, almost to gallop down a graveled lane over which the wheels spit stone; and Jesus Fever, jarred conscious, tugged at the reins: "Whoa, John Brown, whoa!" And the wagon presently came to a spiritless standstill.

A woman slipped down the steps leading from a great porch; delirious white wings sucked round the yellow globe of a kerosene lantern that she carried high. But Joel, scowling at a dream demon, was unaware when the woman bent so intently towards him and peered into his face by the lamp's smoky light.

TWO

falling . . . Falling . . . FALLING! a knifelike shaft, an underground corridor, and he was spinning like a fan blade through metal spirals; at the bottom a yawning-jawed crocodile followed his downward whirl with hooded eyes: as always, rescue came with wakefulness. The crocodile exploded in sunshine. Joel blinked and tasted his bitter tongue and did not move; the bed, an immense four-poster with different rosewood fruits carved crudely on its high headboard, was suffocatingly soft and his body had sunk deep in its feathery center. Although he'd slept naked, the light sheet covering him felt like a wool blanket.

The whisper of a dress warned him that someone was in the room. And another sound, dry and wind-rushed, very much like the beat of bird wings; it was this sound, he realized while rolling over, which had wakened him.

An expanse of pale yellow wall separated two harshly sunlit windows which faced the bed. Between these windows stood the woman. She did not notice Joel, for she was staring across the room at an ancient bureau: there, on top a lacquered box, was a bird, a bluejay perched so motionless it looked like a trophy. The woman turned and closed the only open window; then, with prissy little sidling steps, she started forward.

Joel was wide awake, but for an instant it seemed as if the bluejay and its pursuer were a curious fragment of his dream. His stomach muscles tightened as he watched her near the bureau and the bird's innocent agitation: it hopped around bobbing its blue-brilliant head; suddenly, just as she came within striking distance, it fluttered its wings and flew across the bed and lighted on a chair where Joel had flung his clothes the night before. And remembrance of the night flooded over him: the wagon, the twins, and the little Negro in the derby hat. And the woman, his father's wife: Miss Amy, as she was called. He remembered entering the house, and stumbling through an odd chamber of a hall where the walls were alive with the tossing shadows of candleflames; and Miss Amy, her finger pressed against her lips, leading him with robber stealth up a curving, carpeted stairway and along a second corridor to the door of this room; all a sleepwalker's pattern of jigsaw incidents; and so, as Miss Amy stood by the bureau regarding the bluejay on its new perch, it was more or less the same as seeing her for the first time. Her dress was of an almost transparent grey material; on her left hand, for no clear reason, she wore a matching grey silk glove, and she kept the hand cupped daintily, as if it were crippled. A wispy streak of white zigzagged through the dowdy plaits of her brownish, rather colorless hair. She was slight, and fragile-boned, and her eyes were like two raisins embedded in the softness of her narrow face.

Instead of following the bird directly, as before, she tiptoed over to a fireplace at the opposite end of the huge room, and, artfully twisting her hand, seized hold of an iron poker. The bluejay hopped down the arm of the chair, pecking at Joel's discarded shirt. Miss Amy pursed her lips, and took five rapid, lilting, ladylike steps. . . .

The poker caught the bird across the back, and pinioned it for the fraction of a moment; breaking loose, it flew wildly to the window and cawed and flapped against the pane, at last dropping to the floor where it scrambled along dazedly, scraping the rug with its outspread wings.

Miss Amy trapped it in a corner, and scooped it up against her breast.

Joel pressed his face into the pillow, knowing that she would look in his direction, if only to see how the racket had affected him. He listened to her footsteps cross the room, and the gentle closing of the door.

He dressed in the same clothes he'd worn the previous day: a blue shirt, and bedraggled linen trousers. He could not find his suitcase anywhere, and wondered whether he'd left it in the wagon. He combed his hair, and doused his face with water from a washbasin that sat on a marble-topped table beside the rosewood four-poster. The rug, which was bald in spots and of an intricately oriental design, felt grimy and rough under his bare feet. The stifling room was musty; it smelled of old furniture and the burned-out fires of wintertime; gnat-like motes of dust circulated in the sunny air, and Joel left a dusty imprint on whatever he touched: the bureau, the chiffonier, the washstand. This room had not been used in many years certainly; the only fresh things here were the bedsheets, and even these had a yellowed look.

He was lacing up his shoes when he spied the bluejay feather. It was floating above his head, as if held by a spider's thread. He plucked it out of the air, carried it to the bureau, and deposited it in the lacquered box, which was lined with red plush; it also occurred to him that this would be a good place to store Sam Radclif's bullet. Joel loved any kind of souvenir, and it was his nature to keep and catalogue trifles. He'd had many grand collections, and it pained him sorely that Ellen persuaded him to leave them in New Orleans. There had been magazine photos and foreign coins, books and no-two-alike rocks, and a wonderful conglomeration he'd labeled simply Miscellany: the feather and bullet would've made good items for that. But maybe Ellen would mail his stuff on, or maybe he could start all over again, maybe . . .

There was a rap at the door.

It was his father, of that he was sure. It must be. And what should he say: hello, Dad, Father, Mr Sansom? Howdyado, hello? Hug, or shake hands, or kiss? Oh why hadn't he brushed his teeth, why couldn't he find the Major's suitcase and a clean shirt? He whipped a bow into his shoelace, called, "Yeah?" and straightened up erect, prepared to make the best, most manly impression possible.

The door opened. Miss Amy, her gloved hand cradled, waited on the threshold; she nodded sweetly, and, as she advanced, Joel noticed the vague suggestion of a mustache fuzzing her upper lip.

"Good morning," he said, and, smiling, held out his hand. He was of course disappointed, but somehow relieved, too.

She stared at his outstretched hand, a puzzled look contracting her puny face. She shook her head, and skirted past him to a window where she stood with her back turned. "It's after twelve," she said.

Joel's smile felt suddenly stiff and awkward. He hid his hands in his pockets.

"Such a pity you arrived last night at so late an hour: Randolph had planned a merrier welcome." Her voice had a weary, simpering tone; it struck the ear like the deflating whoosh of a toy balloon. "But it's just as well, the poor child suffers with asthma, you know: had a wretched attack yesterday. He'll be ever so peeved I haven't let him know you're here, but I think it best he stay in his room, at least till supper."

Joel rummaged around for something to say. He recalled Sam Radclif having spoken of a cousin, and one of the twins, Florabel, of a Cousin Randolph. At any rate, from the way she talked, he supposed this person to be a kid near his own age.

"Randolph is our first cousin, and a great admirer of yours," she said, turning to face him. The hard sunshine emphasized the pallor of her skin, and her tiny eyes, now fixing him shrewdly, were alert. There was lack of focus in her face, as though, beneath the uningratiating veneer of fatuous refinement, another personality, quite different, was demanding attention; the lack of focus gave her, at unguarded moments, a panicky, dismayed expression, and when she spoke it was as if she were never precisely certain what every word signified. "Have you money left from the check my husband sent Mrs Kendall?"

"About a dollar, I guess," he said, and reluctantly offered his change purse. "It cost a good bit to stay at that café."

"Please, it's yours," she said. "I was merely interested in whether you are a wise, thrifty boy." She appeared suddenly irritated. "Why are you so fidgety? Must you use the bathroom?"

"Oh, no." He felt all at once as though he'd wet his pants in public. "Oh, no."

"Unfortunately, we haven't modern plumbing facilities. Randolph is opposed to contrivances of that sort. However," and she nodded toward the washstand, "you'll find a chamber pot in there . . . in the compartment below."

"Yes'm," said Joel, mortified.

"And of course the house has never been wired for electricity. We have candles and lamps; they both draw bugs, but which would you prefer?"

"Whichever you've got the most of," he said, really wanting candles, for they brought to mind the St. Deval Street Secret Nine, a neighborhood detective club of which he'd been both treasurer and Official Historian. And he recalled club get-togethers where tall candles, snitched from the five 'n' dime, flamed in Coca-Cola bottles, and how Exalted Operative Number One, Sammy Silverstein, had used for a gavel an old cow bone.

She glanced at the firepoker which had rolled halfway under a wing chair. "Would you mind picking that up and putting it over by the hearth? I was in here earlier," she explained, while he carried out her order, "and a bird flew in the window; such a nuisance: you weren't disturbed?"

Joel hesitated. "I thought I heard something," he said. "It woke me up."

"Well, twelve hours sleep should be sufficient." She lowered herself into the chair, and crossed her toothpick legs; her shoes were low-heeled and white, like those worn by nurses. "Yes, the morning's gone and everything's all hot again. Summer is so unpleasant." Now despite her impersonal manner, Joel was not antagonized, just a little uncomfortable. Females in Miss Amy's age bracket, somewhere between forty-five and fifty, generally displayed a certain tenderness toward him, and he took their sympathy for granted; if, as had infrequently happened, this affection was withheld, he knew with what ease it could be guaranteed: a smile, a wistful glance, a courtly compliment: "I want to say how pretty I think your hair is: a *nice* color."

The bribe received no clear-cut appreciation, therefore: "And how much I like my room."

And this time he hit his mark. "I've always considered it the finest room in the house. Cousin Randolph was born here: in that very bed. And Angela Lee . . . Randolph's mother: a beautiful woman, originally from Memphis . . . died here, oh, not many years ago. We've never used it since." She perked her head suddenly, as if to hear some distant sound; her eyes squinted, then closed altogether. But presently she relaxed and eased back into the chair. "I suppose you've noticed the view?"

Joel confessed that no, he hadn't, and went obligingly to a window. Below, under a fiery surface of sun waves, a garden, a jumbled wreckage of zebrawood and lilac, elephant-ear plant and weeping willow, the lace-leafed limp branches shimmering delicately, and dwarfed cherry trees, like those in oriental prints, sprawled raw and green in the noon heat. It was not a result of simple neglect, this tangled oblong area, but rather the outcome, it appeared, of someone having, in a riotous moment, scattered about it a wild assortment of seed. Grass and bush and vine and flower were all crushed together. Massive chinaberry and waterbay formed a rigidly enclosing wall. Now at the far end, opposite the house, was an unusual sight: like a set of fingers, a row of five white fluted columns lent the garden the primitive, haunted look of a lost ruin: Judas vine snaked up their toppling slenderness, and a yellow tabby cat was sharpening its claws against the middle column.

Miss Amy, having risen, now stood beside him. She was an inch or so shorter than Joel.

"In ancient history class at school, we had to draw pictures of some pillars like those. Miss Kadinsky said mine were the best, and she put them on the bulletin board," he bragged.

"The pillars . . . Randolph adores them, too; they were once part of the old side porch," she told him in a reminiscing voice. "Angela Lee was a young bride, just down from Memphis, and I was a child younger than you. In the evening we would sit on the side porch, sipping cherryade and listen to the crickets and wait for the moonrise. Angela Lee crocheted a shawl for me: you must see it sometime, Randolph uses it in his room as a ta-blescarf: a waste and a shame." She spoke so quietly it was as though she intended only herself to hear.

"Did the porch just blow away?" asked Joel.

"Burned," she said, rubbing a clear circle on the dusty glass with her gloved hand. "It was in December, the week before Christmas, and at a time when there was no man on the place but Jesus Fever, and he was even then very old. No one knows how the fire started or ended; it simply rose out of nothing, burned away the dining room, the music room, the library . . . and went out. No one knows."

"And this garden is where the part that burned up was?" said Joel. "Gee, it must've been an awful big house."

She said: "There, by the willows and goldenrod . . . that is the site of the music room where the dances were held; small dances, to be sure, for there were few around here Angela Lee cared to entertain. . . . And they are all dead now, those who came to her little evenings; Mr Casey, I understand, passed on last year, and he was the last."

Joel gazed down on the jumbled green, trying to picture the music room and the dancers ("Angela Lee played the harp," Miss Amy was saying, "and Mr Casey the piano, and Jesus Fever, though he'd never studied, the violin, and Randolph the Elder sang; had the finest male voice in the state, everyone said so"), but the willows were willows and the goldenrod goldenrod and the dancers dead and lost. The yellow tabby slunk through the lilac into tall, concealing grass, and the garden was glazed and secret and still.

Miss Amy sighed as she slipped back into the shade of the room. "Your suitcase is in the kitchen," she said. "If you'll come downstairs, we'll see what Missouri has to feed you."

❧❧❧

A dormer window of frost glass illuminated the long top-floor hall with the kind of pearly light that drenches a room when rain is falling. The wallpaper had once, you could tell, been blood red, but now was faded to a mural of crimson blisters and maplike stains. Including Joel's, there were four doors in the hall, impressive oak doors with massive brass knobs, and Joel wondered which of them, if opened, might lead to his father.

"Miss Amy," he said, as they started down the stairs, "where is my dad? I mean, couldn't I see him, please, ma'am?"

She did not answer. She walked a few steps below him, her gloved hand sliding along the dark, curving bannister, and each stairstep remarked the delicacy of her footfall. The strand of grey winding in her mousy hair was like a streak of lightning.

"Miss Amy, about my father . . ."

What in hell was the matter with her? Was she a little deaf, like his cousin Louise? The stairs sloped down to the circular chamber he remembered from the night, and here a full-length mirror caught his reflection bluely; it was like the comedy mirrors in carnival houses; he swayed shapelessly in its distorted depth. Except for a cedar chest supporting a kerosene lantern, the chamber was bleak and unfurnished. At the left was an archway, and a large crowded parlor yawned dimly beyond; to the right hung a curtain of lavender velvet that gleamed in various rubbed places like frozen dew on winter grass. She pushed through the parted folds. Another hall, another door.

The kitchen was empty. Joel sat down in a cane-bottom chair at a large table spread with checkered oilcloth, while Miss Amy went out on the backsteps and stood there calling, "Yoo hoo, Missouri, yoo hoo," like an old screech owl.

A rusty alarm clock, lying face over on the table, ticktucked, ticktucked. The kitchen was fair-sized, but shadowed, for there was a single window, and by it the furry leaves of a fig tree met darkly; also, the planked walls were the somber bluegray of an overcast sky, and the stove, a woodburning relic with a fire pulsing in it now, was black with a black chimney flute rising to the low ceiling. Worn linoleum covered the floor, as it had in Ellen's kitchen, but this was all that reminded Joel of home.

And then, sitting alone in the quiet kitchen, he was taken with a terrible idea: what if his father had seen him already? Indeed, had been spying on him ever since he arrived, was, in fact, watching him at this very moment? An old house like this would most likely be riddled with hidden passages, and picture-eyes that were not eyes at all, but peepholes. And his father thought: that runt is an impostor; my son would be taller and stronger and handsomer and smarter-looking. Suppose he'd told Miss Amy: give the little faker something to eat and send him on his way. And dear sweet Lord, where would he go? Off to foreign lands where he'd set himself up as an organ grinder with a little doll-clothed monkey, or a blind-boy street singer, or a beggar selling pencils.

"Confound it, Missouri, why can't you learn to light in one place longer than five seconds?"

"I gotta chop the wood. Ain't I gotta chop the wood?"

"Don't sass me."

"I ain't sassin nobody, Miss Amy."

"If that isn't sass, what is it?"

"Whew!"

Up the steps they came, and through the back screen door, Miss Amy, vexation souring her white face, and a graceful Negro girl toting a load of kindling which she dropped in a crib next to the stove. The Major's suitcase, Joel saw, was jammed behind this crib.

Smoothing the fingers of her silk glove, Miss Amy said: "Missouri belongs to Jesus Fever; she's his grandchild."

"Delighted to make your acquaintance," said Joel, in his very best dancing-class style.

"Me, too," rejoined the colored girl, going about her business. "Welcome to," she dropped a frying pan, "the Landin."

"If we aren't more careful," stage-whispered Miss Amy, "we're liable to find ourselves in serious difficulty. All this racket: Randolph will have a conniption."

"Sometime I get so tired," mumbled Missouri.

"She's a good cook . . . when she feels like it," said Miss Amy. "You'll be taken care of. But don't stuff, we have early supper on Sundays."

Missouri said: "You comin to Service, Ma'am?"

"Not today," Miss Amy replied distractedly. "He's worse, much worse."

Missouri placed the pan on a rack and nodded knowingly. Then, looking square at Joel: "We countin on you, young fella."

It was like the exasperating code-dialogue which, for the benefit and bewilderment of outsiders, had often passed between members of the St. Deval Street Secret Nine.

"Missouri and Jesus hold their own prayer meeting Sunday afternoons," explained Miss Amy.

"I plays the accordion and us sings," said Missouri. "It's a whole lota fun."

But Joel, seeing Miss Amy was preparing to depart, ignored the colored girl, for there were certain urgent matters he wanted settled. "About my father . . ."

"Yes?" Miss Amy paused in the doorway.

Joel felt tongue-tied. "Well, I'd like to . . . to see him," he finished lamely.

She fiddled with the doorknob. "He isn't well, you know," she said. "I don't think it advisable he see you just yet; it's so hard for him to talk." She made a helpless gesture. "But if you want, I'll ask."

❦

With a cut of cornbread, Joel mopped bone-dry the steaming plate of fried eggs and grits, sopping rich with sausage gravy, that Missouri had set before him.

"It sure do gimme pleasure to see a boy relish his vittels," she said. "Only don't spec no refills cause I gotta pain lickin my back like to kill me: didn't sleep a blessed wink last night; been sufferin with this pain off and on since I'm a wee child, and done took enough medicine to float the whole entire United States Navy: ain't nona it done me a bita good nohow. There was a witch woman lived a piece down the road (Miz Gus Hulie) usta make a fine magic brew, and that helped some. Poor white lady. Miz Gus Hulie. Met a terrible accident: fell into an ol Injun grave and was too feeble for to climb out." Tall, powerful, barefoot, graceful, soundless, Missouri Fever was like a supple black cat as she paraded serenely about the kitchen, the casual flow of her walk beautifully sensuous and haughty. She was slant-eyed, and darker than the charred stove; her crooked hair stood straight on end, as if she'd seen a ghost, and her lips were thick and purple. The length of her neck was something to ponder upon, for she was almost a freak, a human giraffe, and Joel recalled photos, which he'd scissored once from the pages of a *National Geographic,* of curious African ladies with countless silver chokers stretching their necks to improbable heights. Though she wore no silver bands, naturally, there was a sweat-stained blue polka-dot bandanna wrapped round the middle of her soaring neck. "Papadaddy and me's countin on you for our Service," she said, after filling two coffee cups and mannishly straddling a chair at the table. "We got our own little place backa the garden, so you scoot over later on, and we'll have us a real good ol time."

"I'll come if I can, but this being my first day and all, Dad will most likely expect me to visit with him," said Joel hopefully.

Missouri emptied her coffee into a saucer, blew on it, dumped it back into the cup, sucked up a swallow, and smacked her lips. "This here's the Lord's day," she announced. "You believe in Him? You got faith in His healin power?"

Joel said: "I go to church."

"Now that ain't what I'm speakin of. Take for instance, when you thinks bout the Lord, what is it passes in your mind?"

"Oh, stuff," he said, though actually, whenever he had occasion to remember that a God in heaven supposedly kept his record, one thing he thought of was money: quarters his mother had given him for each Bible stanza memorized, dimes diverted from the Sunday School collection plate to Gabaldoni's Soda Fountain, the tinkling rain of coins as the cashiers of the church solicited among the congregation. But Joel didn't much like God, for He had betrayed him too many times. "Just stuff like saying my prayers."

"When I thinks bout Him, I thinks bout what I'm gonna do when Papadaddy goes to his rest," said Missouri, and rinsed her mouth with a big swallow of coffee. "Well, I'm gonna spread my wings and fly way to some swell city up north like Washington, D.C."

"Aren't you happy here?"

"Honey, there's things you too young to unnerstand."

"I'm thirteen," he declared. "And you'd be surprised how much I know."

"Shoot, boy, the country's just fulla folks what knows everythin, and don't unnerstand nothin, just fullofem," she said, and began to prod her upper teeth: she had a flashy gold tooth, and it occurred to Joel that the prodding was designed for attracting his attention to it. "Now one reason is, I get lonesome: what I all the time say is, you ain't got no notion what lonesome is till you stayed a spell at the Landin. And there ain't no mens round here I'm innersted in, leastwise not at the present: one time there was this mean buzzard name of Keg, but he did a crime to me and landed hisself on the chain gang, which is sweet justice considerin the lowdown kinda trash he was. I'm only a girl of fourteen when he did this bad thing to me." A fist-like knot of flies, hovering over a sugar jar, dispersed every whichaway as she swung an irritated hand. "Yessir, Keg Brown, that's the name he go by." With a fingertip she shined her gold tooth to a brighter luster while her slanted eyes scrutinized Joel; these eyes were like wild foxgrapes, or two discs of black porcelain, and they looked out intelligently from their almond slits. "I gotta longin for city life poisonin my blood cause I was brung up in St. Louis till Papadaddy fetched me here for to nurse him in his dyin days. Papadaddy was past ninety then, and they say he ain't long for this world, so I come. That be thirteen year ago, and now it look

to me like Papadaddy gonna outlive Methusaleh. Make no mistake, I love Papadaddy, but when he gone I sure aimin to light
out for Washington, D.C., or Boston, Coneckikut. And that's
what I thinks bout when I thinks bout God."

"Why not New Orleans?" said Joel. "There are all kinds of
good-looking fellows in New Orleans."

"Aw, I ain't studyin no New Orleans. It ain't only the mens,
honey: I wants to be where they got snow, and not all this sunshine. I wants to walk around in snow up to my hips: watch it
come outa the sky in gret big globs. Oh, pretty . . . pretty. You
ever see the snow?"

Rather breathlessly, Joel lied and claimed that he most certainly had; it was a pardonable deception, for he had a great
yearning to see bona fide snow: next to owning the Koh-i-noor
diamond, that was his ultimate secret wish. Sometimes, on flat
boring afternoons, he'd squatted on the curb of St. Deval Street
and daydreamed silent pearly snowclouds into sifting coldly
through the boughs of the dry, dirty trees. Snow falling in August and silvering the glassy pavement, the ghostly flakes icing
his hair, coating rooftops, changing the grimy old neighborhood
into a hushed frozen white wasteland uninhabited except for
himself and a menagerie of wonder-beasts: albino antelopes,
and ivory-breasted snowbirds; and occasionally there were humans, such fantastic folk as Mr Mystery, the vaudeville hypno-
tist, and Lucky Rogers, the movie star, and Madame Veronica,
who read fortunes in a Vieux Carré tearoom. "It was one stormy
night in Canada that I saw the snow," he said, though the far-
thest north he'd ever set foot was Richmond, Virginia. "We were
lost in the mountains, Mother and me, and snow, tons and tons
of it, was piling up all around us. And we lived in an ice-cold
cave for a solid week, and we kept slapping each other to stay

awake: if you fall asleep in snow, chances are you'll never see the light of day again."

"Then what happened?" said Missouri, disbelief subtly narrowing her eyes.

"Well, things got worse and worse. Mama cried, and the tears froze on her face like little BB bullets, and she was always cold. . . ." Nothing had warmed her, not the fine wool blankets, not the mugs of hot toddy Ellen fixed. "Each night hungry wolves howled in the mountains, and I prayed. . . ." In the darkness of the garage he'd prayed, and in the lavatory at school, and in the first row of the Nemo Theatre while duelling gangsters went unnoticed on the magic screen. "The snow kept falling, and heavy drifts blocked the entrance to the cave, but uh . . ." Stuck. It was the end of a Saturday serial that leaves the hero locked in a slowly filling gas chamber.

"And?"

"And a man in a red coat, a Canadian mountie, rescued us . . . only me, really: Mama had already frozen to death."

Missouri denounced him with considerable disgust. "You is a gret big story."

"Honest, cross my heart," and he x-ed his chest.

"Uh uh. You Mama die in the sick bed. Mister Randolph say so."

Somehow, spinning the tale, Joel had believed every word; the cave, the howling wolves, these had seemed more real than Missouri and her long neck, or Miss Amy, or the shadowy kitchen. "You won't tattle, will you, Missouri? About what a liar I am."

She patted his arm gently. "Course not, honey. Come to think, I wish I had me a two-bit piece for every story I done told. Sides, you tell good lies, the kind I likes to hear. We gonna get along just elegant: me, I ain't but eight years older'n you, and you been to the school." Her voice, which was like melted chocolate, was warm and tender. "Les us be friends."

"O.K.," said Joel, toasting her with his coffee cup, "friends."

"And somethin else is, you call me Zoo. Zoo's my rightful name, and I always been called by that till Papadaddy let on it stood for Missouri, which is the state where is located the city of St. Louis. *Them*, Miss Amy 'n Mister Randolph, they so proper: Missouri this 'n Missouri t'other, day in, day out. Huh! You call me Zoo."

Joel saw an opening. "Does my father call you Zoo?"

She dipped down into the blouse of her gingham dress, and withdrew a silver compact. Opening it, she took a pinch of snuff, and sniffed it up her wide nose. "Happy Dip, that's the bestest brand."

"Is he awful sick—Mister Sansom?" Joel persisted.

"Take a pinch," she said, extending her compact.

And he accepted, anxious not to offend her. The ginger-colored powder had a scalding, miserable taste, like devil's pepper; he sneezed, and when water sprang up in his eyes he covered his face ashamedly with his hands.

"You laughin or cryin, boy?"

"Crying," he whimpered, and this came close to truth. "Everybody in the house is stone deaf."

"I ain't deaf, honey," said Zoo, sounding sincerely concerned. "Have the backache and stomach jitters, but I ain't deaf."

"Then why does everybody act so queer? Gee whiz, every time I mention Mister Sansom you'd think . . . you'd think . . . and in the town . . ." He rubbed his eyes and peeked at Zoo. "Like just now, when I asked if he was really ill . . ."

Zoo glanced worriedly at the window where fig leaves

pressed against the glass like green listening ears. "Miss Amy done tol you he ain't the healthiest man."

The flies buzzed back to the sugar jar, and the ticktuck of the defective clock was loud. "Is he going to die?" said Joel.

The scrape of a chair. Zoo was up and rinsing pans in a tub with water from a well-bucket. "We friends, that's fine," she said, talking over her shoulder. "Only don't never ax me nothin bout Mister Sansom. Miss Amy the one take care of him. Ax her. Ax Mister Randolph. I ain't in noways messed up with Mister Sansom; don't even fix him his vittels. Me and Papadaddy, us got our own troubles."

Joel snapped shut the snuff compact, and revolved it in his hands, examining the unique design. It was round and the silver was cut like a turtle's shell; a real butterfly, arranged under a film of lime glass, figured the lid; the butterfly wings were the luminously misty orange of a full moon. So elegant a case, he reasoned, was never meant for ordinary snuff, but rare golden powders, precious witch potions, love sand.

"Yessir, us got our own troubles."

"Zoo," he said, "where'd you get this?"

She was kneeling on the floor cursing quietly as she shoveled ashes out of the stove. The firelight rippled over her black face and danced a yellow light in her foxgrape eyes which now cut sideways questioningly. "My box?" she said. "Mister Randolph gimme it one Christmas way long ago. He make it hisself, makes lotsa pretty dodads long that line."

Joel studied the compact with awed respect; he would've sworn it was store-bought. Distastefully he recalled his own attempts at hand-made gifts: necktie racks, tool kits, and the like; they were mighty sorry by comparison. He comforted himself with the thought that Cousin Randolph must be older than he'd supposed.

"I usta been usin it for cheek-red," said Zoo, advancing to claim her treasure. She dipped more snuff before re-depositing it down her dress-front. "But seein as I don't go over to Noon City no more (ain't been in two years), I reckoned it'd do to keep my Happy Dip good 'n dry. Sides, no sense paintin up less there's mens round a lady is innerested in . . . which there ain't." A mean expression pinched her face as she gazed at the sunspots freckling the linoleum. "That Keg Brown, the one what landed on the chain gang cause he did me a bad turn, I hope they got him out swingin a ninety-pound pick under this hot sun." And, as if it were sore, she touched her long neck lightly. "Well," she sighed, "spec I best get to tendin Papadaddy: I'm gonna take him some hoecake and molasses: he must be powerful hungry."

Joel watched apathetically while she broke off a cold slab of cornbread, and poured a preserve jar half-full of thick molasses. "How come you don't fix yourself a sling-shot, and go out and kill a mess of birds?" she suggested.

"Dad will probably want me in a minute," he told her. "Miss Amy said she'd see, so I guess I'd better stick around here."

"Mister Randolph likes the dead birds, the kinds with pretty feathers. Won't do you no good squattin in this dark ol kitchen." Her naked feet were soundless as she moved away. "You be at the Service, you hear?"

❦

The fire had waned to ashes, and, while the old broken clock ticked like an invalid heart, the sunspots on the floor spread and darkened; the shadows of the fig leaves trellising the walls swelled to an enormous quivering shape, like the crystal flesh of a jellyfish. Flies skittered along the table, rubbing their restless hair-feet, and zoomed and sang round Joel's ears. When, two hours later, two that seemed five, he raised the clock off its battered face it promptly stopped beating and all sense of life faded from the kitchen; three-twenty its bent hands recorded: three, the empty, middle hour of an endless afternoon. She was not coming. Joel plowed his fingers through his hair. She was not coming, and it was all some crazy trick.

His leg had gone numb from resting so long in one position, and it tingled bloodlessly as he got up and limped out of the kitchen, and down the hall, calling plaintively: "Miss Amy. Miss Amy."

He swished the lavender curtains apart, and moved into the bleak light filling the barren, polished chamber towards his image floating on the watery-surfaced lookingglass; his formless reflected face was wide-lipped and one-eyed, as if it were a heat-softened wax effigy; the lips were a gauzy line, the eyes a glaring bubble. "Miss Amy . . . anybody!"

Somewhere in a school textbook of Joel's was a statement contending that the earth at one time was probably a white hot sphere, like the sun; now, standing in the scorched garden, he remembered it. He had reached the garden by following a path which led round from the front of the house through the rampart of interlacing trees. And here, in the overgrown confusion, were some plants taller than his head, and others razor-sharp with thorns; brittle sun-curled leaves crackled under his cautious step. The dry, tangled weeds grew waist high. The sultry smells of summer and sweet shrub and dark earth were heavy, and the itchy whirr of bumblebees stung the silence. He could hardly raise his eyes upward, for the sky was pure blue fire. The wall of the house rising above the garden was like a great yellow cliff, and patches of Virginia creeper greenly framed all its eight overlooking windows.

Joel trampled down the tough undergrowth till he came up flat against the house. He was bored, and figured he might as well play Blackmail, a kind of peeping-tom game members of the Secret Nine had fooled around with when there was absolutely nothing else to do. Blackmail was practiced in New Orleans only after sunset, inasmuch as daylight could be fatal for a player, the idea being to approach a strange house and peer invisibly through its windows. On these dangerous evening patrols, Joel had witnessed many peculiar spectacles, like the night he'd watched a young girl waltzing stark naked to victrola music; and again, an old lady drop dead while puffing at a fairyland of candles burning on a birthday cake; and most puzzling of all, two grown men standing in an ugly little room kissing each other.

The parlor of Skully's Landing ran the ground-floor's length; gold draperies tied with satin tassels obscured the greater part of its dusky, deserted interior, but Joel, his nose mashed against a pane, could make out a group of heavy chairs clustered like fat dowagers round a tea-table. And a gilded loveseat of lilac velvet, an Empire sofa next to a marble fireplace, and a cabinet, one of three, the others of which were indistinct, gleaming with china figurines and ivory fans and curios. On top of a table directly before him were a Japanese pagoda, and an ornate shepherd lamp, chandelier prisms dangling from its geranium globe like jeweled icicles.

He slipped away from the window and crossed the garden to the slanting shade of a willow. The diamond glitter of the afternoon hurt his eyes, and he was as slippery with sweat as a greased wrestler; it stood to reason such weather would have to break. A rooster crowed beyond the garden, and it had for him the same sad, woebegone sound as a train whistle wailing late at night. A train. He sure wished he were aboard one headed far from here. If he could get to see his father! Miss Amy, she was a mean old bitch. Stepmothers always were. Well, just let her try and lay a hand on him. He'd tell her off soon as look at her, by God. He was pretty brave. Who was it licked Sammy Silverstein to a frazzle a year ago come next October? But gee, Sammy was a good kid, kind of. And he wondered what devilment old Sammy was up to right this minute. Probably sitting in the Nemo Theatre stuffing his belly with popcorn; yeah, that's where you'd find him, because this was the matinee they were going to show that spook picture about a batty scientist changing Lucky Rogers into a murderous gorilla. Of all the pictures he would have to miss that one. Hell! Now supposing he did suddenly decide to make dust tracks on the road? Maybe it would be fun to own a barrel organ and a monkey. And there was always the soda-jerking business: anybody that liked ice-cream sodas as much as he did ought to be able to make one. Hell!

"Ra ta ta ta," went his machine gun as he charged toward the five broken porch columns. And then, midway between the pillars and a clump of goldenrod, he discovered the bell. It was a bell like those used in slave-days to summon fieldhands from work; the metal had turned a mildewed green, and the platform on which it rested was rotten. Fascinated, Joel squatted Indian-style and poked his head inside the bell's flared mouth; the lint of withered spiderwebs hung everywhere, and a delicate green lizard, racing liquidly round the rusty hollow, swerved, flicked its tongue, and nailed its pinpoint eyes on Joel, who withdrew in disordered haste.

Rising, he glanced up at the yellow wall of the house, and speculated as to which of the top-floor windows belonged to him, his father, Cousin Randolph. It was at this point that he saw the queer lady. She was holding aside the curtains of the left corner window, and smiling and nodding at him, as if in greeting or approval; but she was no one Joel had ever known: the hazy substance of her face, the suffused marshmallow features, brought to mind his own vaporish reflection in the wavy chamber mirror. And her white hair was like the wig of a character from history: a towering pale pompadour with fat dribbling curls. Whoever she was, and Joel could not imagine, her sudden appearance seemed to throw a trance across the garden: a butterfly, poised on a dahlia stem, ceased winking its wings, and the rasping F of the bumblebees droned into nothing.

When the curtain fell abruptly closed, and the window was again empty, Joel, reawakening, took a backward step and stumbled against the bell: one raucous, cracked note rang out, shattering the hot stillness.

THREE

"Hey, Lord!" STAMP. "Hey, Lord!" STAMP. "Don't wanna ride on the devil's side ... jus wanna ride with You!"

Zoo squeezed the music from a toylike accordion, and pounded her flat foot on the rickety cabin-porch floor. "Oh devil done weep, devil done cried, cause he gonna miss me on my last lonesome ride." A prolonged shout: the fillet of gold glistened in the frightening volcano of her mouth, and the little mail-order accordion, shoved in, shoved out, was like a lung of pleated paper and pearl shell. "Gonna miss me ..."

For some time the rainbird had shrilled its cool promise from an elderberry lair, and the sun was locked in a tomb of clouds, tropical clouds that nosed across the low sky, massing into a mammoth grey mountain.

Jesus Fever sat surrounded by a mound of beautiful scrapquilt pillows in a rocker fashioned out of old barrel-staves; his reverent falsetto quavered like a broken ocarina-note, and occasionally he raised his hands to give a feeble, soundless clap.

"... on my ride!"

Perched on a toadstool-covered stump growing level with the porch, Joel alternated his interest between Zoo's highjinks and the changing weather; the instant of petrified violence that sometimes foreruns a summer storm saturated the hushed yard, and in the unearthly tinseled light rusty buckets of trailing fern which were strung round the porch like party lanterns appeared illuminated by a faint green inward flame. A damp breeze, tuning in the boles of waterbays, carried the fresh mixed scent of rain, of pine and June flowers blooming in far-off fields. The cabin door swung open, banged closed, and there came the muffled rattle of the Landing's window-shutters being drawn.

Zoo mashed out a final gaudy chord, and put the accordion aside. She had varnished her upended hair with brilliantine, and exchanged the polka-dot neckerchief for a frayed red ribbon. Different colored threads darned her white dress in a dozen spots, and she'd jeweled her ears with a pair of rhinestone earrings.

"If you gotta thirst, and the water done gone, PRAY to the Lord, pray on and on." Outstretching her arms, balanced like a tightrope walker, she stepped into the yard, and strutted round Joel's tree stump. "If you gotta lover, and the lover done gone, PRAY to the Lord, pray on and on."

High in chinaberry towers the wind moved swift as a river, the frenzied leaves, caught in its current, frothed like surf on the sky's shore. And slowly the land came to seem as though it were submerged in dark deep water. The fern undulated like seafloor plants, the cabin loomed mysterious as a sunken galleon hulk, and Zoo, with her fluid, insinuating grace, could only be, Joel thought, the mermaid bride of an old drowned pirate.

"If you gotta hunger, and the food done gone, PRAY to the Lord, pray on and on."

A yellow tabby loped across the yard, and sprang nimbly into Jesus Fever's lap; it was the cat Joel had seen skulking in the garden lilac. Clambering to the old man's shoulder, it smooched its crafty mug next to the puny cheek, its tawny astonished eyes blazing at Joel. It rumbled as the little Negro stroked the striped belly. Minus his derby hat, Jesus Fever's skull, except for sparse sprouts of motheaten wool, was like a ball of burnished metal; a black suit double his size sagged dilapidatedly on his delicate frame, and he wore tiny high-button shoes of orange leather. The spirit of the service was rousing him mightily, and, from time to time, he honked his nose between his fingers, tossing the discharge into the fern.

The rhythmic chain of Zoo's half-sung, half-shouted phrases rose and fell like her pounding foot, and her earrings, dangling with the sway of her head, shot flecks of sparkle. "Listen oh Lord when us pray, kindly hear what us has to say...."

Silent lightning zigzagged miles away, then another bolt, this a dragon of crackling white, now not too distant, was followed by a crawling thunder-roll. A bantam rooster raced for the safety of a well-shed, and the triangular shadow of a crow flock cut the sky.

"I cold," complained Jesus petulantly. "Leg all swole up with rain. I cold...." The cat curled in his lap, its head flopped over his knee like a wilted dahlia.

The off-on flash of Zoo's gold tooth made Joel's heart suddenly like a rock rattling in his chest, for it suggested to him a certain winking neon sign: *R. R. Oliver's Funeral Estb.* Darkness. *R. R. Oliver's Funeral Estb.* Darkness. "Downright tacky, but they don't charge too outlandish," that's what Ellen had said, standing before the plate window where a fan of gladiolas blushed livid under the electric letters publicizing a cheap but decent berth en route to the kingdom and the glory. Now here again he'd locked the door and thrown away the key: there was conspiracy abroad, even his father had a grudge against him, even

God. Somewhere along the line he'd been played a mean trick. Only he didn't know who or what to blame. He felt separated, without identity, a stone-boy mounted on the rotted stump: there was no connection linking himself and the waterfall of elderberry leaves cascading on the ground, or, rising beyond, the Landing's steep, intricate roof.

"I cold. I wants to wrap up in the bed. It gonna storm."

"Hold your tater, Papadaddy."

Then an unusual thing occurred: as if following the directions of a treasure map, Zoo took three measured paces toward a dingy little rose bush, and, frowning up at the sky, discarded the red ribbon binding her throat. A narrow scar circled her neck like a necklace of purple wire; she traced a finger over it lightly.

"When the time come for that Keg Brown to go, Lord, just you send him back in a hound dog's nasty shape, ol hound ain't nobody wants to trifle with: a haunted dog."

It was as though a brutal hawk had soared down and clawed away Joel's eyelids, forcing him to gape at her throat. Zoo. Maybe she was like him, and the world had a grudge against her, too. But christamighty he didn't want to end up with a scar like that. Except what chance have you got when there is always trickery in one hand, and danger in the other. No chance whatsoever. None. A coldness went along his spine. Thunder boomed overhead. The earth shook. He leaped off the stump, and made for the house, his loosened shirt-tail flying behind; run, run, run, his heart told him, and wham! he'd pitched headlong into a briar patch. This was a kind of freak accident. He'd seen the patch, known it for an obstacle, and yet, as though deliberately, he'd thrown himself upon it. But the stinging briar scratches seemed to cleanse him of bewilderment and misery, just as the devil, in fanatic cults, is supposedly, through self-imposed pain, driven from the soul. Realizing the tender concern in Zoo's face as she helped him to his feet, he felt a fool: she was, after all, his friend, and there was no need to be afraid. "Here, little old bad boy," she said kindly, plucking briar needles off his breeches, "how come you act so ugly? Huh, hurt me and Papadaddy's feelins." She took his hand, and led him to the porch.

"Hee hee hee," cackled Jesus, "I tumble thataway, I bust every bone."

Zoo picked up her accordion and, reclining against a porchpole, presently, with careless effort, produced a hesitant, discordant melody. And her grandfather, in a disappointed child's wheedling singsong, reiterated his grievances: he was about to perish of chill, but what matter; who gave a goldarn whether he lived or died? and why didn't Zoo, inasmuch as he'd performed his Sabbath duty, tuck him in his good warm bed and leave him in peace? oh there were cruel folk in this world, and heartless ways.

"Hush up and bow that head, Papadaddy," said Zoo. "We gonna end this meetin proper-like. We gonna tell Him our prayers. Joel, honey, bow that head."

The trio on the porch were figures in a woodcut engraving; the Ancient on his throne of splendid pillows, a yellow pet relaxed in his lap gazing gravely in the drowning light at the small servant bowed at its master's feet, and the arms of the black arrow-like daughter lifted above them all, as if in benediction.

But there was no prayer in Joel's mind; rather, nothing a net of words could capture, for, with one exception, all his prayers of the past had been simple concrete requests: God, give me a bicycle, a knife with seven blades, a box of oil paints. Only how,

how, could you say something so indefinite, so meaningless as this: God, let me be loved.

"Amen," whispered Zoo.

And in this moment, like a swift intake of breath, the rain came.

FOUR

"Can't we be more specific?" said Randolph, languidly pouring a glass of sherry. "Was she fat, tall, lean?"

"It was hard to tell," said Joel.

Outside in the night, rain washed the roof with close slanted sounds, but here kerosene lamps spun webs of mellow light in the darkest corner, and the kitchen window mirrored the scene like a golden lookingglass. So far Joel's first supper at the Landing had gone along well enough. He felt very much at ease with Randolph, who, at each conversational lag, introduced topics which might interest and flatter a boy of thirteen: Joel found himself holding forth exceedingly well (he thought) on Do Human Beings Inhabit Mars? How Do You Suppose Egyptians Really Mummified Folks? Are Headhunters Still Active? and other controversial subjects. It was due more or less to an overdose of sherry (disliking the taste, but goaded by the hope of getting sure enough drunk ... now wouldn't he have something to write Sammy Silverstein! ... three thimble glasses had been drained) that Joel mentioned the Lady.

"Heat," said Randolph. "Exposing one's bare head to the sun occasionally results in minor hallucinations. Dear me, yes. Once, some years ago, while airing in the garden, I seemed quite distinctly to see a sunflower transformed into a man's face, the face of a scrappy little boxer I admired at one point, a Mexican named Pepe Alvarez." He fondled his chin reflectively, and wrinkled his nose, as if to convey that this name had for him particular implications. "Stunning experience, so impressive I cut the flower, and pressed it in a book; even now, if I come across it, I fancy . . . but that is neither here nor there. It was the sun, I'm sure. Amy, dearest, what do you think?"

Amy, who was brooding over her food, glanced up, rather startled. "No more for me, thank you," she said.

Randolph frowned in mock annoyance. "As usual, out picking the little blue flower of forgetfulness."

Her narrow face softened with pleasure. "Silver-tongued devil," she said, unreserved adoration brightening her sharp little eyes, and making them, for an instant, almost beautiful.

"To begin at the beginning, then," he said, and burped ("*Excusez-moi, s'il vous plaît.* Blackeyed peas, you understand; most indigestible"). He patted his lips daintily. "Now where was I, oh yes . . . Joel refuses to be persuaded we at the Landing aren't harboring spirits."

"That isn't what I said," Joel protested.

"Some of Missouri's chatter," was Amy's calm opinion. "Just a hotbed of crazy nigger-notions, that girl. Remember when she wrung the neck off every chicken on the place? Oh, it isn't funny, don't laugh. I've sometimes wondered what would happen if it got into her head *his* soul inhabited one of us."

"Keg?" said Joel. "You mean Keg's soul?"

"Don't tell me!" cried Randolph, and giggled in the prim, suffocated manner of an old maid. "Already?"

"I didn't think it was so funny," said Joel resentfully. "He did a bad thing to her."

Amy said: "Randolph's only cutting up."

"You malign me, angel."

"It wasn't funny," said Joel.

Squinting one eye, Randolph studied the spokes of amber light whirling out from the sherry as he raised and revolved his glass. "Not funny, dear me, no. But the story has a certain bizarre interest: would you care to hear it?"

"How unnecessary," said Amy. "The child's morbid enough."

"All children are morbid: it's their one saving grace," said Randolph, and went right ahead. "This happened more than a decade ago, and in a cold, very cold November. There was working for me at the time a strapping young buck, splendidly proportioned, and with skin the color of swamp honey." A curious quality about Randolph's voice had worried Joel from the first, but not till now could he put a finger on it: Randolph spoke without an accent of any kind: his weary voice was free of regional defects, yet there was an emotional undercurrent, a caustic lilt of sarcasm which gave it a rather emphatic personality.

"He was, however, a little feeble-minded. The feeble-minded, the neurotic, the criminal, perhaps, also, the artist, have unpredictability and perverted innocence in common." His expression became smugly remote, as though, having made an observation he thought superior, he must pause and listen admiringly while it reverberated in his head. "Let's compare them to a Chinese chest: the sort, you remember, that opens into a second box, another, still another, until at length you come upon the last . . . the latch is touched, the lid springs open to reveal . . . what unsuspected cache?" He smiled wanly, and tasted the sherry. Then, from the breastpocket of the taffy-silk pyjama top that he wore, he extracted a cigarette, and struck a match. The cigarette had a strange, medicinal odor, as though the tobacco had been long soaked in the juice of acid herbs: it was the smell that identifies a house where asthma reigns. As he puckered his lips to blow a smoke ring, the pattern of his talcumed face was suddenly complete: it seemed composed now of nothing but circles: though not fat, it was round as a coin, smooth and hairless; two discs of rough pink colored his cheeks, and his nose had a broken look, as if once punched by a strong angry fist; curly, very blond, his fine hair fell in childish yellow ringlets across his forehead, and his wide-set, womanly eyes were like sky-blue marbles.

"So they were in love, Keg and Missouri, and we had the wedding here, the bride all clothed in family lace . . ."

"Nice as any white girl, I'll tell you," said Amy. "Pretty as a picture."

Joel said: "But if he was crazy . . ."

"She was never one for reasoning," sighed Randolph. "Only fourteen, of course, a child, but decidedly stubborn: she wanted to marry, and so she did. We lent them a room here in the house the week of their honeymoon, and let them use the yard to have a fishfry for their friends."

"And my dad . . . was he at the wedding?"

Randolph, looking blank, tapped ash onto the floor. "But then one night, very late . . ." Lowering his eyelids sleepily, he drew a finger round the rim of his glass. "Does Amy, by chance, recall the very *original* thing I did when we heard Missouri scream?"

Amy couldn't make up her mind whether she did or not. Ten years, after all, was a long time.

"We were sitting like this in the parlor, doesn't that come back? And I said: it's the wind. Of course I knew it wasn't." He paused, and sucked in his cheeks, as though the memory proved too exquisitely humorous for him to maintain a straight face.

He aimed a gun-like finger at Joel, and cocked his thumb: "So I put a roller in the pianola, and it played the 'Indian Love Call.'"

"Such a sweet song," said Amy. "So sad. I don't know why you never let me play the pianola any more."

"Keg cut her throat," said Joel, a mood of panic bubbling up, for he couldn't follow the peculiar turn Randolph's talk had taken; it was like trying to decipher some tale being told in a senseless foreign language, and he despised this left-out feeling, just when he'd begun to feel close to Randolph. "I saw her scar," he said, and all but shouted for attention, "that's what Keg did."

"Uh yes, absolutely."

"It went like this," and Amy hummed: "When I'm calling yoo hoo de da dum de da . . ."

". . . from ear to ear: ruined a roseleaf quilt my great-great aunt in Tennessee lost her eyesight stitching."

"Zoo says he's on the chain gang, and she hopes he never gets off: she told the Lord to make him into an old dog."

"Will you answer da de de da . . . that isn't quite the tune, is it, Randolph?"

"A little off-key."

"But how should it go?"

"Haven't the faintest notion, angel."

Joel said: "Poor Zoo."

"Poor everybody," said Randolph, languidly pouring another sherry.

❦

Greedy moths flattened their wings against the lamp funnels. Near the stove rain seeped through a leak in the roof, dripping with dismal regularity into an empty coal scuttle. "It's the kind of thing that happens when you tamper with the smallest box," observed Randolph, the sour smoke from his cigarette spiraling toward Joel, who, with discreet handwaves, directed it elsewhere.

"I do wish you'd let me play the pianola," said Amy wistfully. "But I don't suppose you realize how much I enjoy it, what a comfort it is."

Randolph cleared his throat, and grinned, dimples denting his cheeks. His face was like a round ripe peach. He was considerably younger than his cousin: somewhere, say, in his middle thirties. "Still, we haven't exorcized Master Knox's ghost."

"It wasn't any ghost," muttered Joel. "There isn't any such of a thing: this was a real live lady, and I saw her."

"And what did she look like, dear?" said Amy, her tone indicating her thoughts were fastened on less farfetched matters. It reminded Joel of Ellen and his mother: they also had used this special distant voice when suspicious of his stories, only allowing him to proceed for the sake of peace. The old trigger-quick feeling of guilt came over him: a liar, that's what the two of them, Amy and Randolph, were thinking, just a natural-born liar, and believing this he began to elaborate his description embarrassingly: she had the eyes of a fiend, the lady did, wild witch-eyes, cold and green as the bottom of the North Pole sea; twin to the Snow Queen, her face was pale, wintry, carved from ice, and her white hair towered on her head like a wedding cake. She had beckoned to him with a crooked finger, beckoned . . .

"Gracious," said Amy, nibbling a cube of watermelon pickle. "You really saw such a person!"

While talking, Joel had noticed with discomfort her cousin's amused, entertained expression: earlier, when he'd given his first flat account, Randolph had heard him out in the colorless way one listens to a stale joke, for he seemed, in some curious manner, to have advance knowledge of the facts.

"You know," said Amy slowly, and suspended the watermelon pickle midway between plate and mouth, "Randolph, have you been . . ." she paused, her eyes sliding sideways to confront the smooth, amused peach-face. "Well, that *does* sound like . . ."

Randolph kicked her under the table; he accomplished this maneuver so skillfully it would have escaped Joel altogether had Amy's response been less extreme: she jerked back as though lightning had rocked the chair, and, shielding her eyes with the gloved hand, let out a pitiful wail: "Snake a snake I thought it was a snake bit me crawled under the table bit me foot you fool never forgive bit me my heart a snake," repeated over and over the words began to rhyme, to hum from wall to wall where giant moth shadows jittered.

Joel went all hollow inside; he thought he was going to wee wee right there in his breeches, and he wanted to hop up and run, just as he had at Jesus Fever's. Only he couldn't, not this time. So he looked hard at the window where fig leaves tapped a wet windy message, and tried with all his might to find the far-away room.

"Stop it this instant," commanded Randolph, making no pretense of his disgust. But when she could not seem to regain control he reached over and slapped her across the mouth. Then gradually she tapered off to a kind of hiccuping sob.

Randolph touched her arm solicitously. "All better, angel?" he said. "Dear me, you gave us a fright." Glancing at Joel, he added: "Amy is so very highstrung."

"So very," she agreed. "It was just that I thought . . . I hope I haven't upset the child."

But the walls of Joel's room were too thick for Amy's voice to penetrate. Now for a long time he'd been unable to find the far-away room; always it had been difficult, but never so hard as in the last year. So it was good to see his friends again. They were all here, including Mr Mystery, who wore a crimson cape, a plumed Spanish hat, a glittery monocle, and had all his teeth made of solid gold: an elegant gentleman, though given to talking tough from the side of his mouth, and an artist, a great magician: he played the vaudeville downtown in New Orleans twice a year, and did all kinds of eerie tricks. This is how they got to be such buddies. One time he picked Joel from the audience, brought him up on the stage, and pulled a whole basketful of cotton-candy clean out of his ears; thereafter, next to little Annie Rose Kuppermann, Mr Mystery was the most welcome visitor to the other room. Annie Rose was the cutest thing you ever saw. She had jet black hair and a real permanent wave. Her mother kept her dressed in snow white on Sundays and all clear down to her socks. In real life, Annie Rose was too stuck up and sassy to even tell him the time of day, but here in the far-away room her cute little voice jingled on and on: "I love you, Joel. I love you a bushel and a peck and a hug around the neck." And there was someone else who rarely failed to show up, though seldom appearing as the same person twice; that is, he came in various costumes and disguises, sometimes as a circus strongman, sometimes as a big swell millionaire, but always his name was Edward Q. Sansom.

Randolph said: "She seeks revenge: out of the goodness of my heart I'm going to endure a few infernal minutes of the pianola. Would you mind, Joel, dear, helping with the lamps?"

Like the kitchen, Mr Mystery and little Annie Rose Kuppermann slipped into darkness when the lifted lamps passed through the hall to the parlor.

❧❦❧

Ragtime fingers danced spectrally over the upright's yellowed ivories, the carnival strains of "Over the Waves" gently vibrating a girandole's crystal prism-fringe. Amy sat on the piano stool, cooling her little white face with a blue lace fan which she'd taken from the curio cabinet, and rigidly watched the mechanical thumping of the pianola keys.

"That's a parade song," said Joel. "I rode a float in the Mardi Gras once, all fixed up like a Chink with a long black pigtail, only a drunk man yanked it off, and set to whipping his lady-friend with it right smack in the street."

Randolph inched nearer to Joel on the loveseat. Over his pyjamas he wore a seersucker kimono with butterfly sleeves, and his plumpish feet were encased in a pair of tooled-leather sandals: his exposed toenails had a manicured gloss. Up close, he had a delicate lemon scent, and his hairless face looked not much older than Joel's. Staring straight ahead, he groped for Joel's hand, and hooked their fingers together.

Amy closed her fan with a reproachful snap. "You never thanked me," she said.

"For what, dearheart?"

Holding hands with Randolph was obscurely disagreeable, and Joel's fingers tensed with an impulse to dig his nails into the hot dry palm; also, Randolph wore a ring which pressed painfully between Joel's knuckles. This was a lady's ring, a smoky rainbow opal clasped by sharp silver prongs.

"Why, the feathers," reminded Amy. "The nice bluejay feathers."

"Lovely," said Randolph, and blew her a kiss.

Satisfied, she spread the fan and worked it furiously. Behind her, the girandole quivered, and shedding lilac, loosened by the ragged pounding of the pianola, scattered on a table. A lamp had been placed by the empty hearth, so that it glowed out like a wavery ashen fire. "This is the first year a cricket hasn't visited," she said. "Every summer one has always hidden in the fireplace, and sang till autumn: remember, Randolph, how Angela Lee would never let us kill it?"

Joel quoted: "Hark to the crickets crying in grass, Hear them serenading in the sassafras."

Randolph bent forward. "A charming boy, little Joel, dear Joel," he whispered. "Try to be happy here, try a little to like me, will you?"

Joel was used to compliments, imaginary ones originating in his head, but to have some such plainly spoken left him with an uneasy feeling: was he being poked fun at, teased? So he questioned the round innocent eyes, and saw his own boy-face focused as in double camera lenses. Amy's cousin was in earnest. He looked down at the opal ring, touched and sorry he could've ever had a mean thought like wanting to dig his nails into Randolph's palm. "I like you already," he said.

Randolph smiled and squeezed his hand.

"What are you two whispering about?" said Amy jealously. "I declare you're rude." Suddenly the pianola was silent, the trembling girandole still. "May I play something else, Randolph, oh please?"

"I think we've had quite enough . . . unless Joel would care to hear another."

Joel bided time, tasting his power; then, recalling the miserable lonesome afternoon, spitefully gave a negative nod.

Amy pursed her lips. ". . . the last chance you'll ever have to humiliate me," she told Randolph, flouncing over to the curio

cabinet, and replacing her blue fan. Joel had inspected the contents of this cabinet before supper, and had yearned to have as
his own such treasures as a jolly Buddha with a fat jade belly, a
two-headed china crocodile, the program of a Richmond ball
dated 1862 and autographed by Robert E. Lee, a tiny wax Indian in full war regalia, and several plush-framed daintily
painted miniatures of virile dandies with villainous mustaches.
"It's your house, I'm perfectly aware . . ."

But a queer sound interrupted: a noise like the solitary thump
of an oversized raindrop, it drum-drummed down the stairsteps. Randolph stirred uneasily. "Amy," he said, and coughed
significantly. She did not move. "Is it the lady?" asked Joel, but
neither answered, and he was sorry he'd drunk the sherry: the
parlor, when he did not concentrate hard, had a bent tilted look,
like the topsy-turvy room in the crazyhouse at Pontchartrain.
The thumping stopped, an instant of quiet, then an ordinary
red tennis ball rolled silently through the archway.

With a curtsy, Amy picked it up, and, balancing it in her
gloved hand, brought it under close scrutiny, as if it were a fruit
she was examining for worms. She exchanged a troubled glance
with Randolph.

"Shall I come with you?" he said, as she hurried out.

"Later, when you've sent the boy to bed." Her footsteps re-
sounded on the black stairs; somewhere overhead a doorlatch
clicked.

Randolph turned to Joel with a desperately cheerful expression. "Do you play parcheesi?"

Joel was still puzzling over the tennis ball. He concluded, finally, that it would be best just to pretend as though it were the
most commonplace thing in the world to have a tennis ball
come rolling into your room out of nowhere. He wanted to

laugh. Only it wasn't funny. He couldn't believe in the way things were turning out: the difference between this happening, and what he'd expected was too great. It was like paying your fare to see a wild-west show, and walking in on a silly romance picture instead. If that happened, he would feel cheated. And he felt cheated now.

"Or shall I read your fortune?"

Joel held up a clenched hand; the grimy fingers unfurled like the leaves of an opening flower, and the pink of his palm was dotted with sweat-beads. Once, thinking how ideal a career it would make, he'd ordered from a concern in New York City a volume called *Techniques of Fortune-Telling*, authored by an alleged gypsy whose greasy earringed photo adorned the jacket; lack of funds, however, cut short this project, for, in order to become a bonafide fortune-teller, he had to buy, it developed, a generous amount of costly equipment.

"Sooo," mused Randolph, drawing the hand out of shadow nearer lamplight. "Is it important that I see potential voyages, adventure, an alliance with the pretty daughter of some Rockefeller? The future is to me strangely unexciting: long ago I came to realize my life was meant for other times."

"But it's the future I want to know," said Joel.

Randolph shook his head, and his sleepy sky-blue eyes, contemplating Joel, were sober, serious. "Have you never heard what the wise men say: all of the future exists in the past."

"At least may I ask a question?" and Joel did not wait for any judgment: "There are just two things I'd like to know, one is: when am I going to see my dad?" And the quietness of the dim parlor seemed to echo when? when?

Gently releasing the hand, Randolph, a set smile stiffening his face, rose and strolled to a window, his loose kimono swaying about him; he folded his arms like a Chinaman into the butterfly sleeves, and stood very still. "When you are quite settled," he said. "And the other?"

Eyes closed: a dizzy well of stars. Open: a bent tilted room where twin kimonoed figures with curly yellow hair glided back and forth across the lopsided floor. "I saw that Lady, and she was real, wasn't she?" but this was not the question he'd intended.

Randolph opened the window. The rain had stopped, and cicadas were screaming in the wet summer dark. "A matter of viewpoint, I suppose," he said, and yawned. "I know her fairly well, and to me she is a ghost." The night wind blew in from the garden, flourishing the drapes like faded gold flags.

FIVE

Wednesday, after breakfast, Joel shut himself in his room, and went about the hard task of thinking up letters. It was a hot dull morning, and the Landing, though now and again Randolph's sick cough rattled behind closed doors, seemed, as usual, too quiet, too still. A fat horsefly dived toward the Red Chief tablet where Joel's scrawl wobbled loosely over the paper: at school this haphazard style had earned him an F in penmanship. He twitched, twirled his pencil, paused twice to make water in the china slopjar so artistically festooned with pink-bottomed cupids clutching watercolor bouquets of ivy and violet; eventually, then, the first letter, addressed to his good friend Sammy Silverstein, read, when finished, as follows:

"You would like the house I am living in Sammy as it is a swell house and you would like my dad as he knows all about airplanes like you do. He doesn't look much like your dad though. He doesn't wear specs or smoke cigars, but is tall like Mr Mystery (if Mr Mystery comes to the Nemo this summer write and tell all about it) and smokes a pipe and is very young. He gave me a .22 and when winter comes we will hunt possum and eat possum stew. I wish you could come and visit me as we would have a real good time. One thing we could do is get drunk with my cousin Randolf. We drink alcohol bevrages (sp?) and he is a lot of fun. Its sure not like New Orleans, Sammy. Out here a person old as us is a grown up person. You owe me 20¢. I will forget this det if you will write all news every week. Hello to the gang, remember to write your friend . . ."

and with masterly care he signed his name in a new manner: J.H.K. Sansom. Several times he read it aloud; it had a distinguished, adult sound, a name he could readily imagine prefixed by such proud titles as General, Judge, Governor, Doctor. Doctor J.H.K. Sansom, the celebrated operating specialist; Governor J.H.K. Sansom, the people's choice ("Hello, warden, this is the Governor, just called to say I've given Zoo Fever a reprieve"). And then of course the world and all its folks would love him, and Sammy, well, Sammy could sell this old letter for thousands of dollars.

But searching for i's not dotted, t's uncrossed, it came to him that almost all he'd written were lies, big lies poured over the paper like a thick syrup. There was no accounting for them. These things he'd said, they should be true, and they weren't. At home, Ellen was forever airing unwelcome advice, but now he wished he could close his eyes, open them, and see her standing there. She would know what to do.

His pencil traveled so fast occasional words linked: how sorry he was not to have written sooner; he hoped Ellen was o.k., and ditto the kids . . . he missed them all, did they miss him? "It is nicehere," he wrote, but a pain twinged him, so he got up to walk the floor and knock his hands together nervously. How was he going to tell her? He stopped by the window and looked down at the garden where, except for Jesus Fever's tomcat, parading before the ruined columns, all seemed stagnant, painted: the lazy willows, shadowless in the morning sunshine; the hammered slave-bell muffled in the high weeds. Joel shook his head, as if to rock his thoughts into sensible order, then returned to the table, and, angrily pencilling out "It is nicehere," wrote: "Ellen, I hate this place. I don't know where he is and nobody will tell me. Willyou believe it Ellen when I say I have notseen him? Honest; Amy says he's sick but I don't believe oneword as I don't likeher. She lookslike that mean Miss Addie down the street that use to be making suchalot of unecesary stink. Another thing is, there are no radios, picture shows, funny papers and if you want to take a bath you got to fill a washtub with water from the well. I can't see how Randolf keeps clean as he does. I like him o.k. but I don't like it here onebit. Ellen did mama leave enough $ so as I could go away to a school where you can live? Like a military school. Ellen I miss you. Ellen please tell me what to do. Love from Joel XXXXXXXX."

He felt better now, easier in his mind; say what you will, Ellen had never let him down. He felt so good that, stuffing the letters in their envelopes, he began to whistle, and it was the tune the twins had taught him: *when the north wind doth blow, and we shall have snow* . . . What was her name? And that other one, the tomboy? Florabel and Idabel. There was no reason why he had to mope around here all day: hadn't they invited him to visit? Florabel and Idabel and Joel, he thought, whistling happy, whistling loud.

"Quiet in there," came Randolph's muffled complaint. "I'm desperately, desperately ill . . ." and broke off into coughing.

Ha ha! Randolph could go jump in the lake. Ha ha! Joel

laughed inwardly as he went to the old bureau where the lacquered chest, containing now his bullet, the bluejay feather, and coins amounting to seventy-eight cents, was hidden in the bottom drawer. Inasmuch as he had no stamps, he figured it would be legal simply to put six cents cash money in the r.f.d. box. So he wadded a nickel and a penny in toilet tissue, gathered his letters and started downstairs, still whistling.

Down by the mailbox he ran into Zoo, and she was not alone, but stood talking with a short bullet-headed Negro. It was Little Sunshine, the hermit. Joel knew this, for Monday night at suppertime Little Sunshine had appeared tapping at the kitchen window; he'd come to call on Randolph, for they were, so Randolph said, "dear friends." He was extra-polite, Little Sunshine, and had brought gifts to all the family: a bucket of swamp honey, two gallons of home-brew, and a wreath of pine needles and tiger lilies which Randolph stuck on his head and galavanted around in the whole evening. Even though he lived far in the dark woods, even though he was a kind of hermit, and everybody knows hermits are evil crazy folks, Joel was not afraid of him. "Little Sunshine, he got more purentee sense 'n most anybody," said Zoo. "Tell the truth, honey, if my brain was like it oughta be, why, I'd marry him like a shot." Only Joel couldn't picture such a marriage; in the first place, Little Sunshine was too old, not so ancient as Jesus Fever, to be sure, but old all the same. And ugly. He had a blue cataract in one eye, hardly a tooth in his head, and smelled bad: while he was in the kitchen, Amy kept the gloved hand over her nose like a sachet-handkerchief, and when Randolph had carted him away to his room (from which sounds of drunken conversation came till dawn), she'd breathed a sigh of relief.

Little Sunshine raised his arm: "Hurry, child, make a cross," he said in a trombone voice, "cause you done come up on me in the lighta day." Awed, Joel crossed himself. A smile stretched the hermit's thick wrinkled lips: "Spin round, boy, and you is saved."

Meanwhile Zoo tried unsuccessfully to conceal a necklace-like ornament the hermit had knotted about her giraffish neck. She looked very put out when Joel asked: "What's that you've got on, Zoo?"

"Hit's a charm," volunteered the hermit proudly.

"Hush up," snapped Zoo. "Done just told me it don't work iffen I goes round tellin everbody." She turned to Joel. "Honey, I spec you best run along; got business with the man."

O.K., if that's how she felt. And she was supposed to be his friend! He stalked over to the mailbox, threw up the red flag, and put his letters inside, using the tissue-wrapped coins as a paperweight. Then, determining from memory the general direction of the twins' house, he trudged off down the road.

❧❀❧

Sand dust eddied about his feet where he walked in the misty forest shade skimming the road's edge. The sun was white in a milkglass sky. Passing a shallow creek rushing swift and cool from the woods, he paused, tempted to take off his tight shoes and go wading where soggy leaves rotated wildly in pebbled whirlpools, but then he heard his name called, and it scared him. Turning, he saw Little Sunshine.

The hermit hobbled forward, throwing his weight against a

hickory cane; he carried this cane always, though Joel could not see its necessity since, aside from the fact they were very bowed, nothing seemed wrong with his legs; but his arms were so long his fingertips touched his knees. He wore ripped overalls, no shirt, no hat, no shoes. "Gawd Almighty, you walks fast, boy," he said, panting up alongside. "Else hit's me what ain't use to this daytime; ain't nothin coulda got me out cept Zoo needed that charm mighty bad."

Joel realized that his curiosity was being purposely aroused. So he pretended to be uninterested. And presently, as he expected, Little Sunshine, of his own accord, added: "Hit's a charm guarantee no turrible happenins gonna happen; makes it myself outa frog powder 'n turtle bones."

Joel slackened his gait, for the hermit moved slow as a cripple; in certain ways he was like Jesus Fever: indeed, might have been his brother. But there was about his broad ugly face a slyness the old man's lacked. "Little Sunshine," he said, "would you make *me* a charm?"

The hermit sucked his toothless gums, and the sun shone dull in his gluey blue eye. "They's many kinda charms: love charms, money charms, what kind you speakin of?"

"One like Zoo's," he said, "one that'll keep anything terrible from happening."

"Dog take it!" crowed the hermit, and stopped still in his tracks. He jabbed the road with the cane, and wagged his big bald head. "What kinda troubles a little boy like you got?"

Joel's gaze wandered past the ugly man, who was rocking on his cane, and into the bordering pines. "I don't know," he said, then fixed his eyes on the hermit, trying to make him understand how much this charm meant. "Please, Little Sunshine . . ."

And Little Sunshine, after a long moment, indicated, with a

tilt of his head, that yes, the charm would be made, but: "You gotta come fetch it yoself, cause ain't no tellin when Little Sunshine gonna be up thisaway soon. Sides, thing is, trouble charms won't work noways less you wears them when theys most needed."

But how would Joel ever find the hermit's place? "I'd get lost," he argued, as they continued along the road, the dust rising about them, the sun spinning toward noon.

"Naw you ain't: humans go huntin Little Sunshine, the devil-man guide they feet." He lifted his cane skyward, and pointed to a sailing shark-like cloud: "Lookayonder," he said, "hit travelin west, gonna past right over Drownin Pond; once you gets to Drownin Pond, can't miss the hotel."

All the hermits Joel had ever heard about were unfriendly say-nothings. Not Little Sunshine: he must've been born talking. Joel thought how, on lonesome evenings in the woods, he must chatter to toads and trees and the cold blue stars, and this made him feel tenderly toward the old man, who began now an account of why Drownin Pond had so queer a name.

Years past, sometime before the turn of the century, there had been, he boasted, a splendid hotel located in these very woods, The Cloud Hotel, owned by Mrs Jimmy Bob Cloud, a widow lady bloodkin to the Skullys. Then known as Cloud Lake, the pond was a diamond eye spouting crystal cold from subterranean limestone springs, and Mrs Jimmy Bob's hotel housed gala crowds come immense distances to parade the wide white halls. Mulberry parasols held aloft by silk-skirted ladies drifted all summer long over the lawns rolling round the water. While feather fans rustled the air, while velvet dancing slippers polished the ballroom floor, scarlet-coated house-hands glided in and out among the guests, wine spilling redly on silver trays.

In May they came, October went, the guests, taking with them memories, leaving tall stacks of gold. Little Sunshine, the stable boy who brushed the gleaming coats of their fine teams, had lain awake many a starry night listening to the furry blend of voices. Oh but then! but then! one August afternoon, this was 1893, a child, a creole boy of Joel's years, having taken a dare to dive into the lake from a hundred-foot oak, crushed his head like a shell between two sunken logs. Soon afterwards there was a second tragedy when a crooked gambler, in much trouble with the law, swam out and never came back. So winter came, passed, another spring. And then a honeymoon couple, out rowing on the lake, claimed that a hand blazing with rubies (the gambler had sported a ruby ring) reached from the depths to capsize their boat. Others followed suit: a swimmer said his legs had been lassoed by powerful arms, another maintained he'd seen the two of them, the gambler and the child, seen them clear as day shining below the surface, naked now, and their hair long, green, tangled as seaweed. Indignant ladies snapped their fans, assembled their silks with fearful haste. The nights were still, the lawns deserted, the guests forever gone; and it broke Mrs Jimmy Bob's heart: she ordered a net sent from Biloxi, and had the lake dragged: "Tol her it ain't no use, tol her she ain't never gonna catch them two cause the devilman, he watch over his own." So Mrs Jimmy Bob went to St. Louis, rented herself a room, poured kerosene all over the bed, lay down and struck a match. Drownin Pond. That was the name colored folks gave it. Slowly old creek-slime, filtering through the limestone springs, had dyed the water an evil color; the lawns, the road, the paths all turned wild; the wide veranda caved in; the chimneys sank low in the swampy earth; storm-uprooted trees leaned against the porch; and water-snakes slithering across the strings made night-songs on the ballroom's decaying piano. It was a terrible, strange-looking hotel. But Little Sunshine stayed on: it was his rightful home, he said, for if he went away, as he had once upon a time, other voices, other rooms, voices lost and clouded, strummed his dreams.

The story made for Joel a jumbled picture of cracked windows reflecting a garden of ghosts, a sunset world where twisting ivy trickled down broken columns, where arbors of spidersilk shrouded all.

Miss Florabel Thompkins pulled a comb through her red waist-length hair, the blunt noon-sun paling each strand, and said: "Now don't you know I'm just tickled to see you. Why, only this morning I was telling sister: 'Sister, I got a feeling we're going to have company.' Said, 'So let's wash our hair,' which naturally made no hit whatsoever: never washes nothing, that girl. Idabel? Oh, she's off to the creek, gone to get the melon we've got cooling down there: first of the summer; Papa planted early this year." Florabel wasn't nearly so pretty as moonlight had made her seem. Her face was flat and freckled, like her sister's. She was kind of snaggletoothed, and her lips pouted in prissy discontent. She was half-reclining in a hammock ("Mama made it herself, and she makes all my lovely clothes, except for my dotted swiss, but she doesn't make any for sister: like Mama says, it's better to let Idabel troop around in what-have-you cause she can't keep a decent rag decent: I tell you this frankly, Mister Knox, Idabel's a torment to our souls, Mama's and mine. We could've been so cute dressed alike, but ...") swung between shady pecan trees in a corner of the yard. She picked up a pair of Kress tweezers and, with a pained expression, began plucking her pink eyebrows. "Sister's avowed ... ouch! ... ambition is she wants to be a farmer."

Joel, who was squatting on the grass nibbling a leaf, stretched his legs, and said: "What's wrong with that?"

"Now, Mister Knox, surely you're just teasing," said Florabel. "Whoever heard of a decent white girl wanting to be a farmer? Mama and me are too disgraced. Course I know what goes on in the back of her mind." Florabel gave him a conniving look, and lowered her voice. "She thinks when Papa dies he'll leave her the place to do with like she pleases. Oh, she doesn't fool me one minute."

Joel glanced about at what Idabel hoped to inherit: the house stood far away in a grove of shade trees; it was a nice house, simple, solid-looking, painted a white now turned slightly grey; an open shotgun hall ran front to back, and on the porch were geranium boxes, and a swing. A small shed housing a green 1934 Chevrolet was at one side. Chickens pecked around in the clean yard of flowerbeds and arranged rocks. At the rear was a smoke house, a water-pump windmill, and the first swelling slope of a cottonfield.

"Ouch!" cried Florabel, and tossed the tweezers aside. She gave the hammock a push and swung to and fro, her lips pouting absurdly. "Now me, I want to be an actor . . . or a schoolteacher," she said. "Only if I become an actor I don't know what we'll do about sister. When somebody's famous like that they dig up all the facts on their past life. I really don't want to sound mean about her, Mister Knox, but the reason I bring this matter up is she's got a crush on you . . ." Florabel dropped her gaze demurely, "and, well, the poor child does have a reputation."

Though he would never have admitted it, not even secretly, Joel felt sweetly flattered. "A reputation for what?" he said, careful not to smile.

Florabel straightened up. "Please, sir," she intoned, her old-lady mannerisms frighteningly accurate. "I thought you were a gentleman of the world." Suddenly, looking rather alarmed, she collapsed back in the hammock. Then: "Why, hey there, sister . . . look who's come to call."

"Howdy," said Idabel, surprise or pleasure very absent from her woolly voice. She carried a huge watermelon, and an old black-and-white bird dog trotted close at her heels. She rolled the melon on the grass, rubbed back her cowlicked bangs, and, slumping against a tree, cocked her thumbs in the belt rungs of the dungarees which she wore. She had on also a pair of plowman's boots, and a sweatshirt with the legend DRINK COCA-COLA fading on its front. She looked first at Joel, then at her sister, and, as though making some rude comment, spit expertly between her fingers. The old dog flopped down beside her. "This here's Henry," she told Joel, gently stroking the dog's ribs with her foot. "He's fixing to take a nap, so let's us not talk loud, hear?"

"Pshaw!" said the other twin. "Mister Knox oughta see what happens when I'm trying to get a wink in edgewise: wham bang whomp!"

"Henry feels kinda poorly," explained Idabel. "I'm fraid he's right sick."

"Well, I'm right sick myself. I'm sick of lotsa things."

Joel imagined that Idabel smiled at him. She did not smile in the fashion of ordinary people, but gave one corner of her mouth a cynical crook: it was like Randolph's trick of arching an eyebrow. She hitched up her pants leg and commenced picking the scab off a knee-sore. "How you making out over at the Landing, son?"

"Yes," said Florabel, bending forward with a rather sly smirk, "haven't you *seen* things?"

"Nothing except that it's a nice place," he said discreetly.

"But . . ." Florabel slid out of the hammock, and sat down beside him with her elbow propped against the melon. "But what I mean is . . ."

"Watch out," warned Idabel, "she's only trying to pick you."

And this gave Joel an opportunity to ease the moment with a laugh. Among his sins were lying and stealing and bad thoughts; disloyalty, however, was not part of his nature. He saw how cheap it would be to confide in Florabel, though there was nothing he needed more now than a sympathetic ear. "Does it hurt?" he asked her sister, anxious to show his gratitude by assuming an interest in the sore.

"Why, this old thing?" she said, and clawed the scab. "Shoot, boy, one time I had me a rising on my butt big as a baseball, and didn't pay it any mind whatsoever."

"Hmn, squalled loud enough when Mama smacked you and it busted," reminded Florabel, bunching her lips prissily. She thumped the melon and it made a ripe hollow report. "Hmn, sounds green as grass to me." With her fingernails she scratched her initials on the rind, drew a ragged heart, arrowed it, and carved M.S., which, eyeing Joel coyly, she announced stood for Mysterious Stranger.

Idabel displayed a jackknife. "Look," she demanded, releasing a thin vicious blade. "I could kill somebody, couldn't I?" And with one murderous stab the melon cracked, spraying icy juice as she chopped off generous portions. "Leave Papa a hunk," she said, retiring under the tree to gorge in peace.

"Cold," said Joel, a trickle of red dyeing his shirt. "That creek must be freezing like an icebox; where's it come from: does it flow down from Drownin Pond?"

Florabel looked at Idabel and Idabel looked at Florabel. Neither seemed able to make up her mind which should answer. Idabel spit pulp, and said: "Who told you?"

"Told me?"

"About Drownin Pond?"

A touch of hostility in her tone made him wary. But in this case he could not see where the truth would cost more than a lie. "Oh, the man who lives there. He's a friend of mine."

Idabel responded with a hoarse, sarcastic laugh. "I'm the only person in these parts that'll go anywhere near that creepy hotel; and, son, I've never even got so much as a peek at him."

"Sister's right," added Florabel. "She's always had a hankering to see the hermit; Mama used to say he'd grab us good if we didn't act proper. But lately I've come to think he's just somebody grown people made up."

It was Joel's turn for sarcasm. "If you'd been out on the road an hour ago I would've been glad to introduce you. His name is Little Sunshine, and he's going to make me . . ." but he recalled that to mention the charm was forbidden.

Against such testimony Idabel had no comeback. She was stumped. And jealous. "Huh," she snorted, and shoved a chunk of melon in her mouth.

Rings of sunlight, sifting through the tree, dappled the dark grass like fallen gold fruit; bluebottle flies swarmed over melon rinds, and a cowbell, somewhere beyond the windmill, tolled lazily and long. Henry was having a nightmare. His fretful snores seemed to annoy Florabel; she spit seed into her hand, and, chanting, "Nasty old nasty," hurled them at him.

Idabel did nothing for a moment. Then, rising, she closed the blade of her knife, and stuck it in her pocket. Slowly, without expression, she moved toward her sister, who went quite pink in the face and began to giggle nervously.

Hands on hips, Idabel stared at her with eyes like granite. She did not say a word, but her breathing hissed between clenched teeth, and a vein throbbed in the hollow of her neck. The old dog padded forward, and looked at Florabel reproachfully. Joel inched several feet backwards: he didn't want to become involved in any family fracas.

"You're going to bug-out those eyes too far some day," sassed Florabel. But as the rock-like stare continued her impertinent pose gradually dissolved. "I don't see why you want to take on about that nasty hound thisaway," she said, looping a curl in her strawberry hair, blinking her eyes innocently. "Mama's going to make Papa shoot him anyway cause he's liable to give us all some mortal disease."

Idabel sucked in her breath, and lunged, and over and over they rolled tussling on the grass. Florabel's skirt got hiked up so high Joel's cheeks reddened: then, scratching, kicking, screaming, she managed to break loose. "Sister, please . . . please, sister . . . I beg of you!" She ran behind a pecan tree: like figures on a two-ponied carousel they whirled around the trunk, first one way, then the other. "Mama, get Mama . . . oh, Mister Knox, she's loony . . . DO something!" Henry set up a barking commotion, and commenced to chase his tail. "Mister KNOX . . ."

But Joel was afraid of Idabel himself. She was about the maddest human he ever saw, and the quickest: nobody at home would believe a girl could move this fast. Also, he knew from experience that, if he interfered, the finger of blame would ultimately point in his direction: *he* started the whole thing, that's how the tale would read. Besides, Florabel had no call to throw those seeds: deep in his heart he didn't care if she got the daylight whammed out of her.

She cut across the yard, and made a desperate sprint for the

house, but it was useless, for Idabel hedged her off. Close together they went whooping past Joel, who suddenly became,
like the pecan tree, and through no fault of his own, a shield.
Idabel tried to push him aside: when he did not budge, she
tossed her sweaty hair, and fixed him angrily with her bold
green eyes: "Outa the way, sissy-britches."

Joel thought of the knife in her pocket, and despite Florabel's
pleas, concluded it might be wise to move elsewhere.

So they went off again, running in circles, zigzagging between trees, Florabel's hair jouncing on her back. When they
reached the pecan tree, tallest of two, she began to climb. Idabel
pulled off her clumsy boots. "Ha, won't get far that way," she
hollered, and agile as a monkey shinnied up the trunk.

The branches swayed, broken twigs, torn leaves showered at
Joel's feet: as he darted around hunting a clearer view the sky
seemed to crash bluely through the tree, and the twins, climbing nearer the sun, grew smaller and dizzy bright.

Florabel had gone as far as she could, the top; but it was a safe
and fortified position: here, balanced in the crotch of forked
limbs, she was immune to any assault, for to force the enemy's
retreat she had only to kick.

"I can wait," said Idabel, and straddled a branch. She glanced
down at Joel irritably. "Go on home, you."

"Please disregard her altogether, Mister Knox."

"Go on home and cut out paper dolls, sissy-britches."

Joel stood there hating her, wishing she'd fall from the tree
and bust her neck. Like every other tomboy, Idabel was mean,
just gut-mean: the haircut man in Noon City sure had her number. So did the husky woman with the wart. So did Florabel.
Then he shrugged, and hung his head.

"Come back when *she's* not around," called Florabel as he

started for home. "And Mister Knox, remember what I said about you-know-what. Well, a word to the wise . . ."

❧❧❧

A pair of chicken hawks wheeled with stiffened wings above smoke, dimly yellow in the distance, rising spire-like out the Landing's kitchen chimney: that would be Zoo fixing dinner, he guessed, pausing by the roadside to stampede a colony of ants feeding on a dead frog. He was tired of Zoo's cooking: always the same stuff, collards, yams, blackeyed peas, cornbread. Right now he would like to meet up with the Snowball Man. Every afternoon at home in New Orleans the Snowball Man came pushing his delicious cart, tinkling his delicious bell; and for pennies you could have a dunce-hat of flaked ice flavored with a dozen syrups, cherry and chocolate, grape and blackberry all mingling like a rainbow.

The ants scurried like shooting sparks: thinking of Idabel, he hopped about mashing them underfoot, but this sinful dance did nothing toward lessening the hurt of her insults. Wait! Wait till he was Governor: he'd sic the law on her, have her locked in a dungeon cell with a little trapdoor cut in the ceiling where he could look down and laugh.

But when the Landing came in full view, its rambling outline darkened by foliage, he forgot Idabel.

Like kites being reeled in, the chicken hawks circled lower till their shadows revolved over the slanting shingled roof. The shaft of smoke lifting from the chimney mounted unbroken in the hot windless air; a sign, at least, that people lived here. Joel had known and explored other houses quiet with emptiness, but none so deserted-looking, silent: it was as though the place were captured under a cone of glass; inside, waiting to claim him, was an afternoon of endless boredom: each step, and his shoes were heavy as though soled with stone, carried him closer. A whole afternoon. And how many more for how many months?

Then, approaching the mailbox, seeing its cheerful red flag still upraised, the good feeling came back: Ellen would make things different, she would fix it so he could go away to a school where everybody was like everybody else. Singing the song about snow and the north wind, he stopped and jerked open the mailbox; deep inside lay a thick stack of letters, sealed, as he found, in watergreen envelopes. It was like the stationery his father had used when writing Ellen. And the spidery handwriting was identical: Mr Pepe Alvarez, c/o the postmaster, Monterrey, Mexico. Then Mr Pepe Alvarez, c/o the postmaster, Fukuoka, Japan. Again, again. Seven letters, all addressed to Mr Pepe Alvarez, in care of postmasters in: Camden, New Jersey; Lahore, India; Copenhagen, Denmark; Barcelona, Spain; Keokuk, Iowa.

But his letters were not among these. He certainly remembered putting them in the box. Little Sunshine had seen him. And Zoo. So where were they? Of course: the mailman must've come along already. But why hadn't he heard or seen the mailman's car? It was a half-wrecked Ford and made considerable racket. Then, in the dust at his feet, torn from the toilet-paper wrapping, he saw his coins, a nickel and a penny sparkling up at him like uneven eyes.

At this same instant the sound of bullet fire cracked whiplike on the quiet: Joel, stooping for his money, turned a paralyzed face toward the house: there was no one on the porch, the path, not a sign of life anywhere. Another shot. The wings of the hawks raged as they fled over tree tops, their shadows sweeping across the road's broiling sand like islands of dark.

PART TWO

SIX

"Hold still," said Zoo, her eyes like satin in the kitchen lamp-light. "Never saw such a fidget; best hold still and let me cut this hair: can't have you runnin round here lookin like some ol gal: first thing you know, boy, folks is gonna say you got to wee wee squattin down." Garden shears snipped round the rim of the bowl, a blue bowl fitted on Joel's head like a helmet. "You got such pretty fine molasses hair seems like we oughta could sell it to them wigmakers."

Joel squirmed. "So what did you say after she said that?" he asked, anxious she return to a previous topic.

"Said what?"

"Said you've got a big nerve shooting off rifles when Randolph's so sick."

"Huh," Zoo grunted, "why, I just come right out and tol her, tol her: 'Miss Amy, them hawks fixin to steal the place off our hands less we shoo em away.' Said, 'Done fly off with a dozen fat fryers this spring a'ready, and Mister Randolph, he gonna take mighty little pleasure in his sickness if his stomach stay growl-empty.'"

Removing the bowl, making a telescope of her hands, she roamed around Joel's chair viewing his haircut from all angles.

"Now that's what I calls a good trim," she said. "Go look in the window."

Evening silvered the glass, and his face reflected transparently, changed and mingled with moth-moving lamp yellow; he saw himself, and through himself, and beyond: a night bird whistled in the fig leaves, a whippoorwill, and fireflies sprinkled the blue-flooded air, rode the dark like ship lights. The haircut was disfiguring, for it made him in silhouette resemble those idiots with huge world-globe heads, and now, because of Randolph's flattery, he was self-conscious about his looks. "It's awful," he said.

"Huh," said Zoo, dishing supper scraps into a lard can reserved for pig slop, "you is as ignorant as that Keg Brown. Course he was the most ignorant human in my acquaintance. But you is both ignorant."

Joel, imitating Randolph, arched an eyebrow, and said: "I daresay I know some things I daresay you don't."

Zoo's elegant grace disappeared as she strode about clearing the kitchen: the floor creaked under her animal footfall, and, as she bent to lower the lamp, the hurt sadness of her long face gleamed like a mask. "I daresays," she said, plucking at her neckerchief, and not looking at Joel. "I daresays you is smarter'n Zoo, but I reckon as she knows better about folks feelins; leastwise, she don't go round makin folks feel no-count for no cause whatsoever."

"Aw," said Joel, "aw, I was just joking, honest," and, hugging her, smothered his face against her middle; she smelled sweet, a curious dark sour sweet, and her fingers, gliding through his hair, were cool, strong. "I love you because you've got to love me because you've got to."

"Lord, Lord," said Zoo, disengaging herself, "you is nothin

but a kitty now, but comes the time you is full growed . . . what a Tom you gonna be."

Standing in the doorway he watched her lamp divide the dark, saw Jesus Fever's windows color: here he was, and there she was, and there was all of night between them. It had been a curious evening, for Randolph kept to his room, and Amy, fixing supper trays, one for Randolph and the other, presumably, Mr Sansom's (she'd said: "Mr Sansom won't eat cold peas"), had stopped at the table only long enough to swallow a tumbler of buttermilk. But Joel had talked, and in talking eased away his worries, and Zoo told tales, tall funny sad, and now and again their voices had met and made a song, a summer kitchen ballad.

From the first he'd noticed in the house complex sounds, sounds on the edge of silence, settling sighs of stone and board, as though the old rooms inhaled-exhaled constant wind, and he'd heard Randolph say: "We're sinking, you know, sank four inches last year." It was drowning in the earth, this house, and they, all of them, were submerging with it: Joel, moving through the chamber, imagined moles tracing silver tunnels down eclipsed halls, lank pink sliding through earth-packed rooms, lilac bleeding out the sockets of a skull: Go away, he said, climbing toward a lamp which threw nervous light over the stairsteps, Go Away, he said, for his imagination was too tricky and terrible. But was it possible for a whole house to disappear? Yes, he'd heard of such things. All Mr Mystery had to do was snap his fingers, and whatever was *there* went whisk. And human beings, too. They could go right off the face of the earth. That was what had happened to his father; he was gone, not in a sad respectable way like his mother, but just gone, and Joel had no reason to suppose he would ever find him. So why did they pretend?

Why didn't they say right out, "There is no Mr Sansom, you have no father," and send him away. Ellen was always talking of the decent Christian thing to do; he'd wondered what she meant, and now he knew: to speak truth was a decent Christian thing. He took the steps slowly, awake but dreaming, and in the dream he saw the Cloud Hotel, saw its leaning molding rooms, its wind-cracked windows hung with draperies of blackwidow web, and realized suddenly this was not a hotel; indeed, had never been: this was the place folks came when they went off the face of the earth, when they died but were not dead. And he thought of the ballroom Little Sunshine had described: there nightfall covered the walls like a tapestry, and the dry delicate skeletons of bouquet leaves littering the wavy floor powdered under his dreamed footstep: he walked in the dark in the dust of thorns listening for a name, his own, but even here no father claimed him. The shadow of a grand piano spotted the vaulted ceiling like a luna moth wing, and at the keyboard, her eyes soaked white with moonlight, her wig of cold white curls askew, sat the Lady: was this the ghost of Mrs Jimmy Bob Cloud? Mrs Cloud, who'd cremated herself in a St. Louis boarding house? Was that the answer?

It struck his knee, and all that happened happened quickly: a brief blur of light flashed as a door banged in the hall above, and then he felt something hit him, go past, go bumping down the steps, and it was suddenly as though all his bones had unjoined, as though all the vital parts of him had unraveled like the springs of a sprung watch. A little red ball, it was rolling and knocking on the chamber floor, and he thought of Idabel: he wished he were as brave as Idabel; he wished he had a brother, sister, somebody; he wished he were dead.

Randolph bent over the top banister; his hands were folded

into the sleeves of a kimono; his eyes were flat and glazed, drunk-looking, and if he saw Joel he made no sign. Presently, his kimono rustling, he crossed the hall and opened a door where the eccentric light of candles floated on his face. He did not go inside, but stood there moving his hands in a queer way; then, turning, he started down the stairs and when finally he came against Joel he only said: "Bring a glass of water, please." Without a second word he went back up and into the room, and Joel, unable to move, waited on the stairs a long while: there were voices in the walls, settling sighs of stone and board, sounds on the edge of silence.

❦

"Come in." Amy's voice echoed through the house, and Joel, waiting on the threshold, felt his heart separate.

"Careful there, my dear," said Randolph, lolling at the foot of a canopied bed, "don't spill the water."

But he could not keep his hand from shaking, or focus his eyes properly: Amy and Randolph, though some distance apart, were fused like Siamese twins: they seemed a kind of freak animal, half-man half-woman. There were candles, a dozen or so, and the heat of the night made them lean limp and crooked. A limestone fireplace gleamed in their shine, and a menagerie of crystal chimes, set in motion by Joel's entrance, tinkled on the mantel like brookwater. The air was strong with the smell of asthma cigarettes, used linen, and whiskey breath. Amy's starched face was in coinlike profile against a closed window where insects thumped with a watchbeat's regularity: intent upon embroidering a sampler, she rocked back and forth in a little sewing chair, her needle, held in the gloved hand, stabbing lilac cloth rhythmically. She looked like a kind of wax machine, a life-sized doll, and the concentration of her work was unnatural: she was like a person pretending to read, though the book is upside down. And Randolph, cleaning his nails with a goosequill, was as stylized in his attitude as she: Joel felt as though they interpreted his presence here as somehow indecent, but it was impossible to withdraw, impossible to advance. On a table by the bed there were two rather arresting objects, an illuminated globe of rose frost glass depicting scenes of Venice: golden gondolas, wicked gondoliers and lovers drifting past glorious palaces on a canal of saccharine blue; and a milkglass nude suspending a tiny silver mirror. Reflected in this mirror were a pair of eyes: the instant Joel became aware of them his gaze dismissed all else.

The eyes were a teary grey; they watched Joel with a kind of dumb glitter, and soon, as if to acknowledge him, they closed in a solemn double wink, and turned . . . so that he saw them only as part of a head, a shaved head lying with invalid looseness on unsanitary pillows.

"He wants the water," said Randolph, scraping the quill under his thumb nail. "You'll have to feed him: poor Eddie, absolutely helpless."

And Joel said: "Is that him?"

"Mr Sansom," said Amy, her lips tight as the rosebud she stitched. "It is Mr Sansom."

"But you never told me."

Randolph, clutching the bedpost, heaved to his feet: the kimono swung out, exposing pink substantial thighs, hairless legs. Like many heavy men he could move with unexpected nimbleness, but he'd had more than enough to drink, and as he came toward Joel, a numb smile bunching his features, he looked as if he were about to fall. He stooped down to Joel's size, and whispered: "Tell you what, baby?"

The eyes covered the glass again, their image twitching in the tossing light, and a hand trimmed with wedding gold poked out from under quilts to let go a red ball: it was like a cue, a challenge, and Joel, ignoring Randolph, went briskly forward to meet it.

SEVEN

She came up the road, kicking stones, whistling. A bamboo pole, balanced on her shoulder, pointed toward the late noon sun. She carried a molasses bucket, and wore a pair of toylike dark glasses. Henry, the hound, paced beside her, his red tongue dangling hotly. And Joel, who'd been waiting for the mailman, hid behind a pine tree; just wait, this was going to be good: he'd scare the . . . there, she was almost near enough.

Then she stopped, and took off the sun-glasses, and polished them on her khaki shorts. Shielding her eyes, she looked straight at Joel's tree, and beyond it: there was no one on the Landing's porch, not a sign of life. She shrugged her shoulders. "Henry," she said, and his eyes rolled sadly up, "Henry, I leave it to you: do we want him with us or don't we?" Henry yawned: a fly buzzed inside his mouth and he swallowed it whole. "Henry," she continued, scrutinizing a certain pine, "did you ever notice what funny shadows some trees have?" A pause. "O.K., my fine dandy, come on out."

Sheepishly Joel stepped into the daylight. "Hello, Idabel," he said, and Idabel laughed, and this laugh of hers was rougher than barbed wire. "Look here, son," she said, "the last boy that tried pulling tricks on Idabel is still picking up the pieces." She put back on her dark glasses, and gave her shorts a snappy hitch. "Henry and me, we're going down to catch us a mess of catfish: if you can make yourself helpful you're welcome to come."

"How do you mean helpful?"

"Oh, put worms on the hook . . ." tilting up the bucket, she showed him its white, writhing interior.

Joel, disgusted, averted his eyes; but thought: yes, he'd like to go with Idabel, yes, anything not to be alone: hook worms, or kiss her feet, it did not matter.

"You'd better change clothes," said Idabel; "you're fixed up like it was Sunday."

Indeed, he was wearing his finest suit, white flannels bought for Dancing Class; he'd put them on because Randolph had promised to paint his picture. But at dinner Amy had said Randolph was sick. "Poor child, and in all this heat; it does seem to me if he'd lose a little weight he wouldn't suffer so. Angela Lee was that way, too: the heat just laid her out." As for Angela Lee, Zoo had told him this queer story: "Honey, a mighty peculiar thing happen to that old lady, happen just before she die: she grew a beard; it just commence pouring out her face, real sure enough hair; a yeller color, it was, and strong as wire. Me, I used to shave her, and her paralyzed from head to toe, her skin like a dead man's. But it growed so quick, this beard, I couldn't hardly keep up, and when she died, Miss Amy hired the barber to come out from town. Well, sir, that man took one look, and walked right back down them stairs, and right out the front door. I tell you I mean I had to laugh!"

"It's just my old suit," he said, afraid to go back and change, for Amy might say no he could not go, might, instead, make him read to his father. And his father, like Angela Lee, was paralyzed, helpless; he could say a few words (boy, why, kind, bad, ball, ship), move his head a little (yes, no), and one arm (to drop a tennis ball, the signal for attention). All pleasure, all pain, he communicated with his eyes, and his eyes, like windows in summer, were seldom shut, always open and staring, even in sleep.

Idabel gave him the worm bucket to carry. Crossing a cane field, climbing a thread of path, passing a Negro house where in the yard there was a naked child fondling a little black goat, they passed into the woods through an avenue of bitter wild cherry trees. "We get drunk as a coot on those," she said, meaning cherries. "Greedy old wildcats get so drunk they scream all night: you ought to hear them ... hollering crazy with the moon and cherry juice." Invisible birds prowling in leaves rustled, sang; beneath the still facade of forest restless feet trampled plushlike moss where limelike light sifted to stain the natural dark. Idabel's bamboo pole scraped low limbs, and the hound, eager and suspicious, careened through nets of blackberry bush. Henry, the sentry; Idabel, the guide; Joel, the captive: three explorers on a solemn trek over earth sloping steadily downward. Black, orange-trimmed butterflies wheeled over wheel-sized ponds of stagnant rain water, the glide of their wings traced on green reflecting surfaces; a rattlesnake's cellophane-like sheddings littered the trail, and broken silver spiderweb covered like cauls dead fallen branches. They passed a little human grave: on its splintered headcross was printed a legend: Toby, Killed by the Cat. Sunken, a stretch of sycamore root growing from its depth, it was, you could tell, an old grave. "What's that mean," said Joel, "killed by the cat?"

"It happened before I was born," said Idabel, as if this explained everything. She turned off the path into an area deep with last winter's leaves: a skunk skittered in the distance, and Henry boomed forward. "This Toby, you see, she was a nigger baby, and her mama worked for old Mrs Skully like Zoo does now. She was Jesus Fever's wife, and Toby was their baby. Old Mrs Skully had a big fine Persian cat, and one day when Toby was asleep the cat sneaked in and put its mouth against Toby's mouth and sucked away all her breath."

Joel said he didn't believe it; but if it was true, it was certainly the most horrible tale he'd ever heard. "I didn't know Jesus Fever had ever been married."

"There's lots you don't know. All kinds of strange things . . . mostly they happened before we were born: that makes them seem to me so much more real."

Before birth; yes, what time was it then? A time like now, and when they were dead, it would be still like now: these trees, that sky, this earth, those acorn seeds, sun and wind, all the same, while they, with dust-turned hearts, change only. Now at thirteen Joel was nearer a knowledge of death than in any year to come: a flower was blooming inside him, and soon, when all tight leaves unfurled, when the noon of youth burned whitest, he would turn and look, as others had, for the opening of another door. In the woods they walked the tireless singings of larks had sounded a century, and more, and floods of frogs had galloped in moonlight bands; stars had fallen here, and Indian arrows, too; prancing blacks had played guitars, sung ballads of bandit-buried gold, sung songs grieving and ghostly, ballads of long ago: before birth.

"Not for me: that makes it not so real," said Joel, and stopped, struck still by the truth of this: Amy, Randolph, his father, they were all outside time, all circling the present like spirits: was this why they seemed to him so like a dream? Idabel reached back and jerked his hand. "Wake up," she said. He looked at her, his eyes wide with alarm. "But I can't. I can't." "Can't what?" she said sourly. "Oh, nothing." Early voyagers, they descended together.

❧❧❧

"Take my colored glasses," Idabel offered. "Everything looks a lot prettier."

The grass-colored lenses tinted the creek where nervous minnow schools stitched the water like needles; occasionally, in deeper pools, a chance shaft of sunlight illuminated bigger game: fat clumsy perch moving slowly, blackly below the surface. Idabel's fishline quivered in the midstream current, but now, after an hour, she'd had not even a nibble, so, rooting the pole firmly between two stumps, she leaned back, pillowing her head on a clump of moss. "O.K., give 'em back," she demanded.

"Where did you get them?" he said, wishing he had a pair.

"At the travelin-show," she said. "Travelin-show comes every year in August; it's not such a big one, but they've got a flying jinny, and a ferris wheel. And they've got a two-headed baby inside a bottle, too. The way I got these glasses was I won them; I used to wear them all the time, even nighttime, but Papa, he said I was going to put out my eyes. Want a cigarette?"

There was only one, a crumpled *Wing;* dividing it, she struck a match. "Look," she said, "I can blow one smoke ring through another." The rings mounted in the air, blue and perfect; it was so still, yet all around there was the feeling of movement, subtle, secret, shifting: dragonflies skidded on the water, some sudden unseen motion loosened snowdrop bells brown now all withered and scentless.

Joel said, "I don't think we're going to catch anything."

"I never expect to," said Idabel. "I just like to come here and think about my worries; nobody ever comes hunting for me here. It's a nice place . . . just to lie and take your ease."

"What kind of worries do you worry about?" he asked.

"That's my business. And you know something . . . you're an awful poke-nose. You don't ever catch me prying, hell, no. Anybody else in the country, why, they'd eat you alive, you being a stranger, and living at the Landing and all. Look at Florabel. What a snoop she is."

"I think she's very pretty," said Joel, just to be aggravating.

Idabel made no comment. She flipped away her cigarette, and, forking her fingers between her lips, whistled boylike: Henry, padding along the creek's shallow edge, scrambled up the bank, his coat shining soggy wet. "Pretty on the outside, sure, but it's what's on the inside that counts," she said, hugging the hound. "She keeps telling Papa he ought to do away with Henry, says he's got a mortal disease: that's what she's like on the inside."

The white face of afternoon took shape in the sky; his enemy, Joel thought, was there, just behind those glasslike, smokelike clouds; whoever, whatever this enemy was, his was the face imaged there brightly blank. And in this respect Idabel could be envied; she at least knew her enemies: you and you, she could say, such and such and so and so. "Were you ever afraid of losing your mind?"

"Never thought about it," she said, and laughed. "To hear *them* tell it, I haven't got a mind no ways."

Joel said: "You're not being serious. Here's what I mean: do you ever see things, like people, like whole houses, see them and feel them and know for certain they're real . . . only . . ."

"Only they're not," said Idabel. "The time that snake bit me,

I lived a week in a terrible place where everything was crawling, the floors and walls, everything. Now all that was plain foolishness. But then it was a peculiar thing, because last summer I went with Uncle August (he's the one that's so afraid of girls he won't look at one; he says I'm not a girl; I do love my Uncle August: we're like brothers) . . . we went down to Pearl River . . . and one day we were rowing in this dark place and came on an island of snakes; it was real little, just one tree, but alive with old copperheads: they were even hanging off the branches. I tell you it was right spooky. And when folks talk about dreams-come-true, I guess I know what they mean."

"That's not like what I was saying," said Joel, his voice small, bewildered. "Dreams are different, dreams you can lose. But if you see something . . . a lady, say, and you see her where nobody should be, then she follows you around inside your head. I mean like this: the other night Zoo was scared; she'd heard a dog howl, and she said it was her husband come back, and she went to the window: 'I see him,' she said, 'he's squatting under the fig tree,' she said, 'and his eyes are all yellow in the dark.' But then when I looked there was nothing but nothing."

All this Idabel seemed to find rather unexceptional. "Oh, shoot!" she said, tossing her head, the chopped red hair swishing wonderful fire, "everybody knows Zoo's crazy for true. One time, and it was hot as now, I was passing on the road, and she was there by the mailbox with this dumb look, and she says: 'What a fine snow we had last night.' Always talking about snow, always seeing things, that Zoo, that crazy Zoo."

Joel regarded Idabel with malice: what a mean liar she was. Zoo was not crazy. She was not. Yet he remembered the snow of their first conversation: it fell swiftly all about him: the woods dazzled whitely, and Idabel's voice, speaking now, sounded soft, and snow-hushed: "It's Ivory," she said. "It floats."

"What for?" he said, accepting a cake of soap she'd taken from her pocket.

"To wash with, stupid," she told him. "And don't look so prissy. Everytime I come down here, I always take a scrub. Here, you put your clothes on that stump where the fishpole is."

Joel looked shyly at the designated place. "But you're a girl."

With an exceedingly contemptuous expression, Idabel drew up to her full height. "Son," she said, and spit between her fingers, "what you've got in your britches is no news to me, and no concern of mine: hell, I've fooled around with nobody but boys since first grade. I never think like I'm a girl; you've got to remember that, or we can't never be friends." For all its bravado, she made this declaration with a special and compelling innocence; and when she knocked one fist against the other, as, frowning, she did now, and said: "I want so much to be a boy: I would be a sailor, I would . . ." the quality of her futility was touching.

Joel stood up and began to unbutton his shirt.

He lay there on a bed of cold pebbles, the cool water washing, rippling over him; he wished he were a leaf, like the current-carried leaves riding past: leaf-boy, he would float lightly away, float and fade into a river, an ocean, the world's great flood. Holding his nose, he put his head underwater: he was six years old, and his penny-colored eyes were round with terror: Holy Ghost, the preacher said, pressing him down into baptism water; he screamed, and his mother, watching from a front pew, rushed forward, took him in her arms, held him, whispered softly: my darling, my darling. He lifted his face from the great stillness, and, as Idabel splashed a playful wave, seven years vanished in an instant.

"You look like a plucked chicken," said Idabel. "So skinny and white."

Joel's shoulders contracted self-consciously. Despite Idabel's quite genuine lack of interest in his nakedness, he could not make so casual an adjustment to the situation as she seemed to expect.

Idabel said: "Hold still, now, and I'll shampoo your hair." Her own was a maze of lather-curls like cake icing. Without clothes, her figure was, if anything, more boyish: she seemed mostly legs, like a crane, or a walker on modified stilts, and freckles, dappling her rather delicate shoulders, gave her a curiously wistful look. But already her breast had commenced to swell, and there was about her hips a mild suggestion of approaching width. Joel, having conceived of Idabel as gloomy, and cantankerous, was surprised at how funny and gay she could be: working her fingers rhythmically over his scalp, she kept laughing and telling jokes, some of them quite bawdy: ". . . so the farmer said: 'Sure she's a pretty baby; oughta be, after having been strained through a silk handkerchief.'"

When he did not laugh, she said: "What's the matter? Don't you get it?" Joel shook his head. "And you from the city, too," she sighed.

"What did he mean . . . strained through a silk handkerchief?"

"Skip it, son," said Idabel, rinsing his hair, "you're too young." Joel thought then that the points of Idabel's jokes were even for her none too clear: the manner in which she told them was not altogether her own; she was imitating someone, and, wondering who, he asked: "Where'd you hear that joke?"

"Billy Bob told me," she said.

"Who's that?"

"He's just Billy Bob."

"Do you like him?" said Joel, not understanding why he felt so jealous.

"Sure I like him," she said, rising up and wading toward land; her eyes fixed on the water, she was, moving slowly and with such grace, like a bird in search of food. "Sure: he's practically my best friend. He's awful tough, Billy Bob is. I remember back in fourth grade we had that mean Miss Aikens, and she used to beat Billy Bob's hands raw with a ruler, and he never cried once."

They sat down in a sunny place to dry, and she put on her dark glasses.

"I never cry," Joel lied.

She turned on her stomach, and, fingering moss, said with gentle matter-of-factness: "Well, I do. I cry sometimes." She looked at him earnestly. "But you don't ever tell anybody, hear."

He wanted to say: no, Idabel, dear Idabel, I am your good true friend. And he wanted to touch her, to put his arms around her, for this seemed suddenly the only means of expressing all he felt. Pressing closer, he reached and, with breathtaking delicacy, kissed her cheek. There was a hush; tenuous moods of light and shade seem to pass between them like the leaf-shadow trembling on their bodies. Then Idabel tightened all over. She grabbed hold of his hair and started to pull, and when she did this a terrible, and puzzled rage went through Joel. This was the real betrayal. And so he fought back; tangled and wrestling, the sky turning, descending, revolving, they rolled over, over. The dark glasses fell off, and Joel, falling back, felt them crush beneath and cut his buttocks. "Stop," he panted, "please stop, I'm bleeding." Idabel was astride him, and her strong hands locked his wrists to the ground. She brought her red, angry face close to his: "Give up?"

"I'm bleeding," was all Joel would say.

Presently, after releasing him, she brought water, and washed his cut. "You'll be all right," she said, as if nothing had happened. And, indefinably, it was as if nothing had: neither, of course, would ever be able to explain why they had fought.

Joel said: "I'm sorry about your glasses."

The broken pieces sprinkled the ground like green raindrops. Stooping, she started picking them up; then, seeming to think better of this, she spilled them back. "It's not your fault," she said sadly. "Maybe . . . maybe some day I'll win another pair."

EIGHT

Randolph dipped his brush into a little water-filled vinegar jar, and tendrils of purple spread like some fast-growing vine. "Don't smile, my dear," he said. "I'm not a photographer. On the other hand, I could scarcely be called an artist; not, that is, if you define *artist* as one who sees, takes and purely transmits: always for me there is the problem of distortion, and I never paint so much what I see as what I think: for example, some years ago, this was in Berlin, I drew a boy not much older than yourself, and yet in my picture he looked more aged than Jesus Fever, and whereas in reality his eyes were childhood blue, the eyes I saw were bleary and lost. And what I saw was indeed the truth, for little Kurt, that was his name, turned out to be a perfect horror, and tried twice to murder me . . . exhibiting both times, I must say, admirable ingenuity. Poor child, I wonder whatever became of him . . . or, for that matter, me. Now that is a most interesting question: whatever became of me?" As if to punctuate his sentences he kept, all the while he talked, thrusting the brush inside the jar, and the water, continually darkening, had at its center, like a hidden flower, a rope of red. "Very well, sit back, we'll relax a minute now."

Sighing, Joel glanced about him. It was the first time he'd

been in Randolph's room; after two hours, he still could not quite take it in, for it was so unlike anything he'd ever known before: faded gold and tarnished silk reflecting in ornate mirrors, it all made him feel as though he'd eaten too much candy. Large as the room was, the barren space in it amounted to no more than one foot; carved tables, velvet chairs, candelabras, a German music box, books and paintings seemed to spill each into the other, as if the objects in a flood had floated through the windows and sunk here. Behind his liver-shaped desk unframed foreign postcards crusted the walls; six of these, a series from Japan, were for Joel an education, even though to some extent he knew already the significance of what they depicted. Like a museum exhibit, there was spread out on a long, black, tremendously heavy table a display consisting in part of antique dolls, some with missing arms, legs, some without heads, others whose bead-eyes stared glass-blank though their innards, straw and sawdust, showed through open wounds; all, however, were costumed, and exquisitely, in a variety of velvet, lace, linen. Now set in the center of this table was a little photograph in a silver frame so elaborate as to be absurd; it was a cheap photograph, obviously taken at a carnival or amusement park, for the persons concerned, three men and a girl, were posed against a humorous backdrop of cross-eyed baboons and leering kangaroos; though he was thinner in this scene and more handsome, Joel, without much effort, recognized Randolph, and another of the men looked familiar, too . . . was it his father? Certainly the face was only mildly reminiscent of the man across the hall. The third man, taller than his companions, cut an amazing figure; he was powerfully made and, even in so faded a print, very dark, almost Negroid; his eyes, narrow and sly and black, glittered beneath brows thick as mustaches, and his lips, fuller than any woman's, were caught in a cocky smile which intensified the dashing, rather vaudeville effect of a straw hat he wore, a cane he carried. He had his arm around the girl, and she, an anemic faunlike creature, was gazing up at him with the completest adoration.

"Oh, yes," said Randolph, stretching his legs, lighting a mentholated cigarette, "do not take it seriously, what you see here: it's only a joke played on myself by myself . . . it amuses and horrifies . . . a rather gaudy grave, you might say. There is no daytime in this room, nor night; the seasons are changeless here, and the years, and when I die, if indeed I haven't already, then let me be dead drunk and curled, as in my mother's womb, in the warm blood of darkness. Wouldn't that be an ironic finale for one who, deep in his goddamned soul, sought the sweetly clean-limbed life? bread and water, a simple roof to share with some beloved, nothing more." Smiling, smoothing the back of his hair, he put out the cigarette, and picked up his brush. "Inasmuch as I was born dead, how ironic that I should die at all; yes, born dead, literally: the midwife was perverse enough to slap me into life. Or did she?" He looked at Joel in an amused way. "Answer me: did she?"

"Did she what?" said Joel, for, as usual, he did not understand: Randolph seemed always to be carrying on in an unfathomable vocabulary secret dialogues with someone unseen. "Randolph," he said, "please don't be mad with me: it's only that you say things in such a funny way."

"Never mind," said Randolph, "all difficult music must be heard more than once. And if what I tell you now sounds senseless, it will in retrospect seem far too clear; and when this happens, when those flowers in your eyes wither, irrecoverable as they are, why, though no tears helped dissolve my own cocoon,

I shall weep a little for you." Rising, going to a huge baroque bureau, he dabbed on lemon cologne, combed his polished curls, and, posturing somewhat, studied himself in a mirror; while duplicating him in all essentials, the mirror, full-length and of French vintage, seemed to absorb his color, to pare and change his features: the man in the mirror was not Randolph, but whatever personality imagination desired him to resemble, and he, as if corroborating such a theory, said: "They can romanticize us so, mirrors, and that is their secret: what a subtle torture it would be to destroy all the mirrors in the world: where then could we look for reassurance of our identities? I tell you, my dear, Narcissus was no egotist . . . he was merely another of us who, in our unshatterable isolation, recognized, on seeing his reflection, the one beautiful comrade, the only inseparable love . . . poor Narcissus, possibly the only human who was ever honest on this point."

A shy rap at the door interrupted. "Randolph," said Amy, "is that boy in there with you?"

"We're busy. Go away, go away . . ."

"But Randolph," she whined, "don't you think he ought to come read to his father?"

"I said: go away."

Joel let his face reveal neither relief nor gratitude: to obscure emotion was becoming for him a natural reflex; it helped him sometimes not to feel at all. Still there was one thing he could not do, for there is no known way of making the mind clear-blank, and whatever he obliterated in daytime rose up at night in dreams to sleep beside him with an iron embrace. As for reading to his father, he'd made an odd discovery: Mr Sansom never really listened: a list of prices recited from a Sears Roebuck interested him, Joel had found by experiment, as much as any wild-west story.

"Before it happened," said Randolph, resuming his seat, "before then, Ed was very different . . . very sporting, and, if your standards are not too distinguished, handsome (there, in that photograph you can see for yourself), but, to be truthful, I never much liked him, quite the contrary; for one thing, his owning Pepe, or being, that is, his manager, complicated our relations. Pepe Alvarez, he is the one with the straw hat, and the girl, well, that is Dolores. It is not of course a very accurate picture: so innocent: who could imagine that only two days after it was taken one of us fell down a flight of stairs with a bullet in his back?" Pausing to adjust the drawing board, he stared at Joel, one eye squinting like a watchmaker's. "Careful now, don't speak, I'm doing your lips." Rustling the ribbon-dressed dolls, a breeze came through the windows bringing here in the velvet shade sunshine smells of outside, and Joel wanted to be out there where right now Idabel might be splashing through a field of grass, running with Henry at her heels. The circular composition of Randolph's face lengthened in concentration; he worked silently a great while until at last, and it was as if all that had gone before had indescribably led up to this, he said:

"Let me begin by telling you that I was in love. An ordinary statement, to be sure, but not an ordinary fact, for so few of us learn that love is tenderness, and tenderness is not, as a fair proportion suspect, pity; and still fewer know that happiness in love is not the absolute focusing of all emotion in another: one has always to love a good many things which the beloved must come only to symbolize; the true beloveds of this world are in their lover's eyes lilac opening, ship lights, school bells, a land-scape, remembered conversations, friends, a child's Sunday, lost voices, one's favorite suit, autumn and all seasons, memory, yes, it being the earth and water of existence, memory. A nostalgic list, but then, of course, where could one find a more nostalgic subject? When one is your age most subtleties go unobserved; even so, I imagine you think it incredible, looking at me as I am now, that I should've had ever the innocence to feel such love; nevertheless, when I was twenty-three . . .

"It is the girl in the picture, Dolores. And we met in Madrid. But she was not Spanish; at least I do not believe so, though actually I never knew precisely where she came from: her English was quite perfect. As for me, I had been in Europe then two years, living, as it were, and for the most part, in museums: I wonder really whether anyone ever copied so many Masters? There was almost no painting of which I could not do a most engaging facsimile . . . still, when it came to something of my own, I went quite dead, and it was as though I had no personal perception, no interior life whatever: I was like the wind-flower whose pollen will not mate at all.

"Dolores, on the other hand, was one of those from whom such as I manage occasionally to borrow energy: always with her I knew very much that I was alive, and came finally to believe in my own validity: for the first time I saw things without distortion and complete. That fall we went to Paris, and then to Cuba, where we lived high above the bay of Matanzas in a house . . . how should I describe it? . . . it was cloud-pink stone with rooms strewn like gold and white flowers on a vine of high corridors and crumbling blue steps; with the windows wide and the wind moving through it was like an island, cool and most silent. She was like a child there, and sweet as an orange is sweet, and lazy, deliciously lazy; she liked to sit naked in the sun, and draw tiny little animals, toads and bees and chipmunks, and read astrology magazines, and chart the stars, and wash her hair (this she did no less than three times a day); she was a gambler, too, and every afternoon we went down to the village and bought lottery tickets, or a new guitar: she had over thirty guitars, and played all of them, I must admit, quite horridly.

"And there was this other thing: we very seldom talked; I can never remember having with Dolores a sustained conversation; there was always between us something muted, hushed; still our silence was not of a secret kind, for in itself it communicated that wonderful peace those who understand each other very well sometimes achieve . . . yet neither knew the other truly, for at that time we did not really know ourselves.

"However . . . toward the end of winter I discovered the dream book. Every morning Dolores wrote out her night's dreams in a big scrapbook she kept concealed under a mattress; she wrote them sometimes in French, more often in German or English, but whatever the language, the content was always shockingly malevolent, and I could make no sense of them, for it seemed impossible to identify Dolores with her ruthless dreams. And I was always in them, always fleeing before her, or hiding in the shadow, and each day while she lay naked in the sun I would find the newest page and read how much closer her pursuit had come, for in early dreams she'd murdered in Madrid a lover she called L., and I knew . . . that when she found R. . . . she would kill him, too.

"We slept in a bed with a canopy veil that kept out mosquitoes and sifted the moonlight, and I would lie there awake in the dark watching her sleep, afraid of being trapped in that dream-choked head; and when morning came she would laugh and tease and pull my hair, and presently, after I'd gone, write . . . well, there is this I remember: 'R. is hiding behind a giant clock. Its tick is like thunderstrokes, like the pulsebeat of God, and the hands, shaped like pointing fingers, stand at seventeen past three; come six I will find him, for he does not know it is from me he hides, but imagines it is himself. I do not wish him harm, and I would run away if I could, but the clock demands a sacrifice, or it will never stop, and life must cease somewhere, for who among us can long endure its boom?'

"Aside from all else, there is some truth in that; clocks indeed must have their sacrifice: what is death but an offering to time and eternity?

"Now, oddly enough, our lives were more than ever interlocked: there were any number of times I could have left, gone away, never seen her again; however, to desert would've been to deny love, and if I did not love Dolores, then no emotion of mine has been anything but spurious. I think now she was not altogether human (a trance-child, if such there be, or a dream herself), nor was I . . . though for reasons of youth, and youth is hardly human: it can't be, for the young never believe they will die . . . especially would they never believe that death comes, and often, in forms other than the natural one.

"In the spring we sailed for Florida; Dolores had never been before to the States, and we went to New York, which she did not like, and Philadelphia, which she thought equally tiresome. At last, in New Orleans, where we took a charming patio apartment, she was happy, as indeed was I. And during our peregrinations the dream book disappeared: where she could have hidden it I do not know, for I searched every possible place: it was in a way a relief really not to find it. Then one afternoon, walking home from the market and carrying, if you please, a fine live hen, I saw her talking with a man there in the shade by the cathedral; there was an intimacy in their attitude which made me still inside: this I knew was no simple tourist asking direction, and later, when I told her what I'd seen, she said, oh, very casually, yes, it was a friend, someone she'd met in a café, a prizefighter: would I care to meet him?

"Now after an injury, physical, spiritual, whatever, one always believes had one obeyed a premonition (there is usually in such instances an imagined premonition) nothing would have happened; still, had I had absolute foreknowledge, I should have gone right ahead, for in every lifetime there occur situations when one is no more than a thread in a design willfully woven by . . . who should I say? God?

"It was one Sunday that they came, the prizefighter, Pepe Alvarez, and Ed Sansom, his manager. A mercilessly hot day, as I recall, and we sat in the patio with fans and cold drinks: you could scarcely select a group with less in common than we four; had it not been for Sansom, who was something of a buffoon and therefore distracting, it would all have been rather too tense, for one couldn't ignore the not very discreet interplay between Dolores and the young Mexican: they were lovers, even slow-witted Amy could've perceived this, and I was not surprised: Pepe was so extraordinary: his face was alive, yet dreamlike, brutal, yet boyish, foreign but familiar (as something from childhood is familiar), both shy and aggressive, both sleeping and awake. But when I say he and Dolores were lovers, perhaps I exaggerate: lovers implies, to some extent, reciprocity, and Dolores, as became apparent, could never love anyone, so caught was she within a trance; then, too, other than that they performed a pleasurable function, she had no personal feeling or respect for men or the masculine personality . . . that personality which, despite legend, can only be most sensitively appreciated by its own kind. As it was getting dark in the patio, I looked at Pepe: his Indian skin seemed to hold all the light left in the air, his flat animal-shrewd eyes, bright as though with tears, regarded Dolores exclusively; and suddenly, with a mild shock, I realized it was not she of whom I was jealous, but him.

"Afterwards, and though at first I was careful not to show the quality of my feelings, Dolores understood intuitively what had happened: 'Strange how long it takes us to discover ourselves; I've known since first I saw you,' she said, adding, 'I do not think, though, that he is the one for you; I've known too many Pepes: love him if you will, it will come to nothing.' The brain may take advice, but not the heart, and love, having no geography, knows no boundaries: weight and sink it deep, no matter, it will rise and find the surface: and why not? any love is natural and beautiful that lies within a person's nature; only hypocrites would hold a man responsible for what he loves, emotional illiterates and those of righteous envy, who, in their agitated concern, mistake so frequently the arrow pointing to heaven for the one that leads to hell.

"It was different, this love of mine for Pepe, more intense than anything I felt for Dolores, and lonelier. But we are alone, darling child, terribly, isolated each from the other; so fierce is the world's ridicule we cannot speak or show our tenderness; for us, death is stronger than life, it pulls like a wind through the dark, all our cries burlesqued in joyless laughter; and with the garbage of loneliness stuffed down us until our guts burst bleeding green, we go screaming round the world, dying in our rented rooms, nightmare hotels, eternal homes of the transient heart. There were moments, wonderful moments, when I thought I was free, that I could forget him and that sleepy violent face, but then he would not let me, no, he was always there, sitting in the patio, or listening to her play the guitar, laughing, talking, near but remote, always there, as I was in Dolores' dreams. I could not endure to see him suffer; it was an agony to watch him fight, prancing quick and cruel, see him hit, the glare, the blood and the blueness. I gave him money, bought him cream-colored hats, gold bracelets (which he adored, and wore like a woman), shoes in bright Negro colors, candy silk shirts, and I gave all these things to Ed Sansom, too: how they despised me, both of them, but not enough to refuse a gift, oh never. And Dolores continued with Pepe in her queer compulsive way, not really interested one way or another, not caring whether he stayed or went; like some brainless plant, she lived (existed) beyond her own control in that reckless book of dreams. She could not help me. What we most want is only to be held . . . and told . . . that everything (everything is a funny thing, is baby milk and Papa's eyes, is roaring logs on a cold morning, is hoot-owls and the boy who makes you cry after school, is Mama's long hair, is being afraid and twisted faces on the bedroom wall) . . . everything is going to be all right.

"One night Pepe came to the house very drunk, and proceeded with the boldest abandon to a) beat Dolores with his belt, b) piss on the rug and on my paintings, c) call me horrible hurting names, d) break my nose, e and f and otherwise. And I walked in the streets that night, and along the docks, and talked aloud pleading with myself to go away, be alone again, I said, as if I were not alone, rent another room in another life. I sat in Jackson Square; except for the tolling of train bells, it was quiet and all the Cabildo was like a haunted palace; there was a blond misty boy sitting beside me, and he looked at me, and I at him, and we were not strangers: our hands moved towards each other to embrace. I never heard his voice, for we did not speak; it is a shame, I should so like the memory of it. Loneliness, like fever, thrives on night, but there with him light broke, breaking in the trees like birdsong, and when sunrise came, he loosened his fingers from mine, and walked away, that misty boy, my friend.

"Always now we were together, Dolores, Pepe, Ed and I, Ed and his jokes, we other three and our silences. Grotesque quadruplets (born of what fantastic parent?) we fed upon one another, as cancer feeds upon itself, and yet, will you believe this? there are a medley of moments I remember with the kind of nostalgia reserved usually for sweeter things: Pepe (I see) is lighting a match with his thumbnail, is trying with a bare hand to snatch a goldfish from the fountain, we are at a picture-show eating popcorn from the same bag, he has fallen asleep and leans against my shoulder, he is laughing because I wince at a boxing-cut on his lip, I hear him whistling on the stairs, I hear him mounting toward me and his footsteps are not so loud as my heart. Days, fast fading as snowflakes, flurry into autumn, fall all around like November leaves, the sky, cold red with winter, frightens with the light it sheds: I sleep all day, the shutters closed, the covers drawn above my eyes. Now it is Mardi Gras, and we are going to a ball; everyone has chosen his costume but me: Ed is a Franciscan monk (gnawing a cigar), Pepe is a bandit and Dolores a ballerina; but I cannot think what to wear and this becomes a dilemma of disproportionate importance. Dolores appears the night of the ball with a tremendous pink box: transformed, I am a Countess and my king is Louis XVI; I have silver hair and satin slippers, a green mask, am wrapped in silk pistachio and pink: at first, before the mirror, this horrifies me, then pleases to rapture, for I am very beautiful, and later, when the waltz begins, Pepe, who does not know, begs a dance, and I, oh sly Cinderella, smile beneath my mask, thinking: Ah, if I were really me! Toad into prince, tin into gold; fly, feathered serpent, the hour grows old: so ends a part of my saga.

"Another spring, and they were gone; it was April, the sixth of that rainy lilac April, just two days after our happy trip to Pontchartrain . . . where the picture was taken, and where, in symbolic dark, we'd drifted through the tunnel of love. All right, listen: late that afternoon when I woke up rain was at the window and on the roof: a kind of silence, if I may say, was walking through the house, and, like most silence, it was not silent at all: it rapped on the doors, echoed in the clocks, creaked on the stairs, leaned forward to peer into my face and explode. Below a radio talked and sang, yet I knew no one heard it: she was gone, and Pepe with her.

"Her room was overturned; as I searched through the wreckage, a guitar string broke, its twang vibrating every nerve. I hurried to the top of the stairs, my mouth open but no sound coming out: all the control centers of my mind were numb; the air undulated, and the floor expanded like an accordion. Someone was coming towards me. I felt them like a pressure climbing the steps; unrecognized, they seemed to walk straight into my eyes. First I thought it was Dolores, then Ed, then Pepe. Whoever it was, they shook me, pleading and swearing: that bastard, they said, gone, sonofabitchinbastard, gone, with the car, all the clothes and money, gone, forever and ever and ever. But who was it? I couldn't see: a blinding Jesus-like glow burned around him: Pepe, is it you? Ed? Dolores? I pushed myself free, ran back into the bedroom and shut the door: it was no use: the doorknob began to turn, and suddenly everything was crazy plain: Dolores had at last caught me in her dreams.

"So I found a gun I kept wrapped in an old sock. The rain had stopped. The windows were open, and the room was cool and sweet with lilac. Downstairs the radio was singing, and in my ears there was the roar a seashell makes. The door opened; I fired once, and again, and Jesus dissolved, became nothing but Ed in a dirty linen suit; doubled over, he stumbled toward the stairs, and rolled down the steps loose like a ragdoll.

"For two days he lay crumpled on the couch, bleeding all over himself, moaning and shouting and running a rosary through his fingers. He called for you, and his mother, and the Lord. There was nothing I could do. And then Amy came from the Landing. She was very good. She found a doctor, a little Negro dwarf not too particular. Abruptly the weather was like July, but those weeks were the winter of our lives; the veins froze and cracked with coldness, and in the sky the sun was like a lump of ice. That little doctor, waddling around on his six-inch legs, laughed and laughed and kept the radio playing comedy programs. Every day I woke up saying, 'If I die . . . ,' not realizing how dead I was already, and only a memory tagging along with Dolores and Pepe . . . wherever they were: I grieved for Pepe, not because I'd lost him (yes, that a little), but because in the end I knew Dolores would find him, too: it is easy to escape daylight, but night is inevitable, and dreams are the giant cage.

"To be brief: Ed and Amy were married in New Orleans. It was, you see, her fantasy come true; she was at last what she'd always wanted to be, a nurse . . . with a more or less permanent position. Then we all came back to the Landing; Amy's idea, and the only solution, for he would never be well again. I suppose we shall go on together until the house sinks, until the garden grows up and weeds hide us in their depth."

Randolph, pushing aside his drawing board, slumped over on the desk; dusk had come while he talked, and swept the room bluely; outside, sparrows were calling to roost, their nightfall chatter punctuated by a solemn frog. Pretty soon Zoo would be ringing the supper bell. None of this was apparent to Joel; he was not even aware of any stiffness from having sat so long in one position: it was as though Randolph's voice continued saying in his head things that were real enough, but not necessary to believe. He was confused because the story had been like a movie with neither plot nor motive: had Randolph really shot his father? And, most important of all, where was the ending? What had happened to Dolores and old awful Pepe Alvarez? That is what he wanted to know, and that is what he asked.

"If I knew . . ." said Randolph, pausing, holding a match to a candle; the sudden light flattered his face, made the pink hairless skin more impeccably young. "But, my dear, so few things are fulfilled: what are most lives but a series of incompleted episodes? *'We work in the dark, we do what we can, we give what we have. Our doubt is our passion, and our passion is our task . . .'* It is wanting to know the end that makes us believe in God, or witchcraft, believe, at least, in something."

Joel still wanted to know: "Didn't you ever even try to find out where they got off to?"

"Over there," said Randolph with a tired smile, "is a five-pound volume listing every town and hamlet on the globe; it is what I believe in, this almanac: day by day I've gone through it writing Pepe always in care of the postmaster; just notes, nothing but my name and what we will for convenience call address.

Oh, I know that I shall never have an answer. But it gives me something to believe in. And that is peace."

Downstairs the supper bell sounded. Randolph did not move. His face seemed to contract with a look of sad guilt. "I've been very weak this afternoon, very wicked," he said, rising for Joel to accept an invitation of open arms. "Do forgive me, darling Joel." Then, in a voice as urgent as the bell, he added: "And please, tell me what I want to hear."

Joel remembered. "Everything," he said gently, "everything is going to be all right."

NINE

Jesus Fever was a sick man. For over a week he'd been unable to hold anything on his stomach. His skin was parched like an old leaf, and his eyes, milky with film, saw strange things: Randolph's father, he swore, was lurking in a corner of the cabin; all the funny papers and Coca-Cola pictures plastering the walls were, he complained, crooked and aggravating; a noise like the crack of a whip snapped in his head; a bouquet of sunflowers Joel had brought became suddenly a flock of canaries crazily singing and circling the room; he was worried to frenzy by a stranger staring at him from a gloomy little mirror hung above the mantel. Little Sunshine, arriving to give what aid he could, covered the mirror with a flour sack in order that, as he explained, Jesus Fever's soul could not be trapped there; he hung a charm around the old man's neck, sprinkled magic ginger powder in the air, and disappeared before moonrise. "Zoo, child," said Jesus, "how come you let me freeze thisaway? Fix the fire, child, it's colder'n a well-bottom."

Zoo took a reasoning tone. "Papadaddy, now honey, we all us gonna melt . . . so hot Mister Randolph done change clothes three times today." But Jesus would not listen, and asked for a quilt to wrap around his legs, a wool sock to stretch over his head: the whole house, he argued, was rattling with wind: why, look, there was old Mr Skully, his fine red beard turned white with frost. So Zoo went out in the dark of the yard to find an armful of kindling.

Joel, left in charge, started when Jesus beckoned to him secretively. The old man was sitting in a rattan rocker, a worn scrapquilt of velvet flowers covering his knees. He could not stay in bed: a horizontal position interfered with his breathing. "Rock my rocker, son," he said in a reedy voice, "it's kinda restful like . . . makes me feel I'm ridin in a wagon an got a long way to go." A kerosene lamp burned in the room. The chair, shadowed on the wall, swished a gentle drowsy sound. "Can't you feel the cold, son?"

"Mama was always cold, too," said Joel, prickly chill tingling his spine. Don't die, he thought, and as he pushed the chair back and forth the runners whispered, don't die, don't die. For if Jesus Fever died, then Zoo would go away, and there would be no one but Amy, Randolph, his father. It was not so much these three, however, but the Landing, and the fragile hush of living under a glass bell. Maybe Randolph would take him away: there had been some mention of a trip. And he'd written Ellen again, surely something would come of that.

"Papadaddy," said Zoo, lugging in a bundle of wood, "you is mighty thoughtless makin me hunt round out there in the dark where theys all kinda wild creatures crawlin just hungry for a nip outa tasty me. They is a wildcat smell on the air, they is, I declare. And who knows but what Keg's done runaway from the chain gang? Joel, honey, latch the door."

When the fire commenced to burn Jesus asked that his chair be brought nearer the hearth. "I used to could play the fiddle," he said, wistfully watching the flames slide upward " . . . rheumatism stole all the music outa my fingers." He shook his head, and sucked his gums, and spit into the fire. "Don't fuss with me, child," he complained as Zoo tried to adjust the quilt. "Tell you now, bring me my sword." She returned from the other room bearing a beautiful sword with a silver handle: across the blade there was inscribed, Unsheath Me Not Without Reason— Sheath Me Not Without Honor. "Mister Randolph's grand-daddy gimme this, that be more 'n sixty year ago." In the past days he'd one by one called forth all his treasures: a dusty cracked violin, his derby with the feather, a Mickey Mouse watch, his high-button orange shoes, three little monkeys who neither saw, heard nor spoke evil, these and other precious things lay strewn around the cabin, for he would not allow them to be put again out of sight.

Zoo presented Joel with a handful of pecans and gave him a pair of pliers to crack them with. "I'm not hungry," he said and rested his head in her lap. It was not a comfortable lap like El-len's. You could feel too precisely tensed muscle and sharp bone. But she played her fingers through his hair, and that was sweet. "Zoo," he said softly, not wanting the old man to hear, "Zoo, he's going to die, isn't he?"

"I spec so," she said, and there was little feeling in her voice.

"And then will you go away?"

"I reckon."

At this Joel straightened and looked at her angrily. "But why, Zoo?" he demanded. "Tell me why!"

"Hush, child, speak quiet." A slow moment followed in which she twisted her neckerchief, felt for and found the charm Little Sunshine had given her. "Ain't gonna hold good forever," she said, tapping the charm. "Someday he gonna come back here lookin for to slice me up. I knows it good as anythin. I seen it in my dreams, and the floor don't creak but what my heart stops. Every time a dog howls I think, that's him, that's him on his way, on accounta dogs just naturally hate that Keg and start to holler time they smell him."

"I'd protect you, Zoo," he pleaded. "Honest, I'd never let nobody hurt you."

Zoo laughed, and her laugh seemed to fly around the room like a frightening black bird. "Why, Keg could drop you with just the look of his eyes!" She began to shiver in the suffocating room. "One day he gonna come crawlin through that window, and won't nobody hear nothin; else I'll find him waitin in the dark tween here and the house, gotta long shiny razor: Lawd, I seen it a million times. So I gotta run, gotta go where there's snow and he ain't gonna catch me."

Joel squeezed her wrist. "If you'd let me go with you, Zoo . . . oh, we could have such a lot of fun."

"Don't talk foolishness, baby."

The yellow tabby scooted from under the bed, darted before the fire, arched its back and hissed. "What he see?" cried Jesus, pointing his sword: firelight ran up the gaunt blade like a gold spider. "Answer me, cat, you see somethin?" The cat relaxed on its haunches, and fixed the old man coldly. Jesus giggled. "Try to joke ol Jesus," he said, wagging his finger. "Try to scare him." His blindlike blue-looking eyes closed; he tilted back his head so that the stocking-foot dangled like a Chinese pigtail, sighed and said: "Ain't got no time left for to joke, cat." And then, holding the sword to his chest: "Mister Skully gimme this my weddin day; me and my woman, us just jumped over a broom, and Mister Skully, he say, 'All right now, Jesus, you is married.' Travelin Preacher come tell me and my woman that ain't proper, say the Lawd ain't gonna put up with it: sure enough, the cat done killed Toby, and my woman grieves herself so she hangs on a tree, big cozy lady got the branch bent double: back when I was just so high my daddy cut his switches offen that tree . . ." remembering, it was as if his mind were an island in time, the past surrounding sea.

Joel cracked a pecan, and tossed the hull into the fire. "Zoo," he said, "did you ever hear of anybody called Alcibiades?"

"Who that you say?"

"Alcibiades. I don't know. It's somebody Randolph says I look like."

Zoo considered. "You musta heard wrong, honey. The name he most likely said is Alicaster. Alicaster Jones is a Paradise Chapel boy what used to sing in the choir. Looks like a white angel, so pretty he got the preacher and all kinda mens and ladies lovin him up. Leastwise, that's what folks say."

"I'll bet I can sing better than him," said Joel. "You know, I bet I could sing in vaudeville shows and make a whole lot of money, enough money to buy you a fur coat, Zoo, and dresses like they show in the Sunday papers."

"I want red dresses," said Zoo, entering the spirit. "Look real nice in red, I do. We gonna have us a car?"

Joel was delirious. It seemed so real. There he was bathed by spotlights, and wearing a tuxedo with a gardenia in his lapel. But there was only one song he knew how to sing all the way through. So he said, "Listen, Zoo," and sang, "Silent Night, Holy Night, all is calm, all is bright, round yon Vir . . ." his voice, up to this point high and sweet like a girl's, broke in an ugly, mystifying way.

"Uh huh," Zoo nodded knowingly. "Little tadpole growin to be a fish."

In the fireplace a log, cracking dramatically, sent out a sizzle of sparks; then, with no warning, a nest of newborn chimney sweeps fell into the flames and quite swiftly split with fire: the little birds burned without sound or movement. Joel, somewhat stunned, remained silent, and Zoo's face was blankly surprised. Only Jesus spoke: "In fire," he said, and had it not been so quiet you could not have heard him, "first comes water, and last comes the fire. Don't say no place in the Good Book why we's in tween. Do it? Can't member . . . not nothin. You," his voice rose shrilly, "you-all! It's gettin powerful warm, it's gettin fire!"

TEN

One grey curiously cool afternoon a week later Jesus Fever died. It was as if someone had been tickling his ribs, for he died in a spasm of desperate giggles. "Maybe," as Zoo said, "God done told somethin funny." She dressed him in his little suspender suit, his orange-leather shoes and derby hat; she squeezed a bunch of dogtooth violets in his hand, and put him in a cedar chest: there he remained for two days while Amy, with Randolph's aid, decided the location of his grave: under the moon tree, they said finally. The moon tree, so named for its round ivory blooms, grew in a lonely place far back from the Landing, and here Zoo shoveled away with no one to help but Joel: the mild excavation they managed at last to make reminded him of all the backyard swimming pools dug in summers that seemed now so long ago. Transporting the cedar chest was an arduous business; in the end they hitched a rope to John Brown, the old mule, and he hauled it to the foot of the grave. "Papadaddy would be mighty tickled could he know who it is is pullin him home," said Zoo. "Papadaddy surely did love you, John Brown: trustiest mule he ever saw, he said so many a time: now you member that." At the last minute Randolph sent word he could not be present for the funeral, and Amy, who brought this message, said a prayer in his name, mumbled, that is, a sentence or so, and made a cross: she wore for the occasion a black glove. But for Jesus there were no mourners: the three in the moontree shade were like some distracted group assembled at a depot to wish a friend goodbye, and, as such gatherings long for the whistle of the train that will release them, they wanted to hear the first thud of earth upon the cedar lid. It seemed odd to Joel nature did not reflect so solemn an event: flowers of cottonboll clouds within a sky as scandalously blue as kitten-eyes were offensive in their sweet disrespect: a resident of over a hundred years in so narrow a world deserved higher homage. The cedar chest capsized as they lowered it into the grave, but Zoo said, "Pay no mind, honey, we ain't got the strenth of heathen giants." She shook her head. "Pore Papadaddy, goin to heaven face down." Unfolding her accordion, she spread her legs wide apart, threw back her head, hollered: "Lawd, take him to thy bosom, tote him all around, Lawd don't you never, don't you never put him down, Lawd, he seen the glory, Lawd, he seen the light . . ." Up until now Joel had not altogether accepted Jesus Fever's death; anybody who'd lived that long just couldn't die; way back in his mind he kind of felt the old man was playing possum; but when the last note of Zoo's requiem became stillness, then it was true, then Jesus was really dead.

That night sleep was like an enemy; dreams, a winged avenging fish, swam rising and diving until light, drawing toward daybreak, opened his eyes. Hurriedly buttoning his breeches, he crept down through the quiet house and out the kitchen door. Above, the moon paled like a stone receding below water, tangled morning color rushed up the sky, trembled there in pastel uncertainty.

"Ain't I gotta donkey's load?" cried Zoo, as he crossed the yard to where she stood on the cabin porch. A quilt stuffed fat with belongings bulged on her back; the accordion was tied to her belt and hung there like a caterpillar; aside from this she had a quite large jellyjar box. "Time I gets to Washington D.C. gonna be a humpback," she said, sounding as though she'd swallowed a gallon of wine, and her joy, in the dimness of sunup, was to him disgusting: what right had she to be so happy?

"You can't carry all that. You look like a fool, for one thing."

But Zoo just flexed her arms, and stamped her foot. "Honey, I feels like ninety-nine locomotives; gonna light outa here goin licketysplit: why, I figures to be in Washington D.C. fore dark." She drew back into a kind of pose, and, as if she were about to curtsey, held out her starched calico skirt: "Pretty, huh?"

Joel squinted critically. Her face was powdered with flour, a sort of reddish oil inflamed her cheeks, she'd scented herself with vanilla flavoring, and greased her hair shiny. About her neck she sported a lemon silk scarf. "Turn around," he said; then, after she'd done so, he moved away, pointedly suppressing comment.

She placidly accepted this affront, but said: "How come you gotta go pull such a long face, and take on in any such way? Do seem to me like you'd be glad on my account, us bein friends and all."

He yanked loose a trailing arm of ivy, and this set swinging all the porch-eave pots: bumping against each other they raised a noise like a series of closing doors. "Oh, you're awful funny. Ha ha ha." He gave her one of Randolph's cool arched looks.

"You were never my friend. But after all why should anyone such as me have anything in common with such as you?"

"Baby, baby . . ." said Zoo, her voice rocking in a tender way ". . . baby, I make you a promise: whenever I gets all fixed . . . I'm gonna send for you and take care you all the resta your years. Before the Almighty may He strike me dead if this promise ain't made."

Joel jerked away, flung himself against a porch-pole, embraced it, clung there as though it alone understood and loved him.

"Hold on there now," she told him firmly. "You is almost a growed man; idea, takin on like some little ol gal! Why, you mortify me, I declare. Here was bout to give you Papadaddy's fine handsome sword . . . seen now you is not man enough for to own it."

Parting the curtain of ivy, Joel stepped through and into the yard; to walk straight off, and not look back, that would punish her. But when he reached the tree stump, and still she had not relented, not called him back, he stopped, retraced his steps onto the porch, and, looking seriously into her African eyes, said: "You will send for me?"

Zoo smiled and half picked him up. "Time I gets a place to put our heads." She reached down into her quilt-covered bundle, and brought out the sword. "This here was Papadaddy's proudest thing," she said. "Now don't you bring it no disgrace."

He strapped it to his waist. It was a weapon against the world, and he tensed with the cold grandeur of its sheath along his leg: suddenly he was most powerful, and unafraid. "I thank you kindly, Zoo," he said.

Gathering the quilt, and jellyjar box, she staggered down the steps. Her breath came in grunts, and with every loping movement the accordion, bouncing up and down, sprinkled a rainfall of discordant notes. They walked through the garden wilderness, and to the road. The sun was traveling the green-rimmed distance: as far as you could see daybreak blueness lifted over trees, layers of light unrolled across the land. "I spec to be down past Paradise Chapel fore dew's off the ground: good I got my quilt handy, may be lotsa snow round Washington D.C." And that was the last she said. Joel stopped by the mailbox. "Goodbye," he called, and stood there watching until she grew pinpoint small, lost, and the accordion soundless, gone.

"... no gratitude," Amy sniffed. "Good and kind, that's how we were, always, and what does she do? Runs off, God knows where, leaving me with a houseful of sick people, not one of whom has sense enough to empty a slopjar. Furthermore, whatever else I may be, I'm a lady: I was brought up to be a lady, and I had my full four years at the Normal School. And if Randolph thinks I'm going to play nursemaid to orphans and idiots ... damn Missouri!" Her mouth worked in a furious ugly way. "Niggers! Angela Lee warned me time and again, said never trust a nigger: their minds and hair are full of kinks in equal measure. Still, does seem like she could've stayed to fix breakfast." She took a pan of biscuits from the oven, and, along with a bowl of grits, a pot of coffee, arranged them on a tray. "Here now, trot this up to Cousin Randolph and trot right back: poor Mr Sansom has to be fed too, heaven help us; yes, may the Lord in his wisdom ..."

Randolph was propped up in bed, naked, and with the covers stripped back; his skin seemed translucently pink in the morning light, his round smooth face bizarrely youthful. There was a small Japanese table set across his legs, and on it were a mound of bluejay feathers, a paste pot, a sheet of cardboard. "Isn't this delightful?" he said, smiling up at Joel. "Now put down the tray and have a visit."

"There isn't time," said Joel a little mysteriously.

"Time?" Randolph repeated. "Dear me, I thought that was where we were overstocked."

Pausing between words, Joel said: "Zoo's gone." He was anxious that the announcement should have a dramatic effect. Randolph, however, gave him no satisfaction, for, contrary to Amy, he seemed not at all upset, even surprised. "How tiresome of her," he sighed, "and how absurd, too. Because she can't come back, one never can."

"She wouldn't want to anyway," answered Joel impertinently. "She wasn't happy here; I don't think nothing would make her come back."

"Darling child," said Randolph, dipping a bluejay feather in the paste, "happiness is relative, and," he continued, fitting the feather on the cardboard, "Missouri Fever will discover that all she has deserted is her proper place in a rather general puzzle. Like this." He held up the cardboard in order that Joel could see: there feathers were so arranged the effect was of a living bird transfixed. "Each feather has, according to size and color, a particular position, and if one were the slightest awry, why, it would not look at all real."

A memory floated like a feather in the air; Joel's mental eye saw the bluejay beating its wings up the wall, and Amy's ladylike lifting of a poker. "What good is a bird that can't fly?" he said.

"I beg your pardon?"

Joel was himself uncertain what he meant. "The other one,

the real one, it could fly. But this one can't do anything . . . except maybe look like it was alive."

Tossing the cardboard aside, Randolph lay drumming his fingers on his chest. He lowered his eyelids, and with his eyes closed he looked peculiarly defenseless. "It is pleasanter in the dark," he said, as if talking in his sleep. "Would it inconvenience you, my dear, to bring from the cabinet a bottle of sherry? And then, on tiptoe, mind you, draw all the shades, and then, oh very quietly please, shut the door." As Joel fulfilled the last of these requests, he rose up to say: "You are quite right: my bird can't fly."

Some while later, Joel, his stomach still jittery from having fed Mr Sansom's breakfast to him mouthful by mouthful, sat reading aloud in rapid flat tones. The story, such as it was, involved a blonde lady and a brunette man who lived in a house sixteen floors high; most of the stuff the lady said was embarrassing to repeat: "Darling," he read, "I love you as no woman ever loved, but Lance, my dearest, leave me now while our love is still a shining thing." And Mr Sansom smiled continuously through even the saddest parts; glancing at him, his son remembered a threat Ellen had delivered whenever he'd made an ugly face: "Mark my word," she'd say, "it's going to freeze that way." Such a fate had apparently descended upon Mr Sansom, for his ordinarily expressionless face had been grinning now no less than eight days. Finishing off the beautiful lady and lovely man, who were left honeymooning in Bermuda, Joel went on to a recipe for banana custard pie: it was all the same to Mr Sansom, romance or recipe, he gave each of them staring unequaled attention.

What was it like almost never to shut your eyes, always to be forever reflecting the same ceiling, light, faces, furniture, dark? But if the eyes could not escape you, neither could you avoid them; they seemed indeed sometime to permeate the room, their damp greyness covering all like mist; and if those eyes were to make tears they would not be normal tears, but something grey, perhaps green, a color at any rate, and solid, like ice.

Downstairs in the parlor was a collection of old books, and exploring there Joel had come upon a volume of Scottish legends. One of these concerned a man who compounded a magic potion unwisely enabling him to read the thoughts of other men and see deep into their souls; the evil he saw, and the shock of it, turned his eyes into open sores: thus he remained the rest of his life. It impressed Joel to the extent that he was half-convinced Mr Sansom's eyes knew exactly what went on inside his head, and he attempted, for this reason, to keep his thoughts channeled in impersonal directions. ". . . mix sugar, flour, salt and add egg yolks. Stir constantly while pouring on scalded milk . . ." Every once in a while he was tantalized by a sense of guilt: he ought to feel more for Mr Sansom than he did, he ought to try and love him. If only he'd never seen Mr Sansom! Then he could have gone on picturing him as looking this and that wonderful way, as talking in a kind strong voice, as being really his father. Certainly this Mr Sansom was not his father. This Mr Sansom was nobody but a pair of crazy eyes. ". . . turn into baked pieshell. Cover with . . . it says meringay or something like that . . . and bake. Makes nine-inch pie." He put down the magazine, a journal for females to which Amy subscribed, and began straightening Mr Sansom's pillows. Mr Sansom's head lolled back and forth, as if saying no no no; actually, and his voice sounded prickly as though a handful of pins were lodged in his throat, he said, "Boy kind kind boy kind," over and over, "ball kind ball," he said, dropping one of his red tennis balls, and, as Joel retrieved it, his set smile became more glassy: it ached on his grey skeleton face. Then all at once a whistle broke through the shut windows. Joel turned to listen. Three short blasts and a hoot-owl wail. He went to the window. It was Idabel; she was in the garden below, and Henry was with her. The window was stuck, so he signaled to her, but she could not see him, and he hurried to the door. "Bad," said Mr Sansom, and let go every tennis ball in the bed, "boy bad bad!"

Detouring into his room long enough to strap on his sword, he ran downstairs, outside and into the garden. For the first time since he'd known her Joel felt Idabel was glad to see him: a look of serious relief cleared her face, and for a moment he thought she might embrace him: her arms lifted as if to do so, then instead she stooped and hugged Henry, squeezed his neck until the old hound whined. "Is something wrong?" he said, for she had not spoken, nor, in a sense, taken notice of him, not enough, that is, even to mention his sword, and when she said, "We were scared you weren't home," all the rough spirit seemed to have drained from her voice. Joel felt stronger than she, and sure of himself as he'd never been with that other Idabel, the tomboy. He squatted down beside her there in the shade of the house where tulip stalks leaned around, and elephant leaves, streaked with silver snail tracks, hung above their heads like parasols. She was pale beneath her freckles, and a ridge of fingernail-scratch stood out across her cheek. "How'd you get that?" he said.

Her lips whitened, she spit the answer: "Florabel. That damned bastard."

"A girl can't be a bastard," he said.

"Oh, she's a bastard all right. But I didn't mean her." Idabel pulled the hound onto her lap; sleepily submissive, he lay there allowing her to pick fleas off his belly. "I meant that old bastard daddy of mine. We had us a knock-down drag-out fight, him and me and Florabel. On account of he tried to shoot Henry here; Florabel put him up to it . . . says Henry's got a mortal disease, which is a low-down lie from start to finish. I figure I broke her nose and some teeth, too; leastwise, she was bleeding like a pig when me and Henry took off. We been walking around in the dark all night." Suddenly she laughed in her woolly familiar way. "And up around sunrise, know who we saw? Zoo Fever. She couldn't hardly breathe, she was carrying so much junk: golly, we were right sorry to hear about Jesus. It's funny for that old man to die and nobody hear a word. But like I told you, who knows what goes on at the Landing?"

Joel thought: who knows what goes on anywhere? Except Mr Sansom. He knew everything; in some trick way his eyes traveled the whole world over: they this very instant were watching him, of that he had no doubt. And it was probable, too, that, if he had a mind, he could reveal to Randolph Pepe Alvarez's whereabouts.

"Don't you fret none, Henry," said Idabel, popping a flea. "They'll never lay a hand on you."

"But what are you going to do?" Joel asked. "You've got to go home sometime."

She rubbed her nose, and considered him with eyes exaggeratedly wide and appealing: if it had been anyone but Idabel, Joel would've thought she was making up to him. "Maybe," she said, "and maybe not; that's what I came to see you for." Abruptly businesslike, she shoved the dog off her lap, and took a hearty comrade-grip on Joel's shoulders: "How would you like to run away?" But before he could say what he'd like she hurried on: "We could go to town tonight when it's dark. The travelin-show's in town, and there'll be a big crowd. I do want to see the travelin-show one more time; they've got a ferris wheel this year somebody said, and . . ."

"But where would we go?" he said.

Idabel's mouth opened, closed. Apparently she hadn't given this much thought, and with the wide world to choose from, all she could find to say was: "Outside; we'll just walk around outside till we come on a nice place."

"We could go to California and pick grapes," he suggested. "Out West you don't have to be but twelve years old to get married."

"I don't want to get married," said Idabel, coloring. "Who the hell said I wanted to get married? Now you listen, boy: you behave decent, you behave like we're brothers, or don't you behave at all. Anyway, we don't want to do no sissy thing like pick grapes. I thought maybe we could join the navy; else we could teach Henry tricks and get in the circus: say, couldn't you learn magic tricks?"

Which reminded him: he'd never gone after the charm Little Sunshine had promised; certainly, if he were running off with Idabel, they would need this magic, and so he asked if she knew the way to the Cloud Hotel. "Kind of," she said, "down through the woods and the sweetgum hollow and then across the creek where the mill is . . . oh, it's a long way. Why'd we want to go anyhow?" But of course he could not say, for Little Sunshine had warned him never to mention the charm. "I've got important business with the man there," he said, and then, wanting a little to frighten her: "Otherwise something terrible will happen to us."

They both jumped. "Don't hide, I know you're out there, I heard you." It was Amy, and she was calling from a window directly above: she could not see them, though, for the elephant leaves were a camouflage. "The idea, leaving Mr Sansom in this fix, are you completely out of your mind?" They crawled from under the leaves, crept along the side of the house, then raced for the road, the woods. "I know you're there, Joel Knox, come up this instant, sir!"

Deep in the hollow, dark syrup crusted the bark of vine-roped sweetgums; like pale apple leaves green witch butterflies sank and rose there and there; a breezy lane of trumpet lilies (Saints and Heroes, these alone, or so old folks said, could hear their mythical flourish) beckoned like hands lace-gloved and ghostly. Idabel kept waving her arms, for the mosquitoes were fierce: everywhere, like scraps of a huge shattered mirror, mosquito pools of marsh water gleamed and broke in Henry's jogging path.

"I've got some money," said Idabel. "Fact is, I've got near about four bits." Joel thought of the change he'd stored away in the box, and bragged that he had more than that. "We'll spend it all at the travelin-show," she said, and took a froggish jump over a crocodile-looking log. "Who needs money anyhow? Least-wise, not right aways we don't . . . except for dopes. We ought to save enough so as we can have a dope every day cause my brains get fried if I can't have myself an ice-cold dope. And cigarettes. I surely do appreciate a smoke. Dopes and smokes and Henry are the onliest things I love."

"You like me some, don't you?" he said, without meaning really to speak aloud. In any case, Idabel, chanting ". . . the big baboon by the light of the moon was combing his auburn hair . . ." did not answer.

They stopped to scrape off chews of sweetgum, and while they stood there she said: "My daddy'll be out rooting up the country for me; I bet he'll go down and ask Mr Bluey for the loan of his old bloodhound." She laughed and sweetgum juice trickled out the corners of her mouth; a green butterfly lighted on her head, held like a ribbon to a lock of her hair. "One time they were hunting for an escaped convict (right here in this very hollow), Mr Bluey and his hound and Sam Radclif and Roberta Lacey and the Sheriff and all those dogs from the farm; when it got dark we could see their lamps shining way off here in the woods, and hear the dogs howling; it was like a holiday: daddy and all the men and Roberta Lacey got hollering drunk, you could hear old Roberta's hee-haw clear to Noon City and back . . . and you know, I was real sorry for that convict, and afraid for him: I kept thinking I was him and he was me and it was both of us they were out to catch." She spit the gum like tobacco, and hooked her thumbs in the belt rungs of her khaki shorts. "But he got away. They never did find him. Some folks hold that he's still about . . . hiding in the Cloud Hotel, maybe, or living at the Landing."

"There *is* someone living at the Landing," Joel said excitedly, and then, with some disappointment, added: "Except it's not a convict, it's a lady."

"A lady? You mean Miss Amy?"

"Another lady," he told her, and regretted mentioning the matter. "She has a tall white wig, and wears a lovely old-time dress, but I don't know who she is or even if she is real." But Idabel just looked at him as if he were a fool, so he smiled uneasily and said: "I'm only joking, I only wanted to scare you." And, not wanting to answer questions, he ran a little ahead, the sword spanking his thigh. It seemed to him they had come a far way, and he played with the notion that they were lost: probably there was no such place as this hotel whose name evoked a kind of mist-white palace floating foglike through the woods. Then, facing a fence of brambles, he unsheathed his sword and cut an opening. "After you, my dear Idabel," he said, bowing low, and Idabel, whistling for Henry, stepped through. Off a short distance on the other side lay a roughly pebbled beach along which the creek, here rather more of a river, ran sluggishly. A yellowed cane-break obscured at first the sight of a broken dam, and, below this, a queer house straddling the water on high stilts: it was made of unpainted plank gone grey now, and had a strange unfinished look, as though its builder had been frightened and fled his job midway. Three sunning buzzards sat hunched on what remained of the roof, butterflies went in and out of blue sky-bright windows. Joel was sorely let-down, for he thought this alas was the Cloud Hotel, but then Idabel said no, it was an old forsaken mill, a place where, years since, farmers had brought corn to be ground. "There used to be a road, one that went to the Cloud Hotel; nothing but woods now, not even a path to show the way." She seized a rock, and threw it up at the buzzards; they glided off the roof, glided over the beach, their shadows making there lazy interlocking circles.

The water, deeper here than where he and Idabel had taken their bath, was also darker, a muddy bottomless olive, and when he knew they did not have to swim over, his relief gave him courage enough to travel down under the mill where there was a heavy but rotting beam on which they might cross.

"I'd better go first," said Idabel. "It's pretty old and liable to bust."

But Joel pushed in front of her and started over; after all, no matter what Idabel said, he was a boy and she was a girl and he was damned if she were going to get the upper hand again. "You and Henry come after me," he called, his voice hollow in the sudden cellar-like dark. Luminous water-shadows snaked up the cracked and eaten columns supporting the mill-house; copper waterbugs swung on intricate trapezes of insect's thread, and fungus flowered fist-size on the wet decrepit wood. Joel, stepping gingerly, using his sword to balance, made his eyes avoid the dizzy deep creek moving so closely below, kept them, instead, aimed on the opposite bank where, in sunshine, laden gourdvine burst from red clay green and promising. Still all at once he felt he would never reach the other side: always he would be balanced here suspended between land, and in the dark, and alone. Then, feeling the board shake as Idabel started across, he remembered he had someone to be together with. Only. And his heart turned over, skipped: every part of him went like iron.

Idabel shouted: "What's wrong? What're you stopping for?"

But he could not tell her. Nor bring himself to make any sound, motion. For piled no more than a foot beyond was a cotton-mouth thick as his leg, long as a whip; its arrow-shaped head slid out, the seed-like eyes alertly pointed, and all over Joel began to sting, as though already bitten. Idabel, coming up behind him, looked over his shoulder. "Jesus," she breathed, "oh Jesus," and at the touch of her hand he broke up inside: the creek froze, was like a horizontal cage, and his feet seemed to sink, as though the beam on which they stood was made of quicksand. How did Mr Sansom's eyes come to be in a moccasin's head?

"Hit him," Idabel demanded. "Hit him with your sword."

It was this way: they were bound for the Cloud Hotel, yes, the Cloud Hotel, where a man with a ruby ring was swimming

underwater, yes, and Randolph was looking through his almanac and writing letters to Hongkong, to Port-o'-Spain, yes, and
poor Jesus was dead, killed by Toby the cat (no, Toby was a
baby), by a nest of chimney sweeps falling in a fire. And Zoo:
was she in Washington yet? And was it snowing? And why was
Mr Sansom staring at him so hard? It was really very, very rude
(as Ellen would say), really very rude indeed of Mr Sansom
never to close his eyes.

The snake, unwinding with involved grace, stretched toward
them in a rolling way, and Idabel screamed, "Hit him, hit him!"
but Joel of course was concerned only with Mr Sansom's stare.

Spinning him around, and pushing him safely behind her,
she pulled the sword out of his hand. "Big granddaddy bastard,"
she jeered, thrusting at the snake. For an instant it seemed paralyzed; then, invisibly swift, and its whole length like a wire sing-
ingly tense, it hooked back, snapped forward. "Bastard," she
hollered, closing her eyes, swinging the blade like a sickle, and
the cotton-mouth, slapped into the air, turned, plunged, flattened on the water: belly up, white and twisted, it was carried by
the current like a torn lily root. "No," said Joel when, some
while later, Idabel, calm in her triumph, tried to coax him on
across. "No," he said, for what use could there be now in finding
Little Sunshine? His danger had already been, and he did not
need a charm.

ELEVEN

During supper Amy announced: "It is my birthday. Yes," she said, "it is indeed, and not a soul to remember. Now if Angela Lee were here, I should've had an immense cake with a prize in every slice: tiny gold rings, and a pearl for my add-a-pearl, and little silver shoe-buckles: oh when I think!"

"Happy birthday," said Joel, though what he wished her was hardly happiness, for when he'd come home she'd rushed down the hall with every intention, or so she'd said, of breaking an umbrella over his head; whereupon Randolph, throwing open his door, had warned her, and very sincerely, that if ever she touched him he'd wring her damned neck.

Randolph went right on chewing a pig's knuckle, and Amy, ignoring Joel, glared at him, her eyebrows going up and up, her lips pursed and trembling. "Eat, go on and eat, get fat as a hog," she said, and slammed down her gloved hand: hitting the table it knocked like wood, and the old alarm clock, touched off by this commotion, began to ring: all three sat motionless until it whined itself silent. Then, the lines of her face becoming prominent as veins, Amy, with a preposterously maudlin sob, broke into tears and hiccups. "You silly toad," she panted, "who else has ever helped you? Angela Lee would sooner have seen you hanged! But no, I've given up my life." Spouting intermittent pardon-me's, she hiccuped in succession a dozen times. "I tell you this, Randolph, I would sooner go off and clean house for a bunch of tacky niggers than stay here another instant; don't think I couldn't earn my way, the mothers of any town in America would send their children to me and we would play organized games, blind man's bluff and musical chairs and pin the tail, and I would charge each child ten cents: I could make a good living. No, I need not depend on you; in fact, if I had a particle of sense I'd sit down and write a letter to the Law."

Randolph crossed his knife and fork, and patted his lips with his kimono sleeve. "I'm sorry, my dear," he said, "but I'm afraid I haven't been following: exactly where is it you fancy me at fault?"

His cousin shook her head, took a deep, nervous breath; the tears stopped coming, the hiccups ceased, and all at once she turned on a shy smile. "It's my birthday," she said, her voice reduced to a waver.

"How very odd. Joel, does it seem to you peculiarly warm for January?"

Joel was listening for sounds above their voices: three short whistles and a hoot-owl wail, Idabel's signal. In his impatience it was as if the clock, having unwound, had stopped time altogether.

"January, yes; and you, my dear, were born (if one believes a family Bible, though I'll admit one never should, so many weddings being listed an erroneous nine months early) one January New Year's."

Amy's neck dipped turtlewise into shoulders timidly contracting, and her hiccups racked up again, but less indignant

now, more mournful. "But Randolph . . . Randolph I *feel* as
though it was my birthday."

"A little wine, then," he said, "and a song on the pianola; look
in the cupboard, too, I'm certain you'll find a box of stale animal
crackers with little silver worms in every crumb." Carrying
lamps, they moved into the parlor, and Joel, sent upstairs to
fetch the wine, crossed Randolph's room quickly, and raised the
window. Below, bonfires of newly bloomed roses burned like
flower-eyes in the August twilight, their sweetness filling the air
like a color. He whistled, whispered, "Idabel, Idabel," and with
Henry she appeared between the leaning columns. "Joel," she
said, unsure, and behind her it was as though the falling night
slipped a glove over the five stone fingers which, curling in
shadow, seemed bendingly to reach her; when he answered, she
hurried beyond their grasp, came safely under the window. "Are
you ready?" She'd plaited a collar of white roses for Henry, and
there was a rose hung awkwardly in her hair. Idabel, he thought,
you look real beautiful. "Go to the mailbox," he said, "I'll meet
you there." It was too dark now to maneuver without light. He
lit a candle on Randolph's desk, and went to the cabinet, searching there until he located an unopened bottle of sherry. Stooping to extinguish the candle, he noticed a sheet of green
tissue-thin stationery, and on it, in a handwriting daintily familiar, was written only a salutation: "My dearest Pepe." Randolph,
then, had composed the letters to Ellen, but how could he have
supposed that Mr Sansom could ever have written a word? In
the black hall, lamplight rimmed Mr Sansom's door, which, as
he waited, a cross-draft commenced to swing open, and it was as
though he were seeing his father's room through reversed bin-
oculars, for, in its yellow clarity, it was like a miniature: the hand

with the wedding ring slouched over the bed's side; scenes of Venice, projected by the frost-glass globe, tinted the walls, the crocheted spread, and there in the mirror whirled his eyes, his smile. Joel entered on tiptoe and went on his knees beside the bed. Downstairs the pianola had begun pounding its raggedy carnival tune, yet somehow it did not interfere with the stillness and secrecy of this moment. Tenderly he took Mr Sansom's hand and put it against his cheek and held it there until there was warmth between them; he kissed the dry fingers, and the wedding ring whose gold had been meant to encircle them both. "I'm leaving, Father," he said, and it was, in a sense, the first time he'd acknowledged their blood; slowly he rose up and pressed his palms on either side of Mr Sansom's face and brought their lips together: "My only father," he whispered, turning, and, descending the stairs, he said it again, but this time all to himself.

He set the bottle of sherry on the hall-tree in the chamber, and, hidden by a curtain, peered into the parlor; neither Amy nor Randolph had heard him come down the stairs: she was sitting on the pianola stool, studiously working an ivory fan, tiresomely tapping her foot, and Randolph, bored to limpness, was staring at the archway where Joel was scheduled presently to present himself. He was gone now, and running toward the mailbox, Idabel, outside. The road was like a river to float upon, and it was as if a roman-candle, ignited by the sudden breath of freedom, had zoomed him away in a wake of star-sparks. "Run!" he cried, reaching Idabel, for to stop before the Landing stood forever out of sight was an idea unendurable, and she was racing before him, her hair pulling back in windy stiffness: as the road humped into a hill it was as though she mounted the sky on a moon-leaning ladder; beyond the hill they came to a standstill, panting, tossing their heads. "Was they chasing us?" asked Idabel, petals from her hair-rose shedding in the air, and he said: "Nobody will catch us now never." Staying to the road, even when they passed close by her house, they walked with Henry between them: roses, strewn from the wreath about the dog's neck, soaked the colors of a stony moon, and Idabel said she was hungry enough to eat a rose, "or grass and toadstools." Well, he said, well, when they reached town he'd splurge and treat her to a barbecue at R. V. Lacey's Princely Place. And they talked of the night he'd first come along this road and heard her in the distance singing with her sister. His eyes nailed down with stars, an old wagon had carried him over a ledge of sleep, a wintry slumber dispelled in the exhilaration of recent waking: meantime, there had taken place a dream, from whose design, unraveling now swifter than memory could reweave it, only Idabel remained, all else and others having dimmed-out as shadows do in dark. "I remember," she said, "and I thought you was a mess just like Florabel; to be honest to God, I never did much change-mind till today." Seeming then ashamed, she scampered down the road-bank, and scooped up drinks of water from a thread of creek which trickled there; abruptly she straightened, and, with a finger to her lips, motioned for Joel to join her. "Hear it?" she whispered. Behind the foliage, a bull-toned voice, and another, this like a guitar, blended as raindrops caress to sound a same rhythm; an intricate wind of rustling murmurs, small laughter followed sighs not sad and silences deeper than space. Moss cushioned their footsteps as they moved through the leafy thickness, and came to pause at the edge of an opening: two Negroes, caught in a filmy skein of moon and fern, lay unclothed and enfolded, the man's caramel-colored body braceleted with his darker lover's arms, legs, his lips nuzzling her nipples: oo-we, oo-we, sweet Simon, she sighed, love shivering her voice, love rolling through her like thunder; easy, Simon, sweet Simon, easy honey, she crooned, and tensed then, her arms lifting as if to embrace the moon; her lover sank across her, and there together, limbs akimbo, they made on the bloom of moss a black fallen star. Idabel retreated with splashful, rowdy haste, and Joel, trying to keep up, went shh! shh!, thinking how wrong to frighten the lovers, and wishing, too, that she'd waited longer, for watching them it had been as if his heart were beating all over his body, and all undefined whisperings had gathered into one yearning roar: he knew now, and it was not a giggle or a sudden white-hot word; only two people with each other in withness, and it was as though a tide had receded leaving him dry on a beach white as bone, and it was good at last to have come from so grey so cold a sea. He wanted to walk with Idabel's hand in his, but she had them doubled like knots, and when he spoke to her she looked at him mean and angry and scared; it was as if their positions of the afternoon had somehow reversed: she'd been the hero under the mill, but now he had no weapon with which to defend her, and even if this were not true he wouldn't have known what it was she wanted killed.

A whirl of ferris-wheel lights revolved in the distance; rockets rose, burst, fell over Noon City like showering rainbows; gawky kids and their elders, all beautiful in their Sunday summer finest, traipsed back and forth with reflections of the carnival starring their eyes; a young Negro watched sadly from the isolation of the jail, and a rhinestoned colored girl, red-silk stockings flashing on her legs, swished by shouting lewdly up at him. On the porch of the cracked ancient house old people recalled traveling-shows in other years, and little boys, going behind hedges to pee, lingered to laugh and pinch each other. Ice-cream cones slipped from grimy fingers, crackerjack spilt and so did tears, but nobody was unhappy, nobody thought of chores beyond the moment.

Hiya, Idabel—Watcha say, Idabel? but not a soul spoke to him, he was no part of them, they did not know him; only R. V. Lacey remembered. "Look, babylove!" she said, when they appeared in the door of her Princely Place, and those assembled there, beribboned sassy-faced town-tarts and rednecked farmboys with cow-dumb eyes, paused in their jukebox shuffling; one girl advanced to tickle him under the chin. "Where'd you find this, Idabel? He's cute."

"Mind your own business, punk," Idabel said, seating herself at the counter.

Miss Roberta Lacey wagged her finger. "Idabel Thompkins, I warned you time and again, none of that gangster talk in my establishment. Furthermore, I have many times put into words the fact you are not to set foot inside my place, acting as you do like Baby Face Floyd, and dressing as you do in no proper way befitting a young lady: now skidaddle, and take that filthy hound with you."

"Please, Miss Roberta," said Joel, "Idabel's awful hungry."

"Then she oughta be home learning to fix a man his vittels (laughter); besides which this here's a grown-folks café (applause). Romeo, remind me to put up a sign to that effect. Whatismore, Idabel, your daddy has been round here inquirin as to your whereabouts, and it is my serious opinion he means to burn up that saucy little butt of yours (laughter)."

Idabel leveled a slant-eyed look at the proprietress, then, as though this seemed to her the most expressive retort, she spit on the floor, shoved her hands in her pockets and swaggered out. Joel started to follow, but R. V. Lacey clamped a hand on his shoulder. "Babylove," she said, toying with the long black hair extending from her chin-wart, "Angelboy, you're keeping kinda peculiar company. Idabel's daddy said she's done broke her pretty sweet little sister's nose, and knocked out most her teeth." Grinning, scratching under her armpits like a baboon, she added, "Now don't go saying Roberta's a hard woman; she's soft on you," and handed him a bag of salted peanuts. "No charge."

Idabel told him what he could do with those old Roberta goobers, but she relented, to be sure, and devoured the sack solo. She let him take her arm, and they descended on the gala beehive acre where the traveling-show buzzed. The merry-go-round, a sorry battered toy, turned to a jingling sound of bells, and colored folks, who were not allowed to ride, stood clustered at a distance getting more fun from its magical whirl than those astride saddles. Idabel shelled out 35¢ at the dart-throw game, all in order to win a pair of dark glasses like the ones Joel had broken, and what a ruckus she raised when the straw-hat man tried to palm off a walking cane! You bet she got those specs, but, being too large for her, they kept sliding down her nose. At the 10¢ Tent they saw a four-legged chicken (stuffed), and the two-headed baby floating in a glass tank like a green octopus: Idabel studied it a long while, and when she turned away her eyes were moist: "Poor little baby," she said, "poor little thing." The Duck Boy cheered her up; he sure was a comedy all right, quack-quack-quacking, making dopey faces and flapping his hands, the fingers of which were webbed together; at one point he opened his shirt to reveal a white feathery chest. Joel preferred Miss Wisteria, a darling little girl, he thought, and so did Idabel; they did not quite believe she was a midget, though Miss Wisteria herself claimed to be twenty-five years old, and just back from a grand tour of Europe where she'd appeared before all the crowned heads: her own sweet little gold head sported a twinkling crown; she wore elegant silver slippers (it was a marvel the way she could walk on her toes); her dress was a drape of purple silk tied about the middle with a yellow silk sash. She hopped and skipped and giggled and sang a song and said a poem, and when she came off the platform, Idabel, more excited than Joel had ever seen her, rushed up and asked, please, wouldn't she have some sodapop with them. "Charmed," said Miss Wisteria, twisting her gold sausage curls, "charmed." Idabel humbled herself; she bought cokes, found them a place to sit, and made Henry keep his distance, for Miss Wisteria confessed to a fear of animals. "Frankly," she lisped, "I do not think God intended them." Except for rouged kewpie-doll lips, her baby-plump face was pale, enameled; her hands flitted about so that they seemed to have a separate life of their own, and she glanced at them now and again as if they deeply puzzled her; they were smaller than a child's these hands, but thin, mature, and the fingernails were painted. "Well, this is surely a treat," she said. "Now lots of show-people are just plain put-ons, but I don't hold with any put-on, I like to bring my art to the people . . . lots of whom don't see how come I jog around with an outfit like this . . . look, they say to me, there you were out in Hollywood pulling down a thousand dollars a week as Shirley Temple's stand-in . . . but I say to them: the road to happiness isn't always a highway." Draining her coke, she took out a lipstick and reshaped her kewpie-bow; then a queer thing happened: Idabel, borrowing the lipstick, painted an awkward clownish line across her mouth, and Miss Wisteria, clapping her little hands, shrieked with a kind of sassy pleasure. Idabel met this merriment with a dumb adoring smile. Joel could not understand what had taken her. Unless it was that the midget had cast a spell. But as she continued to fawn over tiny yellow-haired Miss Wisteria it came to him that Idabel was in love. No, she would not consider leaving, there was a world of time. "Charmed," said Miss Wisteria to a suggestion they ride the ferris-wheel, "charmed."

A rash of lightning rattled the stars; Miss Wisteria's royal headgear caught fire in this brief tinseled burst, the glass jewels glittering roselike in the pink lights of the ferris-wheel, and Joel, left below, could see her white winglike hands alight on Idabel's hair, flutter away, squeeze the dark as if eating its very substance. They swung low, their laughter rippling like Miss Wisteria's long sash, and, rising toward a new flush of lightning, dissolved; still he could hear the midget's pennyflute voice purring persistent as a mosquito above every fairground noise: Idabel, come back, he thought, thinking he would never see her again, that she would travel on into the sky with Miss Wisteria at her side, Idabel, come back, I love you. So then she was there, telling him, "You can see way off, you can almost touch the sky," so then he was aboard the ferris-wheel, alone with Miss Wisteria, and together they watched Idabel diminish as the rocking rickety car started to climb.

Wind swung them like a lantern; it is wind, Joel thought, for he could see the pennants trembling above the tents, trash-paper scurrying animal-like along the ground, and over there, on the walls of the old house where a Yankee bandit had murdered three women, raggedy posters danced a skeleton jig. The car in front contained a sunbonneted mother and her little girl, who nursed a corncob doll; they waved to a farmer waiting below. "Y'all better get offen that thing," he called back, "hitsa fixin to rain." Around they went, wind rustling Miss Wisteria's purple silk. "Run away, is it?" she said, a smile displaying rabbity teeth. "Well, I said to her, and I say to you: the world is a frightening place." She gestured her arms in an arc, and in that moment she seemed to him Outside, to be, that is, geography, earth and sea and all the cities in Randolph's almanac: her queer little hands, twittering midair, encompassed the globe. "And oh a lonesome place. Once I ran away. I had four sisters (Maudy went to Atlantic City as Miss Maryland, she's that beautiful), tall lovely girls, and my mother, bless her soul, stood nearly six feet in her stockings. We lived in a big house in Baltimore, the nicest on our street, and I never went to school; I was so little I could sit in my mother's sewing basket, and she used to joke that I could crawl through the eye of her needle; there was a beau of Maudy's who could balance me in the palm of his hand, and when I was seventeen I still had to sit in a highchair to eat my supper. They said I need not play alone, there are other little people, they said, go out and find them, they live in flowers. Many's the petal I've peeled but lilac is lilac and no one lives in any rose I ever saw; a spot of grease is all a wishbone leaves, and there is only candy in a Christmas stocking. Then I was twenty, and Mama said it wasn't right I shouldn't have a beau, and she sat right down and wrote a letter to the Sweethearts Matrimonial Agency in Newark, New Jersey. And do you know a man came to marry me: he was much too big, though, and much too ugly, and he was seventy-seven years old; well, even so, I might have married him except when he saw how little I was he said bye-bye and took the train back to from whence he'd come. I never have found a sweet little person. There are children; but I cry sometimes to think little boys must grow tall." Her voice, while making this memoir, had stiffened solemnly, and her hands folded themselves quietly in her lap. Idabel waved, shouted, but wind carried her words another way, and sadly Miss Wisteria said: "Poor child, is it that she believes she is a freak, too?" She placed her hand on his thigh, and then, as though she had no control over them whatsoever, her fingers crept up inside his legs: she stared at the hand with shocked intensity but seemed unable to remove it, and Joel, disturbed but knowing now he wanted never to hurt anyone, not Miss Wisteria, nor Idabel, nor the little girl with the corncob doll, wished so much he could say: it doesn't matter, I love you, I love your hand. The world was a frightening place, yes, he knew: unlasting, what could be forever? or only what it seemed? rock corrodes, rivers freeze, fruit rots; stabbed, blood of black and white bleeds alike; trained parrots tell more truth than most, and who is lonelier: the hawk or the worm? every flowering heart shrivels dry and pitted as the herb from which it bloomed, and while the old man grows spinsterish, his wife assumes a mustache; moment to moment, changing, changing, like the cars on the ferris-wheel. Grass and love are always greener; but remember Little Three Eyes? show her love and apples ripen gold, love vanquishes the Snow Queen, its presence finds the name, be it Rumpelstiltskin or merely Joel Knox: that is constant.

A wall of rain pushed toward them from the distance; you could hear it long before it came, humming like a horde of locusts. The operator of the ferris-wheel began letting off his passengers. "Oh, we'll be last," wailed Miss Wisteria, for they were suspended near the top. The rain-wall leaned over them, and she threw up her hands as if to hold it back. Idabel, everyone, fled as down it toppled like a tidal wave.

Presently only a hatless man stood there in the emptiness below. Joel, his eyes searching so frenziedly for Idabel, did not at first altogether see him. But the carnival lights short-circuited with a crackling flare, and when this happened it was suddenly as though the man turned phosphorescent: he seemed to Joel no more than a hand's space away. "Randolph," he whispered, and the name gripped him at the root of his throat. It was a momentary vision, for the lights all fizzled out, and as the ferris-wheel descended to a last stop, he could not see Randolph anywhere.

"Wait," demanded Miss Wisteria, assembling her drenched costume, "wait for me." But Joel leaped past her, and hurried from one shelter to the next; Idabel was not in the 10¢ Tent: no one was there but the Duck Boy, who was playing solitaire by candlelight. Nor was she in the group huddled on the merry-go-round. He went to the livery stable. He went to the Baptist church. And soon, there being scarcely another possibility, he found himself on the porch of the old house. Leaves, gathering in a coil, spiralled hissingly across its deserted expanse; empty rocking chairs tilted gently back and forth; a Prince Albert poster swept like a bird through the air and struck him in the face: he fought to free himself, but it was as though it were alive, and, struggling with it, it suddenly frightened him more than had the sight of Randolph: he would never rid himself of either. But then, what was there in Randolph to fear? The fact that he'd found him proved he was only a messenger for a pair of telescopic eyes. Randolph would never bring him harm (still, but, and yet). He let down his arms: it was curious, for so soon as he did this, Prince Albert, of his own accord, flew off howling in the hoarse rain. And could he, with equal ease, appease that other fury, the nameless one whose envoy appeared in Randolph's guise? Vine from the Landing's garden had stretched these miles to entwine his wrists, and he saw their plans, his and Idabel's, break apart like the thunder-split sky: not yet, not if he could find her, and he ran into the house: "Idabel, you are here, you are!"

A boom of silence answered him; here, there, a marginal sound: rain like wings in the chimney, mice feet on fallen glass, maidenly steps of her who always walks the stair, and wind, opening doors, closing them, wind conversing sadly on the ceiling, blowing its damp sour breath in his face, breathing out its lungs through the rooms: he let himself be carried in its course: his head was light as a balloon, and as hollow-feeling; ice as eyes, thorns as teeth, flannel as tongue; he'd seen sunrise that morning, but, each step directing him nearing a precipice permanent in shadowed intent (or so it seemed), it was not likely he would see another: sleep was like smoke, he inhaled it deeply, but it went back on the air in rings of color, spots, sparks, whose fire restrained him from falling in a bundle on the floor: warnings, they were, these starry flies, stay awake, Joel, in eskimoland sleep is death, is all, remember? She was cold, his mother, she passed to sleep with dew of snowflakes scenting her hair; if he could have but thawed open her eyes here now she would be to hold him and say, as he'd said to Randolph, "Everything is going to be all right"; no, she'd splintered like frozen crystal, and Ellen, gathering the pieces, had put them in a box surrounded by gladiolas fifty cents the dozen.

Somewhere he owned a room, he had a bed: their promise quivered before him like heat waves. Oh Idabel, why have you done this terrible thing!

There were footsteps on the porch; he could hear the squish-sqush of soggy shoes; abruptly a flashlight beam poked through a parlor window, and for an instant settled on a flecked decaying mantel-mirror: shining there, the mirror was like a slab of jelly, and the figure from outside fumed indistinctly on its surface: no one could've said who it was, but Joel, seeing the light slide away, hearing the steps enter the hall, knew for certain it was

Randolph. And there came over him the humiliating probability that not once since he'd left the Landing had he made a movement unobserved: how amusing his goodbye must've seemed to Mr Sansom!

He crouched behind a door; through the hinged slit he could see into the hall where the light crawled like a burning centipede. It did not matter now if Randolph found him, he would welcome it. Still something kept him from calling out. The squshing steps moved toward the parlor threshold, and he heard, "Little boy, little boy," a whimper of despair.

Miss Wisteria stood so near he could smell the rancid wetness of her shriveled silk; her curls had uncoiled, the little crown had slipped awry, her yellow sash was fading its color on the floor. "Little boy," she said, swerving her flashlight over the bent, broken walls where her midget image mingled with the shadows of things in flight. "Little boy," she said, the resignation of her voice intensifying its pathos. But he dared not show himself, for what she wanted he could not give: his love was in the earth, shattered and still, dried flowers where eyes should be, and moss upon the lips, his love was faraway feeding on the rain, lilies frothing from its ruin. Withdrawing, she went up the stairs, and Joel, who listened to her footfalls overhead as she in her need of him searched the jungle of rooms, felt for himself ferocious contempt: what was his terror compared with Miss Wisteria's? He owned a room, he had a bed, any minute now he would run from here, go to them. But for Miss Wisteria, weeping because little boys must grow tall, there would always be this journey through dying rooms until some lonely day she found her hidden one, the smiler with the knife.

PART THREE

TWELVE

He sentenced himself: he was guilty: his own hands set about to expedite the verdict: magnetized, they found a bullet, the one thefted from Sam Radclif (Mr Radclif, forgive me, please, I never meant to steal) and, inserting it in Major Knox's old Indian pistol (Child, how many times have I told you not to touch that nasty thing?—Mama, don't scold me now, mama, my bones hurt, I'm on fire—The good die cold, the wicked in flames: the winds of hell are blue with the sweet ether of fever-flowers, horned snake-tongued children dance on lawns that are the surface of the sun, all loot from thievery tied to their tails like cat-cans, tokens of a life in crime) and put the bullet through his head: oh dear, there was nothing but a tickling, oh dear, now what? When lo! he was where he'd never imagined to find himself again: the secret hideaway room in which, on hot New Orleans afternoons, he'd sat watching snow sift through scorched August trees: the run of reindeer hooves came crisply tinkling down the street, and Mr Mystery, elegantly villainous in his black cape, appeared in their wake riding a most beautiful boat-like sleigh: it was made of scented wood, a carved red swan graced the front, and silver bells were strung like beads to make a sail: swinging, billowing-out, what shivering melodies it sang as the sleigh, with Joel aboard and warm in the folds of Mr Mystery's cape, cut over snowdeep fields and down unlikely hills.

But all at once his powers to direct adventures in the secret room failed: an ice-wall rose before them, the sleigh raced on to certain doom, that night radios would sadden the nation: Mr Mystery, esteemed magician, and Joel Harrison Knox, beloved by one and all, were killed today in an accident which also claimed the lives of six reindeer who ... r-r-rip, the ice tore like cellophane, the sleigh slid through into the Landing's parlor.

A strange sort of party seemed in progress there. These were among those present: Mr Sansom, Ellen Kendall, Miss Wisteria, Randolph, Idabel, Florabel, Zoo, Little Sunshine, Amy, R. V. Lacey, Sam Radclif, Jesus Fever, a man naked except for boxing-gloves (Pepe Alvarez), Sydney Katz (proprietor of the Morning Star Café in Paradise Chapel), a thick-lipped convict who wore a long razor on a chain around his neck like some sinister crucifix (Keg Brown), Romeo, Sammy Silverstein and three other members of the St. Deval Street Secret Nine. Most were dressed in black, rather formal attire; the pianola was playing Nearer My God to Thee. Not noticing the sleigh, they moved in a leaning black procession around a gladiola-garlanded cedar chest into which each dropped an offering: Idabel her dark glasses, Randolph his almanac, R. V. Lacey the snipped hair from her wart, Jesus Fever his fiddle, Florabel her Kress tweezers, Mr Sansom his tennis balls, Little Sunshine a magic charm, and so on: inside the chest lay Joel himself, all dressed in white, his face powdered and rouged, his goldbrown hair arranged in damp ringlets: Like an angel, they said, more beautiful than Alcibiades, more beautiful, said Randolph, and Idabel wailed: Believe me, I tried to save him, but he wouldn't move, and snakes are so very quick. Miss Wisteria, fitting her little crown upon his head, leaned so far over she nearly fell into the chest: Listen, she whispered, I'm no fool, I know you're alive: unless you give me the answer, I shan't save you, I shan't say a word: are the dead as lonesome as the living? Whereupon the room commenced to vibrate slightly, then more so, chairs overturned, the curio cabinet spilled its contents, a mirror cracked, the pianola, composing its own doomed jazz, held a haywire jamboree: down went the house, down into the earth, down, down, past Indian tombs, past the deepest root, the coldest stream, down, down, into the furry arms of horned children whose bumblebee eyes withstand forests of flame.

He knew too well the rhythm of a rocking-chair; aramp-arump, hour on hour he'd heard one for how long? traveling through space, and the cedar chest became at last confused with its sway: if you fall you fall forever, back and forth together, the ceaseless chair, the cedar chest: he squeezed pillows, gripped the posters of the bed, for on seas of lamplight it rode the rolling rocker's waves whose rocking was the tolling of a bell-buoy; and who was the pirate inching toward him in the seat? His eyes stung as he tasked them to identify: lace masks confounded, frost glass intervened, now the chair's passenger was Amy, now Randolph, then Zoo. But Zoo could not be here; she was walking for Washington, her accordion announcing every step of the way. An unrecognized voice quarreled with him, teased, taunted, revealed secrets he'd scarcely made known to himself: shut up, he cried, and wept, trying to silence it, but, of course, the voice belonged to him: "I saw you under the ferris-wheel," it accused the pirate in the chair; "No," said the pirate, "I never left here, sweet child, sweet Joel, all night I waited for you sitting on the stairs."

Always he was gnawing bitter spoons, or struggling to breathe through scarves soaked in lemon water. Hands coaxed down curtains of slumbering dusk; fingers leanly firm like Zoo's rambled through his hair, and other fingers, too, these with a touch cooler, more spun than sea spray: Randolph's voice, in tones still gentler, augmented their soothing traceries.

One afternoon the rocking-chair became precisely that; scissors seemed to cut round the edges of his mind, and as he peeled away the dead discardings, Randolph, taking shape, shone blessedly near.

"Randolph," he said, reaching out to him, "do you hate me?" Smiling, Randolph whispered: "Hate you, baby?" "Because I went away," said Joel, "went way away and left your sherry on the hall-tree." Randolph took him in his arms, kissed his forehead, and Joel, pained, grateful, said, "I'm sick and so sick," and Randolph replied, "Lie back, my darling, lie still."

❧❦❧

He drifted deep into September; the blissful depths of the bed seemed future enough, every pore absorbed its cool protection. And when he thought of himself he affixed the thought to a second person, another Joel Knox about whom he was interested in the moderate way one would be in a childhood snapshot: what a dumbbell! he would gladly be rid of him, this old Joel, but not quite yet, he somehow needed him still. For long periods each day he studied his face in a hand mirror: a disappointing exercise, on the whole, for nothing he saw concretely affirmed his suspicions of emerging manhood, though about his face there were certain changes: baby-fat had given way to a true shape, the softness of his eyes had hardened: it was a face with a look of innocence but none of its charm, an alarming face, really, too shrewd for a child, too beautiful for a boy. It would be difficult to say how old he was. All that displeased him was the brown straightness of his hair. He wished it were curly gold like Randolph's.

He did not know when Randolph slept; he seemed to vacate the rocking-chair only when it was time for Joel to eat or commit some function; and sometimes, waking with the moon watching at the window like a bandit's eye, he would see Randolph's asthmatic cigarette still pulsing in the dark: though the house had sunk, he was not alone, another had survived, not a stranger, but one more kind, more good than any had ever been, the friend whose nearness is love. "Randolph," he said, "were you ever as young as me?" And Randolph said: "I was never so old." "Randolph," he said, "do you know something? I'm very happy." To which his friend made no reply. The reason for this happiness seemed to be simply that he did not feel unhappy; rather, he knew all through him a kind of balance. There was so little to cope with. The mist which for him overhung so much of Randolph's conversation, even that had lifted, at least it was no longer troubling, for it seemed as though he understood him absolutely. Now in the process of, as it were, discovering someone, most people experience simultaneously an illusion they are discovering themselves: the other's eyes reflect their real and glorious value. Such a feeling was with Joel, and inestimably so because this was the first time he'd ever known the triumph, false or true, of seeing through to a friend. And he did not want any more to be responsible, he wanted to put himself in the hands of his friend, be, as here in the sickbed, dependent upon him for his very life. Looking in the hand-glass became, consequently, an ordeal: it was as if now only one eye examined for signs of maturity, while the other, gradually of the two the more attentive, gazed inward wishing him always to remain as he was.

"There is an October chill in the air today," said Randolph, settling overblown roses in a vase by the bed. "These are the last, I'm afraid, they are quite falling apart, even the bees have lost interest. And here, I've brought an autumn specimen, a sycamore leaf." Another day, and though the air was mild, he built a fire by which they toasted marshmallows and sipped tea from cups two hundred years old. Randolph did imitations. He was Charlie Chaplin to a T, Mae West too, and his cruel take-off on Amy made Joel double up on the bed, finally absorbed in laughter for its own sake, and Randolph said ha! ha! he would show him something really funny: "I'll have to fix up, though," he said, his eyes quickly alive, and made as if to leave the room; then, releasing the doorknob, he looked back. "But if I do … you mustn't laugh." And Joel's answer was a laugh, he couldn't stop, it was like hiccups. Randolph's smile ran off his face like melted butter, and when Joel cried, "Go on, you promised," he sat down, nursing his round pink head between his hands: "Not now," he said wearily, "some other time."

One morning Joel received the first mail he'd ever had at the Landing; it was a picture postcard, and Randolph, appearing with a copy of *Macbeth*, which they'd planned to read aloud, brought it to him. "It's from the little girl down the road," he said, and Joel's breath caught: long-legged and swaggering, Idabel walked from the wall, rocked in the chair. He'd not directly thought of her since the night of the traveling-show, an omission for which he couldn't account, but which did not strike him as freakish: she was, after all, one with the others covered over when the house sank, those whose names concerned the old Joel, whose names now in gnarled October freckling leaves spelled on the wind. Still Idabel was back, a ghost, perhaps, but here, and in the room: Idabel the hoodlum out to stone a one-armed barber, and Idabel with roses, Idabel with sword, Idabel who said she sometimes cried: all of autumn was the sycamore leaf and its red the red of her hair and its stem the rusty color of her rough voice and its jagged shape the pattern, the souvenir of her face.

The card, which showed joyful cottonpickers, was postmarked from Alabama, and it said: "Mrs Collie ½ sister an hes the baptis prechur Last Sunday I past the plate at church! papa and F shot henry They put me to life here. why did you Hide? write to IDABEL THOMPKINS."

Well, frankly, he didn't believe her; she'd put herself to life, and it was with Miss Wisteria, not a baptis prechur. He handed the card to Randolph who, in turn, passed it to the fire; for an instant, as Idabel and her cottonpickers crinkled, he would have lost his hands to retrieve them, but Randolph, adjusting gold reading glasses, began: "First witch. When shall we three meet again In thunder, lightning, or in rain?" and he settled down to listen, he fell asleep and woke up with a holler, for he'd climbed up the chimney after Idabel, and there was only smoke where she'd been, sky. "Hush, now, hush," said Randolph slowly, softly, a voice like dying light, and he was glad for Randolph, calm in the center of his mercy.

So sometimes he came near to speaking out his love for him; but it was unsafe ever to let anyone guess the extent of your feelings or knowledge: suppose, as he often had, that he were kidnapped; in which case the wisest defense would be not to let the kidnapper know you recognized him as such. If concealment is the single weapon, then a villain is never a villain: one smiles to the very end.

And even if he spoke to Randolph, to whom would he be confessing love? Faceted as a fly's eye, being neither man nor woman, and one whose every identity cancelled the other, a grab-bag of disguises, who, what was Randolph? X, an outline in which with crayon you color in the character, the ideal hero: whatever his role, it is pitched by you into existence. Indeed, try to conceive of him alone, unseen, unheard, and he becomes invisible, he is not to be imagined. But such as Randolph justify fantasy, and if a genii should appear, certainly Joel would have asked that these sealed days continue through a century of calendars.

They ended, though, and at the time it seemed Randolph's fault. "Very soon we're going to visit the Cloud Hotel," he said. "Little Sunshine wants to see us; you are quite well enough, I think: it's absurd to pretend you're not." Urgency underscored his voice, an enthusiasm in which Joel could not altogether believe, for he sensed the plan was motivated by private, no doubt unpleasant reasons, and these, whatever they were, opposed Randolph's actual desires. And he said: "Let's stay right here, Randolph, let's don't ever go anywhere." And when the plea was rejected old galling grindful thoughts about Randolph came back. He felt grumpy enough to quarrel; that, of course, was a drawback in being dependent: he could never quarrel with Randolph, for anger seemed, if anything, more unsafe than love: only those who know their own security can afford either. Even so, he was on the point of risking cross words when an outside sound interrupted, and rolled him backward through time: "Why are you staring that way?" said Randolph.

"It's Zoo . . . I hear her," he said: through the evening windows came an accordion refrain. "Really I do."

Randolph was annoyed. "If she must be musical, heaven knows I'd prefer she took up the harmonica."

"But she's gone." And Joel sat up on his knees. "Zoo walked away to Washington . . ."

"I thought you knew," said Randolph, fingering the ribbon which marked the pages of *Macbeth*. "During the worst of it, when you were the most sick, she sat beside you with a fan: can't you remember at all?"

So Zoo was back; it was not long before he saw her for himself: at noon the next day she brought his broth; no greetings passed between them, nor smiles, it was as if each felt too much the fatigued embarrassment of anticlimax. Only with her it was still something more: she seemed not to know him, but stood there as if waiting to be introduced. "Randolph told me you couldn't come back," he said. "I'm glad he was wrong."

In answer there came a sigh so stricken it seemed to have heaved up from the pits of her being. She leaned her forehead on the bed-post, and it was then that with a twinge he realized her neckerchief was missing: exposed, her slanted scar leered like crooked lips, and her neck, divided this way, had lost its giraffe-like grandeur. How small she seemed, cramped, as if some reduction of the spirit had taken double toll and made demands upon the flesh: with that illusion of height was gone the animal grace, arrow-like dignity, defiant emblem of her separate heart.

"Zoo," he said, "did you see snow?"

She looked at him, but her eyes appeared not to make a connection with what they saw; in fact, there was about them a cross-eyed effect, as though they fixed on a solacing inner vision. "Did I see snow?" she repeated, trying hard, it seemed, to understand. "Did I see snow!" and she broke into a kind of scary giggle, and threw back her head, lips apart, like an open-mouthed child hoping to catch rain. "There ain't none," she said, violently shaking her head, her black greased hair waving with a windy rasp like scorched grass. "Hit's all a lotta foolery, snow and such: that sun! it's everywhere."

"Like Mr Sansom's eyes," said Joel, off thinking by himself.

"Is a nigger sun," she said, "an my soul, it's black." She took the broth bowl, and looked down into it, as if she were a gypsy reading tea-leaves. "I rested by the road; the sun poked down my eyes till I'm near-bout blind . . ."

And Joel said: "But Zoo, if there wasn't any snow, what was it you saw in Washington, D.C.? I mean now, didn't you meet up with any of those men from the newsreels?"

". . . an was holes in my shoes where the rocks done cut through the jackodiamonds and the aceohearts; walked all day, an here it seem like I ain't come no ways, an here I'm sittin by the road with my feets afire an ain't a soul in sight." Two tears, following the bony edges of her face, faded, leaving silver stains. "I'm so tired ain't no feelin what tells me iffen I pinch myself, and I go on sittin there in that lonesome place till I looks up an see the Big Dipper: right about now along come a red truck with big bug lights coverin me head to toe." There were four men in the truck, she said, three white boys, and a Negro who rode in back squatting on top of a mountain of watermelons. The driver of the truck got out: "A real low man puffin a cigar like a bull; he ain't wearin no shirt an all this red hair growin even on his shoulders an hands; so quiet he walks through the grass, an looks at me so sweet I reckon maybe he sorry my feets

is cut an maybe's gonna ax me why don't I ride in his fine car?"
Go on, he told her, tapping his cigar so the ash was flung in her
face, go on, gal, get down in the ditch; never mind why, says the
man, and shoved her so she rolled over the embankment, landing on her back helpless as a junebug. "Lord, I sure commenced
to hoop n' holler an this little bull-man says I hush up else he's
gonna bust out my brains." She got up and started to run, but
those other two boys, answering the driver's whistle, jumped
down into the ditch and cut her off at either end; both these
boys wore panama hats, and one had on a pair of sailor pants
and a soldier's shirt: it was he who caught her and called for the
Negro to bring a rifle. "That mean nigger look a whole lot like
Keg, an he put that rifle up side my ear, an the man, he done tore
my pretty dress straight down the front, an tells them panama
boys theys to set to: I hear the Lord's voice talkin down that gun
barrel, an the Lord said Zoo, you done took the wrong road and
come the wrong way, you et of the apple, he said, an hits pure
rotten, an outa the sky my Lord look down an brung comfort,
an whilst them devils went jerkin like billygoats right then and
there in all my shameful sufferin I said holy words: Yea, though
I walk through the valley of the shadow of death, I'll fear no
evil, for you is with me Lord, yea verily, I say, an them fools
laughed, but my Lord took that sailor boy's shape, an us, me an
the Lord, us loved." The boys had removed their panama hats;
now they put them on again, and one said to the driver, well,
what was wrong with him? and the driver sucked his cigar and
scratched behind his ear and said, well, to tell the truth, he
wasn't much one for being watched; O.K., said the boys, and
climbed back up the bank, the Negro following after them, all
three laughing, which made the driver's cheek twitch and his
eyes "go yellow like an ol tomcat; an it was peculiar, cause he

was one scared man." He did not move to touch her, but squatted impotent at her side like a bereaved lover, like an idol, then the truck-horn blew, the boys called, and he bent close: "He pushed that cigar in my bellybutton, Lord, in me was born fire like a child . . ."

Joel plugged his ears; what Zoo said was ugly, he was sick-sorry she'd ever come back, she ought to be punished. "Stop that, Zoo," he said, "I won't listen, I wont . . ." but Zoo's lips quivered, her eyes blindly twisted toward the inner vision; and in the roar of silence she was a pantomime: the joy of Jesus demented her face and glittered like a sweat, like a preacher her finger shook the air, agonies of joy jerked her breast, her lips bared for a lowdown shout: in sucked her guts, wide swung her arms embracing the eternal: she was a cross, she was crucified. He saw without hearing, and it was more terrible for that, and after she'd gone, docilely taking the broth bowl with her, he kept his fingers in his ears till the ringing grew so loud it deafened even the memory of sound.

❧❧❧

They were sure John Brown would never make it up the hill: "If he simply lay down and rolled over on us, I wouldn't blame him," said Randolph, and Joel tightened his muscles, hoping this might make the mule's load lighter. They had a croquer sack for saddle and rope for reins, nevertheless they managed to stay astride, though Randolph wobbled perilously, grunting all the while, and eating endless hardboiled eggs which Joel handed him from a picnic basket he held. "Another egg, my dear, I'm feeling most frightfully seasick again: if you feel something coming up always put something down."

It was a smoky day, the sky like a rained-on tinroof, the sun, when you saw it, fishbelly pale, and Joel, who had been routed out of bed and rushed away with such inconsiderate haste, he'd not had time in which to dress decently, was goosepimpled with cold, for he wore a thin T-shirt (turned inside out), and a pair of summer knickers with most of the buttons busted off the fly. At least he had on regular shoes, whereas Randolph wore only carpet slippers. "My feet have expanded so ominously it's all I can do to squeeze them into these; really, in the light of day what a ghoul I must look: I have the damnedest sensation that every time this sad beast moves my hair falls in floods, and my eyes: are they spinning like dice? Of course I reek of mothballs . . ." The suit he wore gave off their odor like a gas; a shrunken linen suit stiff with starch and ironed shiny, it bulged and creaked like medieval armor, and he handled himself with exaggerated gingerness, for the seams kept announcing bawdy intentions.

Toward twelve they dismounted, and spread their picnic under a tree. Randolph had brought along a fruit-jar of scuppernong wine; he gargled it like mouthwash, and when there was no more, Joel made use of the empty jar to trap ants: The Pious Insect, Randolph called them, and said: "They fill me with oh so much admiration and ah so much gloom: such puritan spirit in their mindless march of Godly industry, but can so anti-individual a government admit the poetry of what is past understanding? Certainly the man who refused to carry his crumb would find assassins on his trail, and doom in every smile. As for me, I prefer the solitary mole: he is no rose dependent upon thorn and root, nor ant whose time of being is organized by the unalterable herd: sightless, he goes his separate way, knowing truth and freedom are attitudes of the spirit." He smoothed his hair, and laughed: at himself, it seemed. "If I were as wise as the mole, if I were free and equal, then what an admirable whorehouse I should be the Madame of; more likely, though, I would end up just Mrs Nobody in Particular, a dumpy corsetless creature with a brickhead husband and stepladder brats and a pot of stew on the stove." Hurriedly, as if bringing an important message, an ant climbed up his neck, and disappeared into his ear. "There's an ant inside your head," said Joel, but Randolph, with the briefest nod, went on talking. So Joel cuddled up to him and, politely as he could, peered into his ear. The idea of an ant swimming inside a human head so enthralled him that it was some while before he became aware of silence, and the tense prolonged asking of Randolph's eyes: it was a look which made Joel prickle mysteriously. "I was looking for the ant," he said. "It went inside your ear; that could be dangerous, I mean, like swallowing a pin."

"Or defeat," said Randolph, his face sinking into sugary folds of resignation.

The gentle jog of John Brown's trot set ajar the brittle woods; sycamores released their spice-brown leaves in a rain of October: like veins dappled trails veered through storms of showering yellow; perched on dying towers of jack-in-the-pulpit cranberry beetles sang of their approach, and tree-toads, no bigger than dewdrops, skipped and shrilled, relaying the news through the light that was dusk all day. They followed the remnants of a road down which once had spun the wheels of lacquered carriages carrying verbena-scented ladies who twittered like linnets in the shade of parasols, and leathery cotton-rich gentlemen gruffing at each other through a violet haze of Havana smoke, and their children, prim little girls with mint crushed in their handkerchiefs, and boys with mean blackberry eyes, little boys who sent their sisters screaming with tales of roaring tigers. Gusts of autumn, exhaling through the inherit-ing weeds, grieved for the cruel velvet children and their virile bearded fathers: Was, said the weeds, Gone, said the sky, Dead, said the woods, but the full laments of history were left to the Whippoorwill.

As seagulls inform the sailor of land's nearness, so a twist of smoke unfurling beyond a range of pines announced the Cloud Hotel. John Brown's hoofs made a sucking sound in the swamp mud as they circled the green shores of Drownin Pond: Joel looked over the water, hoping to glimpse the creole or the gam-bler; alas, those sly and slimy fellows did not show themselves. But anchored off shore was a bent, man-shaped tree with moss streaming from its crown like scarecrow hair; sunset birds, hul-labalooing around this island roost, detonated the desolate scene with cheerless cries, and only catfish bubbles ruffled the level eel-like slickness of the pond: in a burst, like the scream-ing of the birds, Joel heard the lovely laughing splashful girls splashing diamond fountains, the lovely harp-voiced girls, si-lent now, gone to the arms of their lovers, the creole and the gambler.

The hotel rose before them like a mound of bones; a widow's-walk steepled the roof, and leaning over its fence was Little Sunshine, who had a telescope trained upon the path; as they came closer he began a furious gesturing which at first seemed a too frantic welcome, but as his frenzy dissipated not at all, they soon realized he was warning them off. Curbing John Brown, they waited in the seeping twilight while the hermit de-scended through the trapdoor of the widow's-walk, presently reappearing on a slide of steps which tinkled over wastes of feu-dal lawn down to the water's rim. Brandishing his hickory cane, he advanced along the shore with a creeping bowlegged hobble, and Joel's eyes played a trick: he saw Little Sunshine as the old pond-tree come alive.

Still yards away, the hermit stopped and, stooping on his cane, fixed them with a gluey stare. Then Randolph said his name, and the old man, blinking with disbelief, broke into frisky giggles: "Well, now, ain't you the mischief! Can't see worth nothin, an there I was with my ol spyglass axin: who that a-comin where they ain't got no place? Well, now, this be a sweet todo! Step-long, step-long, follow me right careful, plenty quicksand."

They walked single-file, Joel, who led the mule, going last, and wondering, as he followed the sog of Randolph's footprints, why he'd been lied to, for it was plain that Little Sunshine had not been expecting them.

Swan stairs soft with mildewed carpet curved upward from the hotel's lobby; the diabolic tongue of a cuckoo bird, protruding out of a wall-clock, mutely proclaimed an hour forty years before, and on the room clerk's splintery desk stood dehydrated specimens of potted palm. After tying a spittoon onto John Brown's leg, this in order that they could hear him should he wander off, they left him in the lobby, and filed through the ballroom, where a fallen chandelier jeweled the dust, and weather-ripped draperies lay bunched on the waltz-waved floor like curtsying ladies. Passing a piano, over which web was woven like the gauzy covering of a museum exhibit, Joel struck the keys expecting "Chopsticks" in return; instead, there came a glassy rattle of scuttling feet.

Beyond the ballroom, and in what had once been Mrs Cloud's private apartment, were two simply furnished, spacious rooms, both beautifully clean, and this was where Little Sunshine lived:

the evident pride he took in these quarters increased the charm of their surprise, and when he closed the door he made nonexistent the ruin surrounding them. Firelight polished sherry-red wood, gilded the wings of a carved angel, and the hermit, bringing forth a bottle of homemade whiskey, put it where the light could lace its comforting promise. "It is been a mighty long while since you come here, Mister Randolph," he said, drawing chairs about the fire. "You was justa child, like this sweet boy." He pinched Joel's cheek, and his fingernails were so long they nearly broke the skin. "Usta come here totin them drawin books; I wisht you'd come again like that." Randolph inclined his face toward the shadows of his chair: "How silly, my dear; don't you know that if I came here as a child, then most of me never left? I've always been, so to speak, a non-paying guest. At least I hope so, I should so dislike thinking I'd left myself somewhere else." Joel slumped like a dog on the floor before the hearth, and the hermit handed him a pillow for his head; all day, after the weeks in bed, it had been as if he were bucking a whirlpool, and now, lullabyed to the bone with drowsy warmth, he let go, let the rivering fire sweep him over its fall; in the eyelid-blue betweenness the wordy sounds of the whiskey-drinkers spilled distantly: more distinct and real were whisperings behind the walls, above the ceiling: rotate of party slippers answering a violin's demand, and the children passing to and fro, their footsteps linking in a dance, and up and down the stairs going-coming humming heel-clatter of chattering girls, and rolling broken beads, busted pearls, the bored snores of fat fathers, and the lilt of fans tapped in tune and the murmur of gloved hands as the musicians, like bridegrooms in their angel-cake costumes, rise to take a bow. (He looked into the fire, longing to see their faces as well, and the flames erupted an embryo; a veined, vacillating shape, its features formed slowly, and even when complete stayed veiled in dazzle: his eyes burned tar-hot as he brought them nearer: tell me, tell me, who are you? are you someone I know? are you dead? are you my friend? do you love me? But the painted, disembodied head remained unborn beyond its mask, and gave no clue. Are you someone I am looking for? he asked, not knowing whom he meant, but certain that for him there must be such a person, just as there was for everybody else: Randolph with his almanac, Miss Wisteria and her search by flashlight, Little Sunshine remembering other voices, other rooms, all of them remembering, or never having known. And Joel drew back. If he recognized the figure in the fire, then what ever would he find to take its place? It was easier not to know, better holding heaven in your hand like a butterfly that is not there at all.) *Goodnight ladies, sweet dreams ladies, farewell ladies, we're going to leave you now!* Farewell sighs of folding fans, the brute fall of male boots, and the furtive steps of tittering Negro girls tiptoeing through the vast honeycomb snuffing candles and drawing shades against the night: echoes of the orchestra strum a house of sleep.

Then over the floors an unearthly clangclang dragging commenced, and Joel, wide-eyed at this uproar, turned to the others; they'd heard it, too. Randolph, flushed with whiskey and talk, frowned and put down his glass. "It be the mule," said Little Sunshine with an inebriated giggle, "he out there walkin round." And Joel recalled the spittoon they'd tied to John Brown's leg: it banged on the stairs, seemed to pass overhead, become remote, grow near.

"How'd he get up yonder?" said the hermit, worried now. "Ain't no place for him to be: damn fool gonna kill hisself." He held a hunk of kindling in the fire. Using it as a torch, he stumbled out into the ballroom. Joel tagged bravely after him. But Randolph was too drunk to move.

Around the torch swooped white choirs of singing wings which made to leap and sway all within range of the furious light: humped greyhounds hurtled through the halls, their silent shadow-feet trampling flowerbeds of spiders, and in the lobby lizards loomed like dinosaurs; the coral-tongued cuckoo bird, forever stilled at three o'clock, spread wings hawk-wide, falcon-fierce.

They halted at the foot of the stairs. The mule was nowhere to be seen: the banging of the telltale spittoon had stopped. "John Brown . . . John Brown," Joel's voice enlarged the quiet: he shivered to think that in every room some sleepless something listened. Little Sunshine held his torch higher, and brought into view a balcony which overlooked the lobby: there, iron-stiff and still, stood the mule. "You hear me, suh, come down offen there!" commanded the hermit, and John Brown reared back, snorted, pawed the floor; then, as if insane with terror, he came at a gallop, and lunged, splintering the balcony's rail. Joel primed himself for a crash which never came; when he looked again, the mule, hung to a beam by the rope-reins twisted about his neck, was swinging in mid-air, and his big lamplike eyes, lit by the torch's blaze, were golden with death's impossible face, the figure in the fire.

Morning collected in the room, exposing a quilt-wrapped bundle huddled in a corner: Little Sunshine, sound asleep. "Don't wake him," whispered Randolph who, in rising, knocked over three empty whiskey bottles. But the hermit did not stir. As they crept out through the hotel Joel closed his eyes, and let Randolph lead him, for he did not want to see the mule: a sharp intake of breath was Randolph's only comment, and never once did he refer to the accident, nor ask a question: it was as if from the outset they'd planned to return to the Landing on foot. The morning was like a slate clean for any future, and it was as though an end had come, as if all that had been before had turned into a bird, and flown there to the island tree: a crazy elation caught hold of Joel, he ran, he zigzagged, he sang, he was in love, he caught a little tree-toad because he loved it and because he loved it he set it free, watched it bounce, bound like the immense leaping of his heart; he hugged himself, alive and glad, and socked the air, butted like a goat, hid behind a bush, jumped out: Boo! "Look, Randolph," he said, folding a turban of moss about his head, "look, who am I?"

But Randolph would have no part of him. His mouth was set in a queer, grim way. As if he walked the deck of a tossing ship, he lurched forward, leaning from side to side, and his eyes, raw with bloodshot, acted as a poor compass, for he seemed not to know in which direction he was going.

"I am me," Joel whooped. "I am Joel, we are the same people." And he looked about for a tree to climb: he would go right to the very top, and there, midway to heaven, he would spread his arms and claim the world. Running far ahead of Randolph, he shinnied up a birch, but when he reached the middle branches, he clasped the trunk of the tree, suddenly dizzy; from this altitude he looked back and saw Randolph, who was walking in a circle, his hands stretched before him as if he were playing blind man's bluff: his carpet slippers fell off, but he did not notice; now and then he shook himself, like a wet animal. And Joel thought of the ant. Hadn't he warned him? Hadn't he told him it was dangerous? Or was it only corn whiskey swimming in his head? Except Randolph was being so quiet. And drunk folks were never quiet. It was peculiar. It was as though Randolph were in a trance of some kind.

And Joel realized then the truth; he saw how helpless Randolph was: more paralyzed than Mr Sansom, more childlike than Miss Wisteria, what else could he do, once outside and alone, but describe a circle, the zero of his nothingness? Joel slipped down from the tree; he had not made the top, but it did not matter, for he knew who he was, he knew that he was strong.

He puzzled out the rest of the way back to the Landing the best way he could. Randolph did not say a word. Twice he fell down, and sat there on the ground, solemn and baby-eyed, until Joel helped him up. Another time he walked straight into an old stump: after that, Joel took hold of his coat-tail and steered him.

Long, like a cathedral aisle, and weighted with murky leaflight, a path appeared, then a landmark: Toby, Killed by the Cat. Passing the moon tree, beneath which Jesus Fever was buried, no sign marking his grave, they came upon the Landing from the rear, and entered the garden.

A ridiculous scene presented itself: Zoo, crouched near the broken columns, was tugging at the slave-bell, trying, it seemed, to uproot it, and Amy, her hair disarranged and dirt streaking her face like war paint, paced back and forth, directing Zoo's efforts. "Lift it, stupid, lift it . . . why, any child! . . . now try again." Then she saw Randolph; her face contorted, a tick started in her cheek, and she shouted at him: "Don't think you're going to stop me because you're not; you don't own everything; it's just as much mine as it is yours and more so if the truth were known, and I'm going to do just what I please; you leave me alone, Randolph, or I'm going to do something to you. I'll go to the Sheriff,

I'll travel around the country, I'll make speeches. You don't think I will, but I will, I will ..."

Randolph did not look at her, but went on across the garden quite as if he had no idea she was there, and she ran after him, pulling at his sleeve, pleading now: "Let me have it, Randolph, please. Oh, I was so good, I did just what you told me: I said they'd gone away, I said they'd gone off on a long squirrel hunt; I wore my nice grey dress, Randolph, and made little tea-cakes, and the house was so clean, and really she liked me, Randolph, she said she did, and she told me about this store in New Orleans where I could sell my girandoles and the bell and the mirror in the hall: you aren't listening, Randolph!" She followed him into the house.

As soon as she was gone, Zoo spit vindictively on the bell, and gave it such a kick it overturned with a mighty bong. "Ain't nobody gonna pay cash-money for that piece-a mess. She plumb outa sense, the one done told Miss Amy any such of a thing."

Joel tapped the bell like a tomtom. "Who was it that told her?"

"Was ... I don't know who." And it was as if Zoo walked away while standing still; her voice, when she spoke again, seemed slowed down, distant: "Was some lady from New Orleans ... had a ugly little child what wore a machine in her ear: was a little deaf child. I don't know. They went away."

"My cousin Louise, she's deaf," said Joel, thinking how he used to hide her hearing aid, of how mean he'd been to her: the times he'd made that kid cry! He wished he had a penny. But when he saw her again, why, he'd be so kind; he'd talk real loud so that she could hear every word, and he'd play those card games with her. Still, it would be fun to make her mad. Just once. But Ellen had never answered his letters. The hell with

rippling mirrors of cold, seasonal color. Beyond one, someone was watching him. All of him was dumb except his eyes. They knew. And it was Randolph's window. Gradually the blinding sunset drained from the glass, darkened, and it was as if snow were falling there, flakes shaping snow-eyes, hair: a face trembled like a white beautiful moth, smiled. She beckoned to him, shining and silver, and he knew he must go: unafraid, not hesitating, he paused only at the garden's edge where, as though he'd forgotten something, he stopped and looked back at the bloomless, descending blue, at the boy he had left behind.

her. He didn't care any more. His own bloodkin. And she'd made so many promises. And she'd said she loved him. But she forgot. All right, so had he, sure, you forget, o.k., who cares? And she'd said she loved him. "Zoo . . ." he said, and looked up in time to see her retreating through the arbor-vitae hedge, which shivered, and was still.

A sound, as if the bell had suddenly tolled, and the shape of loneliness, greenly iridescent, whitely indefinite, seemed to rise from the garden, and Joel, as though following a kite, bent back his head: clouds were coming over the sun: he waited for them to pass, thinking that when they had, when he looked back, some magic would have taken place: perhaps he would find himself sitting on the curb of St. Deval Street, or studying next week's attractions outside the Nemo: why not? it was possible, for everywhere the sky is the same and it is down that things are different. The clouds traveled slower than a clock's hands, and, as he waited, became thunder-dark, became John Brown and horrid boys in panama hats and the Cloud Hotel and Idabel's old hound, and when they were gone, Mr Sansom was the sun. He looked down. No magic had happened; yet something had happened; or was about to. And he sat numb with apprehension. Before him stood a rose stalk throwing shadow like a sundial: an hour traced itself, another, the line of dark dissolved, all the garden began to mingle, move.

It was as if he had been counting in his head and, arriving at a number, decided through certain intuitions, thought: now. For, quite abruptly, he stood up and raised his eyes level with the Landing's windows.

His mind was absolutely clear. He was like a camera waiting for its subject to enter focus. The wall yellowed in the meticulous setting of the October sun, and the windows were

A NOTE ON THE TYPE

The text of this Modern Library edition
was set in a digitized version of Janson, a typeface that
dates from about 1690 and was cut by Nicholas Kis,
a Hungarian working in Amsterdam. The original matrices have
survived and are held by the Stempel foundry in Germany.
Hermann Zapf redesigned some of the weights and sizes for
Stempel, basing his revisions on the original design.